MARCIA FARRAR AND
MR. WHISKEY
TIME-TRAVEL TO 1997

MARCIA FARRAR AND MR. WHISKEY TIME-TRAVEL TO 1997

A MORTAL COMEDY

Evelyn Somers

STYLITE BOOKS

Boonville, Missouri

Copyright © 2024 by Evelyn Somers Rogers

Library of Congress Control Number: 2024906300
ISBN 979-8-9902405-0-6 (print)
ISBN 979-8-9902405-1-3 (ebook)

Stylite Books
Boonville, MO 65233

Cover and interior design by Jane Raese

COVER PHOTOS: Chicago train by Sawyer Bengtson, Unsplash;
cat by Roman Skrypnyk, Pexels

Marcia Farrar and Mr. Whiskey Time-Travel to 1997: A Mortal Comedy /
Evelyn Somers—1st ed.

IN MEMORY OF MY PARENTS,

JOHN AND TONI

Advice to a ~~Daugther~~ ~~Daugter~~ Daughter
by Dale Farrar

Grow tall as Goofy
And lovely as Lady
Show your spots like Perdita
But keep your mask on like Bandit
Bounce around like Pluto
And act the part like Snoopy
Be a handful like Augie
(Watch out for the likes of Muttley)
Be a hero when necessary
But be humble as Shoeshine Boy
Be laid-back as Manfred
But rowdy as Astro
Laugh often and oftener
But get the villain like Scooby

Don't whine if you can bark
Don't bark if you can howl

Kanz-_ika, officially the Free Republic of Kanz-_ika, is a coastal Eurasian country formed in the postwar partitioning of the Corpus Peninsula. The nation has been governed since the 1980s by the genocidal despot Jaytie Limes. Both Kanz-_ika and Limes are often linked in the same sentence with the name of the country's notorious prison complex, Cor-Spamkeer (an anagram of Corpse Maker), aka the "death prison." Limes considers it to be a construction of lethal genius, in part for its phenomenally efficient execution technology. He has acknowledged, "I'm in the numbers game" and aims to kill more people than anyone in history. Some foreign relations experts have labeled the country a "necro-nation" in light of Limes's genocidal intentions toward his own people.

—THE INFORMATION HATCH 

Chapter 1

Marcia Farrar did not expect seventeen-year-old Orson to die the day before her illegitimate son, Howie, left home and her nest emptied forever. It had been just Marcia, Howie, and Orson. Now, it was just Marcia.

It was a bad time for death and surprise. Orson was a lumpy, homely, furry mutt, spotted and ever diligent in his quest for a piece of steak. He was graying around the muzzle, but he had otherwise given no indication that his time was running out. He'd been healthy all his life, only needing the snip-snip to his privates as a young dog and annual vaccines and occasional flea killer; and, once, a course of antibiotics for an unusual parasite that had lodged in his large intestine. The vet said the parasite lived in ancient yard or basement dirt and was brought into a house on shoes, from where it could get all kinds of places: a hand, some food, a dish, a rag—something Orson had licked. The antibiotics wiped it out, and to keep it from recurring, Marcia and Howie started leaving their shoes on the back porch, like some of the pretentious types Marcia worked for at the college, whose homes were furnished with real Persian rugs not bought at Target. Like Marcia's frenemy and foster sister, Nina.

Marcia had not intended to have a baby with an Italian computer geek or to get a dog, but life assails you, and you are helpless—or, at least, you feel that way. The father, Silvestro, and his accidental demise were things of the past, though. The dog came galloping after Marcia's car one day as she was driving home from the college to the half-Italian baby, by then a precocious boy of four. In the rearview mirror, the dog looked frightened and desperate. Her heart went *thud*. She pulled over and got out, and he ran up between her feet, squealing. He was all dusty spotted coat and wriggles.

"You're all fur. You can't weigh even thirty pounds," she exclaimed and lifted him into the sedan with her garage-sale rejects that she was taking to Goodwill.

At home, she brushed him, fed him a bologna sandwich, and sent the babysitter home with an extra ten dollars to bring dog food the next day. "Chuck Wagon or something," she told Staci, the sitter. "Do they even still make that?" said Staci. "Or anything that doesn't cost more than ten dollars," said Marcia. She had never had a pet and thought dog food was like generic drugs: the formulations were all the same, weren't they?

She sat on the couch with her boy and her dog and began to read them *Charlotte's Web.* This is how life gets full, she thought. You had sex with a persistent Italian. Sperm met egg. Etc. A dog chased you, and you stopped for it, and your eyes met its eyes, and your heart broke. It was all so accidental, just the same as for Fern: a runt pig like Wilbur, a noble rescue, one spider in a million in *that* barn, *that* spring.

"'Radiant,'" repeated Howie. He already loved words. A linguist to be.

"Aroowarooowaraawaroo," whined the dog.

"I am naming you Orson," said Marcia.

FORWARD SIXTEEN YEARS. Precocious Howie had graduated the month before. He was twenty. Spring came late in Round Stone, which was farther north than about half the incorporated communities in the country and farther south than the other half.

"Invite us to graduation?" Nina had asked. So Marcia, reluctantly—but their relationship required these concessions—sent the Noisettes-Pettysaleses one of the scant twenty announcements Howie had ordered. Some people have tiny feet; some have tiny houses. Marcia had a ridiculously tiny family. It was she and Howie. And Orson. Her people were all dead. The Marcos, Silvestro's people, were in Italy and strangely untraceable.

We are so excited to be attending Howie Marco's graduation from Holliday College. Summa cum laude! Nina had posted on her social media the week before. *What a great day for my dear friend, his mom, Marcia, who struggled and sacrificed to get him to this point. All those single moms in dreary low-level campus support positions giving up their lives for their kids and their jobs are truly the unsung heroes of Round Stone. Of every college community!*

Marcia fumed and wondered if Nina might be going to hell eventually. The idea pleased her. "You don't have a clue, do you? Don't you know that I have absolutely no respect for you? None. Zero, zip. Ninguna," she said to Nina in her head. It would do no good to say it to her in person because Nina would not believe it. She was a self-satisfied type with an endless store of condescending quips that made her feel superior to everyone. "Nevertheless, your last name means 'filthy little nuts' in French," Marcia said in her head to Nina.

At commencement, the Noisettes-Pettysaleses were oddly subdued, and Marcia realized they felt like a fifth wheel and might be wondering if they should have had a baby so they, too, could swell with pride at his/her graduation. Nina was in a form-fitting two-tone Vance Corvelle sundress that fell just below the knee, with jacket and shoes that perfectly matched one of the tones in the dress. She carried a statement bag with monkeys on it. Monkeys! Kirk lifted weights, and his polos always looked like something the Hulk would be wearing just before he transformed and the shirt shredded at the seams. He had a spray tan. He sat between Nina and Marcia on the bleachers in the Holliday stadium and put one arm around each of them and hummed "Pomp and Circumstance" with the band and mallet choir as the students marched in. He was half drunk. The May sky was a tinted sheet rippling above. Two geese from the lake nearby were disoriented by the music. They zigzagged over and back and over again, honking, flying yards apart at the two wing-ends of a pointless V.

Kirk began to sway back and forth, causing Marcia and Nina to sway with him. Marcia realized people were staring. This was not how she'd wanted this day to be: she was supposed to be savoring what might be the last public recognition of Howie's talents she would ever attend, but it was impossible to enjoy it, being pushed and pulled and breathed on alcoholically by the drunk, tan, ripped, creepy husband of her fashionista frenemy. Tears streamed down her face. It was through a salty torrent that she watched Howie cross the stage and receive his honors. As he walked down the steps on the other side, Kirk shouted, "Congratulations, Mom!" in Marcia's ear and pounded her on the back, all but knocking the wind out of her.

HOWIE HAD BEEN awarded a selective postbac fellowship: support for a course of fieldwork that, if he completed it successfully, would award him an MA in applied cultural linguistics. He had been personally solicited to apply, and Marcia was proud. She wondered if his being half Italian was part of the reason he was good with languages. In their short time together, Silvestro, who never quite mastered English, used to say, "*È tutto stupido greco per me.*" The young bud of Howie would have heard this in his earliest weeks in utero and perhaps determined to grow up to be nothing like his xenoglossophobic father. (Silvestro didn't know he was a father; he died before Marcia could tell him.)

The bad part about Howie having been accepted into the program was that he had to go away to some remote place where people's language was understudied. Marcia hoped this would turn out to be somewhere fun to visit and within an hour's drive of culture and international transport. Instead his assignment was in a volatile Eurasian state, Kanz-_ika. It was the size of Wyoming and governed by totalitarian president Jaytie Limes. She remembered these details—Kanz-_ika, Wyoming, Jaytie Limes—from an article she'd seen on the Internet. Was it prophetic? Was it because Howie would someday go there that the article had been pinned in her mind like an insect specimen? Or was memory simply that random?

WITH HOWIE READY to go off to the other side of the world, Marcia was glad she'd at least have Orson for company. She said as much to Howie the morning he was packing for his departure.

"I'm glad, too, Mom," he said. He was not a mama's boy; he possessed considerable independence, but he was thoughtful of her out of a natural attentiveness to others that was a lot like his father's. And because the two of them had only each other.

"Orson's an effective crime deterrent," said Howie. "You'll be safer."

"I've got a gun," said Marcia. "That's better than a dog."

"Mom, don't shoot anyone while I'm gone," said Howie.

"I won't," she said (this would turn out to be false, but she didn't know it yet).

"I hope Orson doesn't die on you."

"Why would you say that?" Marcia said. Silvestro had died in a freak accident when she was twenty-two. Her parents had both died suddenly and unexpectedly when she was fourteen. She had never quite gotten past her fear that death could descend on someone she loved with absolutely no warning and leave her bereft—a fear that even, apparently, applied to dogs, because she felt a panic rising in her.

Howie's packing did not take long. Marcia watched him fold briefs into tight squares and check his list to confirm that he had the right number of everything recommended in the PACKING ADVISORY emailed to him by the fellowship coordinator. The coordinator had also sent a waiver for Howie to sign, acknowledging that he understood the risks of fieldwork in a politically unstable region. A persistent fear gnawed at her that she might never see him again, but she had always bent over backward not to overprotect her son.

Howie chose a brown belt over black. Actual handkerchiefs purchased from Stowes over travel packs of Kleenex. She wondered when he had learned to do this. Somewhere between tying his shoes and doing his taxes. A mother was little better than a combination delivery platform and series of YouTube tutorials on basic skills and behaviors, she decided. She'd squeezed Howie out into the world and given him some grounding, and now he was on a linguistic odyssey—she hoped not a perilous one. She was in danger of becoming an unfulfilled empty nester.

"Forget that," she said. "I'll just have to do my own traveling." *Time-travel* came into her head, but she recognized that she was in a labile state and ignored the silly thought.

She wandered off, not teary but still feeling punched in the gut. What if Howie's father, Silvestro, had lived? she wondered. In all these years, she had not thought that once. He'd been a bit of a goof, annoying but sweet, with an accent like a *Godfather* character, and she was not sure it would have lasted—but maybe they would have grown on each other like moss on rotten trees or crystals on a string hung in a glass of salt water for a long, long time. Good thing Orson was still with her. Howie was right about that.

While Howie finished up, she poured a glass of tea and watched the hummingbirds for a while and tried not to worry. They darted and dove and made her grouchy with all their flitting—she was not a fan. The feeder was a gift from Nina, who knew she didn't like them. Gaslighting, passive-aggressive, self-centered Nina. Why did Marcia even have a friend like that? But really, deep down, Marcia felt sorry for Nina—no children, not even a pet of her own, just muscled, spray-tanned Kirk for company. That was why she put up with her.

From upstairs came a loud thump. Howie had dropped his bag. Or maybe a bowling ball.

The thump made her think about fireworks. In no time, it will be July, she thought. Every year, the fireworks made Orson cower and cry until she comforted him and gave him a little piece of steak. Every year, Howie drove out to Stowes and bought a few fancy cones to light in their driveway, and he and Marcia had their Independence Day beer together before he went off to hang with his friends. They had been doing this since he was fifteen. Across from Stowes, the rival store, Floods, set up *its* stand, and Round Stone's two decades-old fireworks enterprises shot bottle rockets back and forth at each other while their patrons held their breath and wondered if a badly aimed firework might hit the merchandise and blow them to pieces. It was an effective strategy by Floods and Stowes to get people to buy a lot of fireworks fast. It might or might not have been small-town seasonal collusion.

This year, though, there would be no fretting about whether Howie would come home in one piece from the fireworks stand; instead, she'd worry about him coming home alive from Kanz-_ ika. There would be no driveway cones, no mother-son beer. She would have to go to Kirk and Nina's and suffer their annual sweaty, drunken barbecue unless she could fabricate a plausible reason not to.

Orson! She'd have to stay home to feed him the steak. She couldn't leave him alone on that night of fire raining in the sky, and Nina, who hated pets, would not allow a visiting dog for even one evening. She was happy that she had thought of this.

She went upstairs to check on Howie's packing. On the way, she saw something unusual in her bedroom. A pile of something loose and spotty.

She poked her head in the door. "Orson?"

"Orson!"

She ran over to his spotted shape stretched out on the carpet and put a hand to his ear. It was warm still, but her slight tug on it elicited no reaction. Alive, he would have bitten her finger.

She put her head to his side and heard nothing but the whine of the ceiling fan above. It was on full speed, and it ruffled, slightly, his fur that would ever after never ruffle in life as it had that first day he came galloping after her.

Yes, he was dead all right.

1974? '75? I can't quite remember the year. But I remember
that the hotel for the gofers and junior assistants was not like
anything I'd experienced. Until I realized that there were
advantages to knowing how the laboring class thought, I was
annoyed at being shuttled to this dump of brown brick. I began
to reconsider whether anything worth my time would come of
this impulsive venture, working as an assistant painter on the
location set of an American space film.

I had come here to test myself and put to rest my fear of
the desert. But I was unprepared for the living conditions:
up to this point in my life, I'd not encountered discomfort in
any great way. My bed looked like someone's failed shop-class
project. The sheets were thin and rough, and the first night,
even though we were at the edge of the desert, a mosquito
whined by my ear all night. Where its progenitors had
found water enough to breed, I had no idea. The other junior
assistants and interns drank cheap alcohol and partied. My
upbringing had protected me from these sorts, so I had no
social skills to interact with them and no inkling yet that they
would find me repulsive and call me names; I hung back.

But I'd made note of an American couple who were
fornicating at every opportunity. Susan Smith and Dale Farrar.
She was not the one who interested me. He was. He had a glow.
No, I did not like men in that way, but Dale was so open and
uncomplicated. He greeted me affably before we'd even been
introduced. I was, against my natural instincts, charmed. All
that friendly good nature balled up and stuffed into one flesh-
and-blood human! He disproved my theory that niceness was a
fiction. He was a new phenomenon—new to me, at any rate. A
nice guy. Through and through. Not a mean bone in his body.
An American.

—MEMOIRS OF SOCRATIES LOVE

Chapter 2

MARCIA HAD BEEN born in the mid-'70s. It was the era of painter pants with Danskin leotards, Jimmy Carter, and *Saturday Night Live.* Rocky Balboa and *Dallas* and wavy-soled Famolares. The whole nation was jogging and eating muesli. Americans were at once cooler (they thought) and more earnestly dorky (in truth) than they might ever be again.

Marcia's parents had met in North Africa, where, thanks to connections (Susan) and chance (Dale), both had secured low-wage opportunities with the location crew of a well-known space epic. Her father was gorgeous and immature. Her mother was at the peak of her moderate looks and fragile orthopedic health; looks and skeletal integrity would both plummet as she passed twenty-seven. They had sex in a shabby hotel near the desert. Susan got pregnant, and Dale, though juvenile, was kind and un-characteristically adult in his determination to be a good father. He married Susan when they got back to the States, on a boat on a recreational lake in a ceremony performed by a friend who was mail-order ordained as a Priest of the Aquarian Age.

When Marcia was a little girl, Dale used to tell her about the people he'd met in Africa and the long evenings they'd spent BS-ing after the sun went down and there was nothing but dead, arid land and the black lath of night, seamed with streaks and glitter-ing with the astrological pantheon of those North African parts. When the conversation lagged those nights, he nudged it back to life by recounting the plots of his favorite cartoons. The desert made a strange setting for comedy, but Dale didn't notice. To a person, the crew were all drawn to gentle, cartoon-loving Dale, and he loved them all. Only one of them didn't fit in: Socraties Love, the rich son of an airline mogul, with delusions of grandeur.

Everyone else thought he was arrogant, rude, and warped; they called him "Sickrabies" behind his back. Dale agreed with them that Socraties—he never called him Sickrabies himself, only sometimes "Soc" for short—was . . . well, a bit creepy. That was what he told Marcia. But despite that, he had gotten on famously with Socraties. He'd made creepy Soc laugh with his funny stories. Dale was no threat to anyone. Everyone, even the people others were universally wary of, thought the world of him. He could have been casual buddies with Hitler and been untainted by it.

What Marcia mostly remembered about her father, though, was not his stories about Socraties Love; it was curling up in his arms and watching Muttley and Bandit and Quick Draw McGraw: all those cartoon animals made him laugh. His favorites were the dogs.

He loved animals but was allergic—thus, the Farrars had no pets. He was crazy about Marcia and had a more restrained love for Susan, and he hated real-life conflict. His beard smelled sweetly and pungently of weed and Dial soap. He could languish on the couch for hours snuggling Marcia until she got hungry and jumped down to ask her mother for a graham cracker. Her father's usefulness was comparable to an old rubber band's—he seemed more liable to break than to hold things together. Years later, she was surprised to discover that he'd had a credit in the space epic as a second junior transportation assistant. He died of exposure at thirty-six after falling down a ravine in some woods behind a friend's house on New Year's Eve and not being found until the next year. His death devastated Marcia, who'd adored him.

Six months later, her mother had surgery for early-onset ankle arthritis and had a fatal reaction to the anesthesia. At fourteen, Marica was an orphan. Her lone relative, Susan's older brother, turned down the job of guardian, but there was a girl she knew slightly at school, Nina Noisettes, who had attached herself to Marcia. Nina's parents offered to foster her, and the court agreed.

If Nina was their treasured gem, Marcia was their charity project. They were half-heartedly good to her in second-rate ways, but Marcia could see the difference in what they thought of her and how they spoiled Nina. So far, her life experience had provided lessons about the wisdom of sex with short-term boyfriends in North African hotels and about the superiority of the dog characters in Hanna-Barbera compared to Looney Tunes (but Looney Tunes artists were better). She'd learned that parents were perishable resources and that diffident altruism was an American middle-class affliction: her temporary residence at the Noisetteses' was the evidence of that. She marked off the days until she would leave Nina's and go out on her own—it didn't make sense to reject a comfortable home and support in the short term. She graduated from high school early and got a full-ride scholarship for orphans to a college in Chicago that was so small the classes all met in one rehabbed warehouse. There she studied history and minored in business. No one she knew had heard of the college, but this only made her feel more independent.

One afternoon in 1997, in the period leading to graduation, Marcia was walking home to her dorm room on one of the warehouse upper stories from her job as counter help at the donut shop. She liked the job, despite Nina's sly comments about it. Nina's parents had sent her to private, exclusive Otterlea College. It was redbrick and ivy, with small classes taught by well-degreed profs. Nina had a job also, collating handouts for her econ professor. "I can put it on my résumé: Senior Research Assistant," she said. "You probably won't want Strikeout Donuts on your résumé when you graduate."

"It's Homerun Donuts," Marcia corrected her.

She had just had that conversation with Nina on the phone the day before, and as she walked home to the dorm, she was thinking about it while trying to stay to her side of the sidewalk and not stare at the well-dressed women of color, of whom there were many in the city. These urban women were some of the most stylish individuals she had ever seen. They were professional and confident and made Marcia feel like a poor white ragpicker when she stood behind them at Marshall Field's or waited on them at the donut shop. They were smart and assured, so at ease in the city, and their leather purses had elegant snaps and buckles that flashed as they extracted bills for their donuts and coffee.

Marcia wondered why Nina wanted to keep up the old relationship now that they were both on separate paths and Marcia was an adult and self-sufficient. Here she was in the city, which she had come to like a great deal: the tall old hotels along the Loop and the sidewalks that were crowded with human variety—but not too crowded, not like Manhattan or Tokyo (she'd seen pictures). The flamboyant old architecture, juxtaposed with modern glass and mirrors, the high gray sky on cool days, and even the bitter bite of wind on subzero days. And always, the lakeshore as a possible destination. She had shared none of these feelings with Nina and didn't intend to, but as she thought about it, an inner eye opened—the one everyone has that stays closed most of the time in most people but, in a handful, opens creakily, like a very worn antique doll's, at unexpected moments and imparts painful objective knowledge. Marcia realized with a shock that it wasn't *family* you couldn't get rid of; it was the connections that accumulate in a life, seemingly randomly but with an insistent stickiness that makes them harder to eradicate than the glue on an old price tag.

In other words, she was bound to Nina. Possibly forever. A notion so upsetting that she was stricken for several minutes, standing weakly on the sidewalk outside a hearing-aid emporium, gazing down through the years to a lifetime's accumulation of jibes about the donut shop or whatever she was going to do when she graduated. A snippet from her freshman Philosophy of

Religion class came back to her: Aelred of Rievaulx, a courtier-turned-monk who said that friendship was eternal—it didn't end even when someone *died*.

Fortunately, in the next minute, three things happened:

1. Her youthful faith in fairness erupted and crushed the nasty thought that she and Nina were handcuffed soul-to-soul until, and unless, Fate chose to stop the entropic carnival of time and everything—spirit and matter and everything—just ended.
2. She turned a corner and was ready to cross at the light, headed back to campus, when an accident occurred nearby and emergency vehicles came wailing through the intersection, preventing everyone from crossing, even though there was a green light and a walk signal.
3. While she was waiting for the sirens to fade and the light to turn green, a voice called out to her from an umbrella table in front of a pizza joint: "Hello! Miss! Wait! What is your name, please?"

In an instant, he was beside her, touching her elbow. "What is your name, please?" he repeated in accented English. Marcia might not have thought Italian if she hadn't seen so many reruns of the last years of *Growing Pains* with Nina, who said Leonardo DiCaprio was the most beautiful male ever created. This person certainly didn't look like Serpico or Rocky, but there was a slight emanation of Leonardo. He was fine-featured. Meaty yet lanky. Light-haired. Darkish of brow but creamy ivory of skin. He wore black plastic glasses and had arrived at her side in a cloud of Armani body splash.

"You are *cute as a bug*," he said, looking at her chest. In his accent, it was something more like "*coot as a bog.*"

People were ignoring and moving around Marcia and her interlocutor to cross the street. No one seemed alarmed for her. He could probably kiss or grope her right here without interference, but he was more genteel than that. He wanted her to have pizza with him. Right now, over *there*, at his umbrella table.

"No," she said. Her epiphany about Nina was fresh in her mind: if she allowed him into her life, she might never get rid of him. "I don't even know your name," she said firmly. "You don't know mine." He was older by about eight years. "You might be married, for all I know." In her mind, she was also narrating the encounter to Nina: "So this guy who was the double of Leonardo DiCaprio wanted to take me out. He said I was cute as a bug."

"My name is Silvestro Marco," he said. "I work in *il settore tecnologico. Non sono sposato.* I am a software engineer *celibe*," he clarified.

Celibate! A celibate software engineer. Marcia amended her communication to Nina: ". . . this guy who was the double of Leonardo DiCaprio. He was celibate, but he was willing to give it all up for me. But I just couldn't get into him."

Silvestro gazed at her with such desperate laser-eye that her skin felt baked. "I am in looove with you," he announced. She had the sudden notion that he was fully in earnest.

"I doubt it," said Marcia drily. Any trepidation she'd had had turned into impatience. No one loved her, except her parents, who were dead. And she had not loved anyone but them. The Noisetteses certainly hadn't loved her, though they'd tried to pretend to. She'd never had a boyfriend, and other than Nina, there were no women she called friends. Love. Love? What did that even mean?

Silvestro failed to pick up on her skepticism. "I am *sincero dal profondo del mio cuore*," he cried. He struck his chest with his fist, miming an arrow going in. "Like that!" he said. "The moment I saw you. A poison arrow has killed me with love!"

Marcia closed her eyes and sighed. A poison arrow? Really? The light had changed twice now, and people were streaming past while Silvestro waxed eloquent about death and arrows and first-sight love. It was the stupidest thing that had happened to her since her mother had expired over a stiff ankle.

Finally she could abide it no more. "I have an afternoon class," she lied and broke away to cross the street, but the yellow light turned red right as she stepped off the curb.

"Oh, you are a student!" he said ecstatically.

She neither confirmed nor denied it. She wasn't about to tell him where—though anyway, the college was off the beaten path and still looked like a warehouse and would be hard for him to find.

A python striking a rodent was not as fast as Silvestro moving in to kiss her on the cheek. He whispered gruffly in her ear, a soft growl—she caught the words and at first could not make sense of them. Then the syllables sorted themselves out, and she understood.

The brisk little white stick man appeared on the traffic light, and she tore herself away and darted across the street.

"Ciao!" he called after her.

What he'd said in her ear—and she was still pondering it even after she'd eaten a bowl of ramen and lain down for a while on her bed, listening to Counting Crows and remembering how handsome her father had been and how he used to tell her cartoon-dog trivia and how he often said how strange it was that even though people loved to laugh, they thought funny things were not important—what Silvestro had said was that she was the most beautiful thing he'd ever seen, and he wanted to give her children and jewels and live with her for the rest of his life.

It was as if he had read the future.

Jaytie (often J. T.) Limes is a Eurasian revolutionary who carved out a political niche as leader of the Advance Liberation Party in the Republic of Kanz-_ika and oversaw the republic's transition from marginal economy to small but aggressive player in the tech revolution. Since the 1980s, he has recruited top talents in military, scientific, technological, architectural, and commercial endeavors from all over the world—all, apparently, with the aim of building the ultimate high-tech death prison, Cor-Spamkeer.

—THE INFORMATION HATCH

Chapter 3

A DAY AND a half after Howie left for his fellowship, he messaged Marcia. *Long flight but safely here. Turns out my fieldwork won't be in Kanz-_ika after all, but on an island off the coast. The island doesn't have an official name. They all call it "What Island." My guide says it's safer than the mainland. You'd like her, Mom. My guide. She seems pretty tough.*

Marcia had done some reading in the interim about Jaytie Limes and his abominable death prison, and lately the international news had featured regular counts of the people he'd executed: a number in the hundreds of thousands that was increasing daily, rapidly. She read Howie's message now and breathed a sigh of relief. Every day she checked her NooNews app for updates about Kanz-_ika. Every day the news alarmed her. But as it turned out, he was somewhere else. Close, but not actually *in* Kanz-_ika. This turn of events reassured her, and she replied playfully, *Be safe and lay low.*

The moment after she hit SEND, her phone rang, and *Nina Nuts* popped up on her screen. Really, Noisettes meant "hazelnuts," but in Marcia's head, it was just Nina Nuts. Kirk's last name, Pettysales, was a corruption of the French *petits salles*, "little rooms," but somewhere along the line, the single t had doubled. Also, the double l had been reduced to a single l, changing "rooms" (*salles*) to "dirty" (*sales*) and the French meaning of Kirk's surname to "dirty little." Together, their hyphenated last name, Noisettes-Pettysales, meant "dirty little nuts," a fact no one else seemed to have noticed or pointed out to them.

"Marsh, how are you *doing*?" said Nina with a tone of condescending pity.

"Great," said Marcia. While she was talking, she wandered down to the basement and opened the chest freezer where she'd put Orson until she decided what to do with him. Stuff, bury, burn. Those were the options. Bronzing would cost a fortune and make him too heavy to move around without a hand truck. She'd wrapped Orson's spotted, furry body in a plush red throw from Stowes but left his head uncovered, placing a pillow beneath it in case it oozed head-goo and stuck to some of the old freezer-burned pork steaks that were still in there from when Howie ate meat. Wrapped and pillowed like this, he looked rigid but regal—ecclesiastical even, like a Catholic cardinal.

"I love how you're always so brave," said Nina. "Even when your life is falling apart."

"'There is something to be learned from a rainstorm. When meeting with a sudden shower, you try not to get wet and run quickly along the road,'" said Marcia, quoting from the *Hagakure*, which Howie had studied in an honors class. In her mind, she said to Nina, "I bet that will have you scratching your head."

Nina didn't say anything. Then she laughed. "Always the optimist, aren't you? I'll have to remember that. 'Try not to get wet and run quickly along the road.'"

Marcia pictured fashionista Nina in a short frock, darting along in a downpour with spray-tanned Kirk trailing.

"Come over for some pinot and girl talk tomorrow night?" said Nina brightly. "Kirk's finishing a big project this week. He'll be holed up in the Finance Building working. So I'm all alone and lonesome."

Marcia thought a minute: Nina was not always easy to take on her own, but pair her with Kirk, and the annoyance factor quadrupled. Sooner or later, she'd have to accept their invitation. It would be better with just Nina. "OK," she said.

She looked down at Orson's stiff, crimson-garbed form. The cold from the open freezer blasted up at her. She closed the lid sadly and felt the suck and settle of the seal.

"Marsh, have you buried Orson yet?" said Nina curiously on the other end of the line.

"Not yet," said Marcia. "I've got him on ice."

"On ice?" she squeaked. "That's such a cute thing to say, in your situation. But I have a suggestion for you. Something I just heard about. I'll tell you about it when you come over. Seven o'clock?"

"Sure," said Marcia.

Dear Mom, wrote Howie in a long and homesick-sounding email that she read on her phone, *I'm here on What Island, and it's not what I thought. In fact, I'm not sure what the heck I'm doing here. The island is very lovely. It's way prettier than the photos I saw of Kanz-_ika. (And it's safer, which you'll be happy about.) There are craggy rocks and cerulean inland pools. There's not a lot of arable land, but what there is is verdant and lush. The ocean is a beautiful blue gray. It dashes against the rocks or laps over the beach, depending on the day and the weather. The waves-bashing sound is so musical—I wish you could hear it.*

The people here are absurdly poor, but it's not really a problem. That's one of the things I can't understand. There is almost no economic development. They don't even trade with the Kanz-_ikan mainland, which is very strange, even as militarized as Kanz-_ika is. Houses are tiny. More like boxes, almost. Materialistic, these folks aren't. Some of them don't even have houses, which is OK right now because at this season it's quite temperate. I've heard that when it gets cold, they move into caves or crevices afforded by the coastal rocks, but how they avoid getting sprayed by the waves, I can't figure out, and I haven't discovered where they put their stuff, either. Though they don't have much stuff. In short, they have resigned themselves to an unheard-of level of poverty, though intellectually they're advanced—a lot of them are super literate and interesting to talk to, yet they don't act like they're bothered by being so poor. Quite the opposite. They're filled with some purpose or mission that they all know but won't talk about. Maybe I'll find out what it is after I've been here longer.

Linguistically, there's nothing to research and document. That's another thing I can't figure out. Why send me here? It would be like doing fieldwork in pig Latin. Most people in Kanz-_ika speak English because Jaytie Limes says it's the lingua franca of high-tech executions. The people here speak English, too, but at some point, there's been a kind of vowel shift. All the "short" vowels (in your layperson's terms) and all the long ones, too, have moved. Take a word like "fat"—you know, a porker. Fat is fête. Fête is fit; fit is pronounced like fought; fought is pronounced like foot; foot is fat. Etc. Same for the long vowels: fute is feet; feet is fight; fight is fote; fote (if there was such a word) would be fute. And fute (again, if it existed), would be fate. Orthographically they've lost c altogether, and voiceless f is usually gh, and silent gh does not exist. So our word fight is spelled ghite but pronounced fote (see previous). Weight is weet. They're allergic to diphthongs, especially the ow sound as in Howie, preferring pure vowels, so my name, which would be Hoey without the vowel shift, becomes Hoo ay (that's the only diphthong they embrace—what you would call long I). So my name is pronounced Who I. Which leaves me perpetually feeling disoriented—is someone asking an ontological question or greeting me?

There are some curious lexical items, too. A movie is an "alphabet," and a book is a "spreadsheet." Most of them don't have phones, though there's some sort of Internet on the island (I guess you figured that out, since I'm emailing). But it's run through a provider you've never heard of. I could theoretically watch movies, but there's so much buffering it would take forever; unlike life back home, people are unconcerned about time, and they don't pay much attention to media. But they love to be read to, so I've been reading them e-books, the free ones. If they're desperate, they'll even ask for fan fiction, and then they walk around lampooning it—American fan fiction is one of their favorite sources of humor. Oh, another weird lexical thing: apple butter is "porridge." They are crazy for apple butter and make kettles and vats of the stuff. Did I say that the food is mostly simple? You would like it, Mom. Bread, leafy greens, sliced boiled eggs with the yolks just a dot soft in the center. No peanut butter, though. I've been eating these almost every day. A signature dessert is "porridge roll" with—you guessed it—apple butter rolled up in a bland, not-sweet spongey stuff and served in thick slices—imagine an applesauce Twinkie. My guide won't let me eat it. She says it's like the produce in Mexico if your system isn't used to the microbes.

I feel like I'm living in a satire of a Jonathan Swift satire. But these people are, overall, unbelievably sweet and kind, I have to admit. They found out my childhood dog died and were very respectful about it. They were curious about how the dead are disposed of back home. I told them that with pets, we usually bury them under a bush but sometimes cremate them, and that more and more people are choosing cremation for themselves these days, and this upset them and made some of them cry.

They won't talk about their pasts, by the way, or if they do, it's obliquely. I'm eager to know more. All my informants so far have had other lives elsewhere, though they won't say where. Some of them were entrepreneurs, which is surprising given how uninvested everyone is here in making money. One owned a pastry shop. One was a pawnbroker. Another was a lawyer. Doctor, auto engineer, pilot, actor, goat farmer, insurance agent, college president, public works—you name it, one of them did it. And now they scavenge for treasures. I'll tell you about the scavenging later—I have to find out more about it.

One weird thing is that no one I've talked to so far is a native What Islander. I'm looking at the possibility that the island was uninhabited until the 1980s—that's about as far back as their history (what little they'll tell me about it) seems to go.

Back to the language thing—it's a disappointment not to be able to study what I came here to study, but as consolation, there are some interesting legends, and although I didn't do the emphasis in folklore, I'm boning up on methodology online and starting to collect some of the stories, which are peculiar and appear to be much older than their presence on the island here, especially some legends about a tribe of powerful dwellers in the Kanz-_ikan desert who are reincarnated spirits and hold the secrets of all time.

I hope you're not worrying. So far it seems safe on What Island, just not on the mainland. But I won't be going there. I'm here on the island for the duration, and I'm sure I'll get a thesis out of it.

P.S., I'm so, so sorry about Orson, Mom. I keep thinking about how quiet the house must be now.

Your kid, "Who I"

MARCIA READ THIS message and felt, suddenly, how heavy an empty nest was. *How like a ponderous boulder, crushing the loveless soul,* she would have said if she were a poet.

She missed her son, and for just a second, she thought maybe it would have been better if she hadn't loved him so much so her anguish would be dilute.

Everything Howie's email had said about What Island was very odd. She found herself puzzling over why the college would sponsor a linguistic fellowship to an island where the population spoke English, or some pig-Latinesque version of it. And why had Howie been invited to apply? Of course, he was a brilliant student, but the invitation had come out of nowhere. He had not heard of the fellowship prior to the invitation, and neither had she, even though, working in an academic department at Holliday College, she knew about most of these opportunities. She had come home from work and found him in the hallway with the letter. "Mom. Mom," he'd said, his eyes ardent with unspoiled dreams, "they want me to apply for this. It's a *big* honor. I think I'm going to do it."

Now Marcia was feeling substantially tilted on her axis. Her son was far away, on a remote, craggy island with eccentric people who lived in caves and cardboard shacks and ate applesauce roll— no, apple *butter*—and wouldn't let him have any. A few miles across the water was a nation governed by an execution-crazed strongman and mired in fear. She wondered if she'd been wrong to encourage him to go.

She went to his bedroom and looked for the letter of invitation to see if there were any clues in it that would make it all make sense, but though Howie was quite organized and habitually filed such things, she couldn't find it.

Dale Farrar. He could have been a young, more rugged and rumpled, dark-eyed Tony Curtis. When I first met him, I thought, Aren't all good-looking people just out for themselves? I was wrong. Dale didn't want anything except to laugh, and to love everyone. If happiness is wanting nothing more than to watch dog cartoons and be friends with people, he was the happiest person alive. He had come along to the film set with a friend on impulse, and when he got there, they hired him to drive. Everyone wanted him for their driver because he was so winsome: impossible to be anything but blissful in his company.

I told him what I was there for: to conquer my fear of the desert and confront something in myself, something frightening that hovered at the edge of darkness. My father was a businessman, never giving me much thought. My mother was stupid. When she wasn't mocking me, she ignored me. From my early years, I'd resented him and hated her, but I'd suppressed these emotions by doing the usual boy things: playing idiotic sports with balls and chopping the legs off small amphibians.

Dale's only fault was that he could bore people—he had the gift of storytelling, but his tales were all rehashings of cartoon plots. Why should I care about these stories of American dogs and their silly predicaments? If a droopy-eyed blue hound liked to sing, off key, an old American folk tune called "Clementine," why would I be amused? If a nighttime relay of barking dogs saved a fleet of spotted puppies or if a bumbling beagle superhero donned a cape, popped a pill, and rescued the perishing, what stake could I possibly have in those plots? I'd not been exposed to humor, and Dale told his tales with a joy that belied the darkness, so I didn't understand how dark they were (Clementine drowns while her lover watches, don't you know; the puppies are slated to be skinned). I had a natural bent toward the macabre that must have come from my mother, and although I was fascinated by Dale, I couldn't quite grasp the appeal of his stories.

But though familiarity can breed contempt, it can also breed affection, and despite or perhaps because of his undaunted positivity, I came to trust him. It was an entirely new experience. In this way, I was a virgin: I had never had a friend before. The feeling grew on me. Over time, I even developed a modest respect for his bottomless repertoire of silly dog stories. There was something in them. I couldn't name it, but they made me smile. And at the same time, oddly, they scratched my dark itch.

—MEMOIRS OF SOCRATIES LOVE

Chapter 4

MARCIA GOT THE job at Homerun Donuts near the end of her freshman year, two and a half years before she met Silvestro. It came about—or so she initially thought—because of something she'd said in one of her history classes.

She had settled on her history major right away. Dale Farrar had liked history, though he hadn't had the money to go to college, or the focus. And after he got her mother pregnant, it was out of the question: from now on, he must work at minimum-wage jobs, many of which were physically taxing, and in the evenings and on weekends lie on the couch with Marcia, mildly stoned, and watch cartoons.

Still, he was quite the history buff. Sometime in his teens, he'd started noticing how eerily the past seemed to foreshadow the future. He wasn't a logical person. But he was curious and inclined to enjoy conspiracy theories, as long as they weren't too dark. He had an adhesive memory, somehow unimpaired by the marijuana, and he wanted to figure it all out. He'd started collecting old textbooks and obsolete volumes of popular history from flea markets and library book sales. When he wasn't watching cartoons with Marcia or working at a series of jobs only a stoner with a high school diploma would want (factory-mattress-seconds delivery; truck-stop convenience-store window washer), he was reading books like *The Search for the Real Barabbas* and *Men Built It out of Wood*. The latter was like a Bible to him. He'd read it so many times it was disintegrating, all taped together with duct tape. (Out of sentiment, Marcia had kept this distressed and taped-together heirloom and still had it, though when she'd left for college and Chicago, she'd discarded most of her childhood possessions—in particular, all the gifts and clothes the Noisetteses had given her over the years.) She'd especially loved to hear Dale talk about the similarities between cartoons and history. "In cartoons, just like in history, the middle is always a muddle, and the ends lead to new episodes. There's more common ground between TV animation and world events than meets the uninitiated eye," he told her. "But the difference is, most people forget the history they've learned. They *remember* cartoons. They don't want to think about bad things. They want to laugh. Believe me, the world will forget the Holocaust before they'll forget their favorite *Scooby-Doo* episode." He said this to her every night before bed, and then he tucked her in and leaned down and gave her head a very gentle Dutch rub.

At the Warehouse College, her history professors were all men. Perhaps her choice of a major was as simple as this: she was searching for the father she had lost prematurely. But there was something missing in each of them. Something her father had possessed in abundance that they lacked, which she couldn't pinpoint at first.

Most of the students at her college were tough urban youths and single moms going back to school to qualify for work promotions. Also non-native speakers of various nationalities who had landed in Chicago and wanted to better their English. She assumed they'd all been drawn there by the same crude but effective recruitment postcard that had lured her. It said, *Come to the only college that meets in a warehouse. We'll give you a scholarship because you're* _____. There was a blank where the admissions office could write something in. In the blank had been written "orphaned." It was a student body comprised mainly of Others and survivors. Marcia sensed that if you said or did the wrong thing around some of them, you might be in trouble, so she kept quiet most of the time.

But one day, in the middle of a Western Civ lecture in which the professor was rambling incoherently about Spengler and Toynbee and the ideology of declinism manifested in the death throes of contemporary Western capitalism, she blurted out, "What about cartoons? In cartoons, the middles are a muddle, but the ends lead to new episodes."

The professor stopped lecturing. "What?"

"History's a lot like that, right?" Marcia continued bravely. "Isn't there more common ground between TV animation and world events than meets the uninitiated eye? Maybe we're just in the middle right now, and that's why we always feel like we're doomed."

A deadly silence. She'd put her foot in it. She didn't want to invoke Dale Farrar and have him mocked in front of her peers, so she said, "It's just that cartoons and history have a lot in common."

The professor looked at her hard. "Good God. Don't tell me you're thinking of that abomination *Peabody's Improbable History.*" (She hadn't been.) "There's really no place where history and cartoons share a space that's not just moronic fictional pap. There," he said, "is your answer, Miss Farrar."

That was how Marcia finally put her finger on the difference between the Warehouse College history faculty and her father: the professors were Negative Neds and Donny Downers. Not a happy man among them. They probably hadn't watched a cartoon since they were two, or read *Men Built It out of Wood,* which was full of cool pictures and delightful tangential anecdotes about wooden basketballs that wouldn't bounce and gas cans that went up in flames. They were nothing like Dale Farrar, who'd laughed often and never met an enemy.

That same day, after class, a student she'd never noticed before, a woman in a White Sox cap with an aggressive, jock-y strut, approached her and said, "I saw how bad you felt when that asshole smacked you down."

"He didn't," said Marcia.

The ball-capped student, who introduced herself as Sheila, pushed back. "Sounded like it to me."

"I try not to think the worst of anyone's motives," said Marcia. "Except for my foster sister, Nina, who despises me."

"What's your foster sister's last name? I know a psycho bitch named Nina, too."

"Noisettes."

"Nope. Wrong Nina."

"Where did you come from?" said Marcia, who was puzzled by the woman's sudden appearance in class today. She was pretty sure she hadn't been there before.

"Someplace hotter and less humid than Chicago."

"Arizona?"

"Maybe not geographically," said Sheila evasively. Then she said, "I know someone you need to meet."

"Why?"

Sheila shrugged. "You just should."

Marcia had not yet had the epiphany about the way personal relationships can become an albatross (e.g., Nina). Nevertheless, she hesitated.

"Come with me," urged Sheila. "You'll like Thomas, I promise."

"Thomas?"

"Thomas Cook."

"I have seminar at five."

"Plenty of time," said Sheila. "We'll be back in a flash."

What the heck? thought Marcia and followed her.

The Warehouse College was near the south edge of Lakeview. They walked north toward the ballpark. It was cool and gusting hard—an intermittent but powerful wet wind that made Marcia's skin feel clammy. A piece of her hair kept blowing against her cheek and sticking to it. Sheila's peat-colored mane was the kind that presented a unified frizz front rather than the independent, peevish strands that Marcia struggled daily to manage with her styling gel. Plus Sheila had the cap, though it didn't come close to covering all the brown frizz. Other than the cap, Sheila was dressed like a normal '90s college girl, in boot-cut jeans and short red leather booties and a moss-colored military-style jacket. Marcia herself was very noticeable. She tried to keep a low profile, but she had inherited a large portion of her father's handsomeness and his jet-black hair, which was straight and glossy, and her mother's vividly blue eyes, noble nose, and tall, hipless, leggy figure; she looked like a busty, blue-eyed Cher, and no matter what she tried, this was hard to cover up and made her awkward at times. (Nina Noisettes, by contrast, was the quintessential American blonde, though she had a nipped-looking little nose like a Hummel figurine's.)

Sheila moved briskly, but Marcia's long legs had no trouble keeping up. When the two women reached West Addison, they turned and went west for a couple more blocks and then crossed the street. And there was a donut shop, Homerun Donuts. Marcia supposed it was named for the baseball stadium.

"Do you like donuts?" said Sheila.

"For breakfast. It's two thirty," said Marcia doubtfully.

Sheila pushed open the shop door, and Marcia stepped in after her. For a weekday afternoon, there were a lot of customers, most of them sitting at the six or eight ice-cream-parlor-style tables with pennant centerpieces. The menu above the counter included pierogi, so that might be what they were eating. The girl at the counter had a nose ring and a ball cap like Sheila's and looked like a high school student. "Whad you want?" she asked.

Sheila waved her hand and said, "We're here to see Thomas." She stepped behind the counter, moving toward the door to the kitchen that said, EMPLOYEES ONLY BEYOND THIS POINT.

"Come on," she said to Marcia, and Marcia looked at the counter girl to see if there was going to be resistance. But the girl was staring out past the tables at something in the street. Sheila pulled her through the door with some urgency. "Come *on!*"

In the kitchen, it was blazing, like they'd dropped right into Hades in July. Two guys about Marcia's age in wifebeaters and do-rags and full-body aprons, glistening with sweat, were cutting holes with a puncher and submerging rows of the dough balls into fryers full of oil in flattish fry baskets. They flaunted their wrist work. A third, who must be Thomas, was tending an industrial mixer that bucked and spun as it mixed a pale periwinkle batter. He was tall and skinny with a face full of acne. He seemed very serious about the mixing. Marcia's heart caught for a second when he looked up and noticed her.

Sheila dragged Marcia over. "Hey, Thomas. This is Marcia. Marcia, Thomas Cook."

From the mixer behind him, Marcia caught the familiar, gag-worthy smell and screwed up her face. "Blueberry cake?" she muttered with revulsion.

He stared at her. For the second time in barely an hour, she felt she had put her foot in it.

"What's wrong with blueberry cake donuts?" he demanded. He had a lilting, intelligent voice. Not deep but not high and squeaky, either.

She didn't know whether to look at his eyes, which seemed like the eyes of a person she wanted to know much better, or the pink hobnailed face full of acne bumps and scars. She focused on the eyes. They were soulful, liquid. They inspired a degree of trust that Marcia did not often feel.

"Well?"

"Do you truly think it's right for blueberry farmers to go to all that work just so people can put them in—" she started to argue.

"You know, I don't like blueberry cake either, but the customers want them," said Thomas. "Anyway, it's artificial flavoring and color, not real blueberries."

Marcia frowned. "That's not the point. It's that someone might think it was OK to waste them in a totally superfluous flavor of *donuts.*"

"I like you," said Thomas. "An idealist."

"I'm not. Just an orphan. And a history major."

"Well, there you go. An orphan. You wouldn't happen to need a job, would you?"

"It would depend. Doing what?" Marcia was pretty sure she didn't want to work in a sugary sweatbox with all men.

"No, not in the kitchen," said Thomas, realizing that was what she thought. "I wouldn't make you do the greasy stuff. You'd end up with a face like mine. I need someone to replace my girl up front. She's just temporary."

"What would I have to do?"

"Ring up sales. Collect money. Dispense donuts. Talk to people. Get here on time. Wear a ball cap and pretend to be a White Sox fan, even if you're not. Learn how to use the 9mm Beretta under the old-fashioneds tray, just in case."

Marcia had started to get drowsy in the heat of the kitchen, but she jerked wide awake at the mention of a gun. She looked around and saw that Sheila had slipped away.

"You probably won't see her again," said Thomas. "But you might hear something about her."

"Is everything all right?" Marcia said, alarmed.

He shrugged. "I guess you could say that. Nothing to worry about right this minute, anyway." He clapped his arm around her shoulders and said amiably, "Think about it. A Homerun Donuts Donut-Dispensing Associate. The work's easy, the money's not terrible. It *smells* great in here. And you'd be safe."

"Safe?"

"Safe. You're *always* safe here. Remember, there's a Beretta under the old-fashioneds, and no matter who's behind the counter, they'll know how to use it."

A Dialogue between Dad and Daughter

"Critical thinking time, Marsh. Why do people have dogs?"

"I don't know. They're good protection?"

"They're unbelievable *friends*. They need their people; and their people need them. How do I know? Because I never had a dog. I had a lot of friends, but not the bare-the-teeth go-for-the-enemy's-throat friendship like between dogs and their people. Only one person, maybe, was almost that close for a while. My friend in North Africa, Socraties Love."

"'Sickrabies'?"

"I shouldn't have told you about that. It was a cruel thing to call him. The other interns and crew members thought he was creepy. But no one deserves meanness, right? He just wanted to be part of things and didn't know how. And he was scared. I found that out later. He was a xerophobe—terrified of deserts. He told everyone he'd come to Africa to learn about working on a film set. Really, it was to face his fear of the desert and try to conquer it. So it was especially cruel that people pushed him away.

"I didn't, though. I made friends with him. Because—you know me—it was something I was good at. He was *that* kind of friend. No one had been decent to him in his whole life, and he needed me. And in a funny way, I needed him, too. It was like we were destined to meet.

"If it hadn't been for you, we might still be hanging out together. But then you came along, and your mom and I got married, and the rest is history—"

. . . after the partitioning of the Corpus Peninsula, Limes enacted a bloody coup in Kanz-_ika. His overthrow of the government was supported by death squads that quelled resistance. Healthy males thirteen and older were forced into military service or sent to Cor-Spamkeer, his "corpse-maker" prison complex. Younger women were trafficked for profit or sent to Cor-Spamkeer, and older ones were "rehomed" to the bordering desert, where they inevitably died. A scant two or three survived and were taken in by the elusive desert dwellers, who have lived there for centuries. ~~They are rumored by some to have extraordinary, even supernatural, abilities.~~ (needs citation)

Curiously, the primary object of Limes's coup appears to have been *not* a power grab but the opportunity to murder, via his death prison, on a scale never before seen in history. To date he has mainly used the increased military personnel to construct Cor-Spamkeer. His goal is to systematically put to death tens of millions. He refers to the continually increasing number of executions as his "More-Tally" (a pun on "mortally") and sees each new death as a step toward his own immortal renown.

—THE INFORMATION HATCH

Chapter 5

THE EVENING AFTER she received Howie's email about vowel shifts and porridge roll and scavenger hunts and impoverished islanders who lived in cardboard houses, Marcia came home from work at the college's Department of High Cultural Endeavors, dreading the wine date with Nina. Earlier, she had read up on Kanz-_ika online and was surprised that nothing Howie had told her about What Island appeared in any of the articles she'd found. Maybe he was right and it hadn't been populated until the '80s—but even so, it ought to merit at least a couple of lines on the Internet somewhere.

She picked up the mail and rolled her stability ball around with her feet for a few minutes to tighten her core. She still had the black hair, cut in a bob now, and long legs, but she had a stubborn porridge roll of her own right below her navel. The stability ball kept it in check.

She ate a leaf of kale spread with Skippy. She put her face to the tap and drank deeply of Round Stone's metallic-tasting water—it saved washing a glass. Nina drank sparkling water from a tumbler and snacked on organic energy knobs that she set out on a hand-forged silver tray, even if she was the only one home and no one was watching. Nina's were those kinds of indulgences, and Nina's was that kind of house. A house with *spaces* and *seating*. Marcia was not opposed to such a home on principle, but she was opposed to the way Nina carried her silver tray of energy knobs around, like she was the doyenne of a castle on a lifestyle show.

Nina's house made Marcia feel bad. Even though Howie's settlement had given them a bit of security, she was still just a single mom with a modest office-support-job income. Howie never complained, but she could tell he felt his difference from the other smart kids—he who'd grown up in a blue-collar neighborhood in the brick-and-siding split-level that she'd bought with the settlement from Silvestro's death.

The settlement had been Howie's, not hers, but he was a minor at the time, so she was able to buy the house for him. The rest of the settlement had provided a reasonable nest egg for his future and, with the trustee's approval, funded Howie's educational and recreational needs: rocket camp, piano lessons, video-game consoles, weekend day trips to local museums and regional fairs in the brown sedan with a picnic lunch and Orson. Whenever Marcia felt the divide between her lifestyle and Nina's, she reminded herself of this: her son hadn't grown up in the fanciest house in Round Stone, but he'd had the opportunities he needed.

Unfortunately, it was precisely because he was accustomed to those "smart kid" extracurriculars that he'd been so eager to apply for the postbac fellowship. If he'd been brought up like a poor dumb kid, he might be safe at home right now, not a short boat ride away from a country governed by a homicidal sociopath intent on executing people. So much for advantages, thought Marcia.

She regretted agreeing to go to Nina's, but she couldn't back out, so she put on tight jeans, a black sweater, a silver chain, and a pair of high clogs. Before she left, she went down to the basement and opened the freezer. Orson was looking a touch shrunken and less fresh, maybe—but so much of him was encased in the red plush throw that it was hard to tell. "I miss you, guy," she said and closed the lid.

She drove to Nina's. She had a handful of fresh-cut flowers from Stowes in a vase from under the sink as a hostess gift. She took it in and set it on Nina's coffee table. Nina gave the flowers a look that slid Marcia into a slot between "widow" and "welfare mother" and carried the flowers to the nook off the kitchen. She put them on the edge of a dry sink there, which could be seen from only two places: right in front of the dry sink or if you were sitting on the toilet in the bathroom across the hall with the door open. "You're so sweet, Marsh," she said as she turned from the flowers and stared at Marcia's clogs. "Do you mind taking those off? You'll make me feel like a munchkin every time you stand up."

Marcia invoked in her brain the little men in suspenders from the movie, shuffling and singing and shoving a giant lollipop at Dorothy. She wished she could do that to Nina and frighten her, but she had no giant lollipop and was required to be gracious, so she stepped out of her clogs. She was still a head taller.

"Come sit with me?" said Nina.

They went into one of the rooms that annoyed Marcia and plopped onto the leather seating across from each other. On the table between them was the same silver tray that Nina used for the energy knobs. Now there was a block of hard white cheese on it, with a cheese knife. There were grapes in a bowl and rice thins and a bottle of wine and two glasses.

"Isn't that the same tray you use for your energy knobs? It's very versatile," said Marcia disingenuously, wanting to make Nina feel good but be secretly unkind in the same breath.

"Energy *bites*," corrected Nina.

"Oh, right." Marcia tried the cheese. It was good, and she was ravenous.

"Manchego," said Nina.

"Delicious. Do they have it at Stowes?"

Nina laughed politely. "It's not Kraft, Marsh. It's imported from Spain." Then she said, "How are you getting along, with Howie in that war zone?"

Before she could respond and explain that he was on an island, not in Kanz-_ika proper, Nina was already on another question. "And what about Orson?"

What could she say? Especially considering that it was Nina, who had no idea what it was like to lose a dog or say goodbye to a son. Orson was dead. Marcia had loved him, been charmed by him, been frustrated by him when he chewed things up or got worms from eating a squirrel carcass that someone tossed in her yard. He'd helped her raise her boy. Given her comfort and been comforted by her. She'd fed him and flea-treated him. He'd pulled on the leash when she walked him, always wanting to say hello to other dogs or sniff things of riveting interest. He'd licked her face. He'd wiggled when he wagged. And now. Now. There *was* no more Orson, only his stiff, frozen body.

"What about him? He's dead," said Marcia dully. "Just dead," she repeated. She thought for a second of her father. He was right; it was better to laugh.

"I know how hard this all must have hit you," Nina said, oozing solicitousness.

Marcia closed her eyes. Before she could open them, she felt Nina's hand on her back. She had come over behind and was patting Marcia's shoulder with creepy little feathery taps. "It's OK, Marsh. It's OK," she murmured in a voice that was high and buttery.

Marcia wanted to scream. She opened her eyes and looked down and pretended to sob. This gave her license to jump up and run to the bathroom for a Kleenex and escape the weird patting.

When she came back, Nina was on the phone with Kirk. It sounded like they were having an argument.

"He's on a big project. It's this Tuition Redefinition," said Nina after she hung up. She offered Marcia more cheese and asked how things were going at the Department of High Cultural Endeavors.

Marcia started to tell her about the new laser printer that was causing a lot of headaches, but Nina circled back to the dog. "About Orson," she said. "Where did you bury him?"

"He's still in the freezer," said Marcia.

"Marsh, Marsh," said Nina, clucking. "It's time to move on. Do you need help? Someone to help bury him?"

"I won't put him in a hole. He's claustrophobic."

"Not anymore," said Nina; but when Marcia started to sob again, she backtracked quickly. "I know what you mean. Cremation, maybe?" She went and retrieved a flyer from the half-moon console in the hallway. "This just came the other day in the mail," she said. "Eternal Paws."

Marcia took the flyer, nodding. She had thought about cremation as a dignified means of disposal with a long, very Eastern and enlightened tradition; plus, you got an urn.

That was how she ended up loading an icy Orson in his stiff red robe into Howie's laundry basket and transporting him to Eternal Paws Pet Resting Place and Cemetery, half an hour away, in a little town called Bixby, across the Sawgash River. The town's economy seemed to be fueled by old animals: there was not much there besides a K-12 rural school, a gas station, and a retired racehorse sanctuary and Eternal Paws. This last occupied several acres of emerald hills dotted with monuments and a sprawling central complex with what she guessed was the crematorium. Marcia drove up and parked.

Toting Orson inside, she felt she had made a mistake bringing him in a laundry basket; Eternal Paws was a nicely appointed facility that demanded something classier.

But then she started to notice that it was, in fact, tacky if you looked past the overall impression of muted, taped music and big furniture. Was that wallpaper or Con-Tact paper above the wainscoting? Hardwood or luxury vinyl planks? Plaster columns? No, plastic! The grief counselor who met her at the door didn't bat an eye at the laundry basket or seem to think it was crass. She gazed upon Orson and whispered reverently, "Oh, my. What a magnificent pup *he* was." She touched the fur of his chin above the red swaddling. "He's quite cold," she remarked.

"I wasn't sure what to do with him at first. So I kept him on ice in the freezer," Marcia admitted with embarrassment.

The woman nodded as if this was quite normal. "Deep freeze? Or refrigerator freezer?"

"Deep freeze. Fortunately, I don't really use it anymore for food, since my son graduated from college and my nest is empty," said Marcia and then wondered why she'd revealed so much to a stranger.

The woman looked into Marcia's eyes and held her gaze with an expression just like the place itself: neither fake nor genuine but oddly unreal. "I'm Lisa," she said. "I'll walk with you through this passage. And I assure you that it won't be as costly as you think." She was forty-sixish and made Marcia think for just a flash of a nun in civilian apparel. Her clothes were business casual, but—this was odd—there were random threads hanging from one of her jacket sleeves, and the material was unusually shiny, like it was not a real jacket but a Halloween costume.

Marcia was having doubts. Still, there were not that many enterprises nearby that dealt with dead pets, and she was here. "How much will it cost to bury him in the cemetery? And how much would cremation be?" Marcia asked pragmatically.

Lisa evinced no judgment as she said, "For a basic burial in an economy casket and flat, engraved marker, the cost for everything, including plot, is $12,634. Of course, we have the option of custom caskets and even a mausoleum. He was a very special animal to you."

"I'm a single mom on a budget," said Marcia.

"Cremation is $84.50. We offer a selection of urns, or you can buy one online."

Marcia considered the phenomenal disparity in price. She almost asked why but was embarrassed to sound cheap. She'd stick with cremation, which had been her original intent, anyway; she'd only been curious about the burial. Orson *would* be claustrophobic in a grave, she felt sure.

"What do the ashes come in if I don't buy an urn?"

"A tasteful resin vessel with his name on a peel-off sticker. And we will take a paw print, too—in case you want to purchase some paw-print fine jewelry. The paw print is free," she emphasized.

"Fine," said Marsha. "I'm not sure about jewelry. Do you keep the print on file?"

"For twenty years," Lisa assured her. "You can order at any time, but the sooner the better, before the price goes up."

"I'll need to think about it," said Marcia. "But I'm sure I can make up my mind in the next twenty years."

Lisa led her to an overstuffed chair with an end table, where Marcia signed a sheaf of paperwork consenting to Orson's cremation, authorizing the paw print, and confirming that she understood the dog was dead.

"Do you want to keep the basket and the wrap?" said Lisa.

"I'd like the basket back. It's my son's. Orson liked the red blanket. He used to shake it around until he wore himself out and then lie down on it and go to sleep. You could just cremate him in it. I think having it around would make me sad."

"It would turn the ashes pink," said Lisa firmly. This seemed to mean no.

"But I don't really need it."

"We can dispose of it respectfully for an eighteen-dollar disposal fee."

"OK. Can you just add that to the cremation charge?" said Marcia, thinking it sounded rather steep for throwing away a blanket. Then Lisa carried the wrapped body into a back room where Marcia assumed there was a cold vault. Soon she returned and made copies of the paperwork. She folded it in thirds to insert in a slim folder, which she handed to Marcia. "You can pay now," she said.

She watched while Marcia wrote out the check. "Did you want to see him one more time?"

"No. I looked at him quite a bit while he was in the freezer," said Marcia. "We had some good one-sided talks."

At this, Lisa smiled and nodded. "We thank you for trusting us with Orson. We will take the very *best* care of him and burn him up with all due ceremony," she said.

Marcia had already handed over the check, and before she could start crying, she quickly grabbed the basket, dropped the folder into it, and was out the door and driving away as fast as possible.

THAT EVENING, STILL feeling quite raw, she tried not to wonder if they'd put Orson in the furnace yet. What would it have mattered if the ashes were pink? Answer: it would not have mattered at all, and Marcia wished she had insisted that he stay in his red wrap.

To keep herself from dwelling on this obsessively, she decided to do some laundry. The empty laundry basket was what made her think of it; jeans and sweats were backing up. She threw some into the basket and topped them off with a towel or two and a bra that hurt her shoulders and that she kept trying to destroy by washing it on the HEAVY-DUTY setting.

At the bottom of the stairs, she turned the corner, but before she made it to the laundry alcove, she dropped the basket in shock.

It could not be.

But it was.

She walked over to the wall and ran her finger through the accumulated cobwebs of the ages and looked at the grounded outlet and then the floor all around for some sign of . . . she wasn't sure what.

Some sign, some bootprint or cigarette butt or empty chew can, some evidential dropped cash-register receipt, some rude note saying this was a joke—*something* that would explain why her freezer was gone.

HOWIE MARCO'S INTERVIEW NOTES
What Island, 9/3/18

Question: What do you know about the Desert People?

Informants 1-4, 15, 22, 27, 33-35, 41-49, 53, 65— unable to answer

Informant 5 (primary school teacher)
"The Desert People are prehistoric. I used to teach a lesson on them. But . . . you know, I've forgotten some of it. They predate the European settlement of the Corpus Peninsula. So, of course, that puts them before Kanz-_ikan independence. The ancient lore ascribes superpowers to them. Omniscience, prophecy, shapeshifting, superhuman sight and hearing. I can't remember the others."

Informant 17 (civil servant)
"The Desert People? They're immortal, aren't they? They're like very powerful ghosts. But they're good. They're good ghosts, but people used to be scared of them. Maybe they were just scared of being removed to the desert. But that would be better than . . . Sorry, I've lost my train of thought."

Informant 31 (child, 8 years)
"They're super old, but not wrinkled. They can fly and read your mind if you lie. They can stretch like rubber."

Informant 12 (occupation unknown)

"They're time-management specialists. Don't ask me what that means. You just said to tell you what I knew. I heard that somewhere."

Informant 61 (CEO, manufacturing)

"I'm trying to remember the name of this group of people that I was telling you about. They were windy sons of bitches. Never shut up. Noisy as fuck. The Desert People rescued them and trained them to fly. I'm new here, so I haven't forgotten everything. But I only knew bits and pieces. People say, 'bits and bobs,' which is snooty, if you ask me. We're not in England. The noise saved those windy sons of bitches' lives—that's what I've heard, but I don't know how, and I can't remember their name. Most of my life, I've worked in bottles. Packaging. I was in pill bottles. Surprising amount of money in pill bottles. The world is full of sick people, you know."

Informant 28 (teen)

"A man and a woman. That's their leaders. They can go anywhere in a flash. We don't talk about them. We're busy, you know, scavenging. They're extremely powerful. They teamed up with those crybabies. The ones who got out. Now they're slaves. If you know what's good for you, stay away from the Desert People. If you're a distraction, they kill you. Watch ooooout!"

Chapter 6

Marcia stood looking at the large rectangle of cleanish concrete where the freezer had sat, and her thoughts went three ways, at 120-degree angles to each other, forming a pattern like the spokes of a steering wheel.

Thought A: Did she need to get more intentional about sweeping the basement? The concrete where the vanished freezer had sat was noticeably cleaner than the floor surrounding and two shades lighter.

Thought B: Call the police?

Thought C: Get the gun.

She immediately dismissed the first idea and toyed with B and C. The Round Stone police were virtuosos at speeding tickets but less skilled at investigation. Only a few days ago, she'd called them because someone had jimmied the back-porch storm door and run amuck in her recycling. It had led to three squad cars arriving and six officers lumbering around the house for a while, hands on weapons, then crouching by the screen door, dragging it open and closed while debating what might have happened to it as they watched the sagging aluminum etch deep gouges in the flooring. Then they kicked through the recycling gingerly with boot tips before announcing that her door was jacked and she ought to get it fixed and get a home security system and quit keeping recycling on her porch. Probably it was a raccoon, they said. But in addition to nearly tearing the door off its hinges—a degree of violence unlikely for a raccoon—whatever or whoever had jimmied the door had also taken a heck of a big piss in the plant saucer on her back step (the officers all walked past it, oblivious) and dropped a Jolly Rancher in it: a colorful cellophane-wrapped sign that she couldn't decipher. *That*, at least, had not been a raccoon. She had not pointed it out to them, having seen how terrible they were at detective work and wanting to get rid of them. Afterward, she'd hosed out the plant saucer and done her best to bend the aluminum back up so the door didn't drag. She'd told no one about this incident: not Nina, not Howie, not even Orson, who was still in the freezer at that time.

So. No police.

But. Yes, the gun. Maybe.

She remembered mentioning it to Howie the day he'd left for What Island. He'd warned her not to shoot anyone, but now it seemed possible that she might. The gun was the Beretta from under the old-fashioneds tray at Homerun Donuts. She had not thought about it in years, but she knew where it was: shoved inside the left of a pair of expensive Langgrønfod boots that Nina had handed down to her after Kirk told her they made her calves look fat. They were indeed wider in the calf than standard boots and did not flatter Nina. But they were useless to Marcia, whose legs were all tendon and lengths of bone; her legs swam in the boots. Nevertheless, the $480 Langgrønfods were a useful hiding place for a gun. Who would look for one there?

She had taken the gun from Homerun sometime in the '90s. It must have been in the '90s because she'd moved to Round Stone not long after birthing Howie, as a condition of his settlement.

This part was strange. She both remembered taking the gun and did not remember it, as though the tape in her mind of having done it had been overwritten with the tape of some other event. Or vice versa. On this semierased tape, someone had told her to take the gun. They'd said, "Do you want to take that gun? You may need it where you're going." "Where am I going?" she'd said, and they'd said, "It's not really a question of where; it's when—" and there the tape ended. The person who was talking to her was not Thomas Cook, though it was Thomas who had taken her for a couple days of practice at a shooting range in the suburbs after he'd hired her. He said he wouldn't be satisfied until she could hit the one shriveled brown dud in a bunch of green grapes. She shot at a square target and got good enough to hit a person in the stomach if they were standing across the counter from her or looming in the Homerun doorway like a yeti.

In her frizzled memory, the person who'd recommended her taking the gun might not even have been a person.

If not a person, then what?

She went upstairs, musing. Why would anyone steal her freezer? It was quite old, and the top had rust freckles from years of basement humidity. In the days of her young motherhood, she'd used it to store breast milk and to stock up on food specials, but in recent times it had sat mostly ignored, holding only old food they'd forgotten about, a few of Howie's boutonnieres from school dances, and the creeping, growing ice amoeba that was the result of her disinterest in defrosting.

She felt forlorn at the triad of disappearances: Howie, Orson, freezer. She wanted to cry.

Instead, she reached for her phone in her pocket and pushed the button to FaceTime Howie.

No answer.

So she messaged him, telling him she was following the news from Kanz-_ika—Jaytie Limes's More-Tally had climbed by another twenty thousand executions in the past two weeks—and missed him and was worried about him. Also, she told him, Orson was ash, or soon to be, and the freezer had been stolen. *Do you think I should load the gun?* she typed and then added, *How long are bullets good for?* She always ended her messages with a string of random emojis—this time a lugubrious gnome face and some cupcakes.

She waited for it to show up as *Delivered*, but no such confirmation appeared. He had turned off his phone. That was not like

Howie, and the small but frantic knot of worry lodged in her gut expanded.

She'd been in the middle of doing laundry when she'd discovered the freezer missing. She remembered now, and she went back down to the basement and threw her clothes into the washer and started it up. At least no one had taken her washer and dryer.

On her way upstairs, her FaceTime signal rang. It was an unfamiliar number, but she accepted the call anyway. From the phone, an echoing tone and a moment of lag, and there he was.

Howie was outside. Behind him, light blue sky and some spidery trees and the edge of a building that looked like a small temple. Marcia had always thought it should be called Big Head Time, not FaceTime, because it made everyone's head the center of the world. Howie's head was quite big relative to the temple.

"Mom," he said in a tinny, lagging voice.

"Howie. Are you OK? I just read about—"

"Mom."

She waited. "Mom, I'm fine. Yes. I can't talk very long. I'm using this borrowed phone and the temple Wi-Fi."

"Is the Wi-Fi spotty?" said Marcia.

"What? No. Maybe. I'm not sure. Yeah, probably. Everything's spotty here. The temple's abandoned." He didn't elaborate.

"Howie," Marcia tried again, "the news—"

"Mom," he interrupted, "I wanted to tell you something pretty cool. I've taught the What Islanders to make mac and cheese. They'd never heard of it, even though they like bland food and from what I've observed don't eat meat.

"Anyway. Mac and cheese. With the vowel shift, it would be 'mek-end-tiize,'—remember, there's no c, so ch sounds are spelled with ti, as in 'fraction'—so I compressed it and took a cue from some of their lexical adaptations and told them it was called 'mekanize.' Get it? Like mechanize. They don't have cheddar here, but they have a soft cheese made from ewe's milk and plant cultures."

"Is it anything like Velveeta?" said Marcia, who disliked the occasional graininess of real cheddar when you melted it.

"No. I *wish*. It's mushy and tastes like grass. But it's the best they've got, so we're making it work. At least they have macaroni. But that's not what they call it. Pasta in any form is 'leather,' and actual leather is just called 'thick brown skin.' If you wanted to ask someone, 'Are those leather boots?' you'd say, 'Er thuz thok broon skon bates?' Remember those Swedish boots Nina gave you?"

With the Beretta in the left one, thought Marcia. "Howie, I'm worried . . ." she began and then stopped and said simply, "I miss you. I'm supposed to go pick up Orson's ashes on Tuesday from Eternal Paws. Nina told me about it."

"Where's that?"

"Bixby. There's a crematorium and a big pet cemetery, too."

"Mom, there's not a pet cemetery *or* a crematorium in Bixby. There's a *people* cemetery and that megachurch—the Pious Body of Formally Doomed Souls."

"Formerly?"

"No, Formally."

"How do you know?"

"I've been there."

"The church?"

"Bixby. But yeah, I've seen the church."

"When?" Marcia's heart was sinking. If it was true . . .

"Last March. For a service project with my fraternity brothers for the retired racehorses," said Howie. "We scooped manure and power-washed horse trailers. Then we oiled tack and then went and checked out the megachurch. Weird place, with that Con-Tact paper and the plastic pillars. They seemed itchy for cash. For a church they did, I mean."

Howie knew what she was thinking. "It's OK, Mom. Pet cremation is probably a side business to help the Pious Body's bottom line. Like I said, they seemed to need money. They asked if we would make a donation, so I gave them six dollars."

"But there was a sign that said ETERNAL—"

He interrupted her to describe his situation. "I can't talk much longer. They watch my every move. Not in a bad way, but there's zero privacy, especially since a lot of people don't have houses, so they just kind of float around. There doesn't seem to be any school, either. There aren't a lot of kids, and I can't figure out if they're homeschooled or what. Shyl won't let me out of her sight for a second. Probably it's because of all the executions in Kanz-_ika. I guess you've been following that?"

"The More-Tally, yes. On NooNews," sighed Marcia.

"Well, don't worry. So far, it's safe here. Shyl acts like a buffer between me and everyone else. Do you know, I'm the first American who has ever been to What Island?"

"Who's Shyl?"

"My guide. But she's more like a bodyguard. She's the one who dragged me out in the middle of nowhere, to this temple. She made me use her phone. Mine doesn't work half the time. I have no idea why. She's connected me with some great informants, though. Since the linguistic study is basically pointless, I'm getting the knack of the folklore methodology. I've been doing a lot of interviews and tapping into the islanders' tacit comprehension of archetypes and motifs and tale types. A collateral discovery is that I think I know what the deal is with porridge roll. None of these people know because their knowledge is subliminal. So they don't know that *I* know, which is a very interesting situation to be in. Kind of like being a mom, right?

"Here's the deal: the chemical combination of island apples, cinnamon, spices, and the flour in the sponge cake keeps them in motion. They need it to keep going. It's like natural speed or something. The people are always super revved and productive, and at the same time, they're really sweet and don't seem to want much. It's an ideal situation: a lot of pumped, totally antimaterialistic people in a state of peaceable near bliss. There's no violence, and they're super-ambitious scavengers. That's why they eat so much porridge roll. The more they eat, the more they're motivated to scavenge. I'm still in the dark about the scavenging, and I might have to go, but I'll know more soon.

"Anyway, Shyl still won't let me try porridge roll. She says it would take *years* for my digestive system to acclimate, so I guess I'll never know what it's like. I'm mostly eating mekanize. The islanders pretend to like it and make it a lot, but then they push it aside and eat more porridge roll.

"You know, I have no idea why they assigned me to come here. Hopefully, I'll still get an MA in *something* for all this research, even though it's research in the wrong field. Shyl says she doesn't know why they sent me here, either, but I think she knows."

He changed the subject. "What's this about the freezer?"

Marcia told him and asked what he thought about her keeping the gun, loaded, by her bed in case of intruders.

"Don't you dare, Mom. You're more likely to shoot yourself." He cited some convincing statistics about accidents with handguns. Then he said, "Shyl's phone's dying. Sorry. Look on the bright side about the freezer: at least Orson wasn't in it. Don't forget to go get him on Tuesday. Also, I know you got a passport, but don't even think about coming here. OK? Promise me?"

"It's hard not to worry," protested Marcia. "And I've got buckets of unused vacation."

"I know. But I'm really busy with this folklore stuff, and you just *can't* come. Shyl says you can't. There's no good transportation to the island."

"This Shyl—is she employed by the fellowship program?"

"I don't know who's paying her," he said, sounding impatient. "She's about your age, but she's nothing like you. She can be pretty badass."

"So can I," said Marcia.

"No, Mom. You're the exact *opposite* of badass, sorry. Wait— Mom? Mom? Oops, I'm about to die."

Then the temple tipped sideways and the phone blurped at her, and Howie froze and shrank and disappeared.

She knew he'd meant the *phone* was dying, but still, she didn't like those last words.

Chapter 7

Monday, at the office, Marcia was distracted. Nina Noisettes kept sending out memos and e-vites regarding a required webinar on the impact of the upcoming Tuition Redefinition. There was nothing in her NooNews feed about Kanz-_ika or the More-Tally, but it didn't make her feel better. Howie had messaged her again, telling her not to worry, that he was still trying to learn about the What Islanders' scavenging habits, but Shyl's protectiveness was making it hard to do independent research. Marcia messaged back, saying she was sorry he felt restricted. But in truth, she was quite happy that he had a vigilant guide looking out for him.

Fortunately, or unfortunately, it was Fire Preparedness Week at Holliday College. Today they were testing the alarms in the Department of High Cultural Endeavors. Marcia had lain awake the night before, agonizing about Howie, and about Orson's cremains, and now she would have been falling asleep but for the alarms that blasted, foghorn-like, at unpredictable moments throughout the day. In her puzzlement about the Eternal Paws thing, she recalled that the "crematory" had featured a number of small statues and candles and other religious goods, which Lisa had explained away with the comment "The loss of a companion animal is an event of great spiritual magnitude, you know."

Also, the more she'd thought about the broken porch door and piss-filled plant saucer, the more obvious it was that someone had been hanging around her house looking for something. The piss in the saucer smacked of a certain degree of fastidiousness and a long stakeout. Whoever her stalker or creeper or searcher was, it was a man, or a woman who could squat with phenomenal aim, and they'd hung around so long they had to go, and for some reason, they chose the saucer rather than the ground. The

Jolly Rancher? Dropped accidentally—and who would retrieve a piece of candy once afloat on the yellow tide? Someone had hoped to find something on her porch or in her basement. The jimmied door and stolen freezer seemed like they could be connected. It had taken her long, sleepless hours to arrive at this conclusion—and now she was exhausted, and the fire alarms kept jolting her awake.

So at first she didn't realize it was her phone beeping—she thought it was another alarm. Then she understood that it was a text.

She picked up her phone. The message was from an unknown number—not the same one Howie had called from, though; this one was local. She opened it anyway.

> Thank you for trusting us with ORSON. We took great delight in preparing his mortal remains for you, and they are now on their way to your place of employment in a convenient temporary resin vessel. His name has been placed in our Eternal Paws registry and in a drawing for a permanent brass urn with a granite caddy. Tap this link for ORSON's delivery details: **2XPX25JGU991Z**

Marcia threw down the phone and burst into tears. The department had a small staff, and usually Marcia worked with one other woman and the two work-study students, but today was not a usual day. There had been some IT issues, so Jerome, the IT guy, was there, and one of Kirk's emissaries from the Finance Office, grilling them about their accounting, and all the maintenance and security staff involved in the alarm testing. Plus the two students. They all stared at Marcia.

Jerome picked up her phone and handed it to her, commending her for having a Phone Mummy. "No cracked screen," he said. "Those Phone Mummies do the job."

Marcia showed him the text.

"Hmm," he said. "Do you know this sender?"

"No."

"Never tap a hyperlink from an unfamiliar number."

"I didn't."

"I can check and see if it's safe," he said. "Who's Orson?"

"Her dog," said the work-study students.

"That's a new one: delivering pet remains," Jerome said. He took the phone again and ran it through some paces and announced that the link was safe. "Tap it?" he said to Marcia.

She shook her head, which he took to mean yes. TAP.

He handed the phone to Marcia. She expected to see an estimated delivery time, like you would with UPS, but the link took her to a livestream of a blue Ford Focus driving down the highway, racing past what Marcia believed were the few miles of flat, infertile land between Bixby and Round Stone. Yes, now it was on the Sawgash River bridge, jolting over the bridge floor. She couldn't tell who was driving or how the video was being shot. A GoPro? The driver had a ponytail. Male? Female? How was this video being streamed, and who was shooting it? It zoomed in now to a magnetic DoorDash sign on the side of the car. You could buy those on the Internet. Anyone could put one on their car.

Jerome and the work-study students were peering over her shoulder. "I didn't know they had DoorDash in Round Stone," said Jerome. "Isn't that just for food?"

"DoorAsh," joked one of the work-study students.

"Hey," said Jerome. "This is her *dog*."

Now the shot shifted to the car's gray cloth interior. How could the camera be both inside and outside the car? The interior was dirty. There were empty paper grocery bags on the back seat, folded flat, and a stapler and a half-full Coke bottle. And the "temporary resin vessel," a rectangular box like a tall Band-Aid container. The camera stayed on the resin vessel for a few seconds, then panned to the back of the driver's head, and then settled on the low brown fields burning by and stayed there.

It had been a long day already, on not enough sleep. It had started much earlier, with Marcia's phone call to Nina at seven fifteen that morning, as she was getting ready for work.

"Marsh! What's wrong? Do you have a flat tire again? Kirk can give you a ride."

"I don't need a ride," Marcia had said. "Did you know that Eternal Paws isn't a real thing? There is no Eternal Paws. It's not in the directory, and it's not online anywhere. I called the number on the flyer and took Orson there, and they acted like they were going to cremate him and took my money, but it's not a pet crematory—it's a church. What did they do with Orson? Throw him in the church dumpster?"

"Oh, Marsh! I'm so sorry. You know, I wondered. It seemed a little off when I read that flyer. You never can tell about things that just get tucked in your door. But we don't have a dog, so I guess I was naive. I'm sure they didn't throw him away. They're probably just cremating pets on the cheap to make ends meet."

"That's what Howie said."

"You talked to Howie? Is he all right? He's got a point about the church trying to make money. With the culture wars and the last gasp of the religious right, no one tithes except old people, and they're all on Social Security, so it can't amount to much. Churches have to generate revenue somehow. And, I mean, *Bixby*. Not exactly thriving."

"Nina! Stop blabbering," Marcia had said sharply.

"Sorry. Sorry. It's my job stress these days; it's giving me hives, there's so much pressure. But, you know, I'm sure they really did cremate Orson. They must have a furnace, at least. Or a firepit."

"*A firepit?* Nina, I hate you!"

"Marcia, you don't. It'll be fine, and you'll have such fun picking out his urn. I saw one that was so clever, where the little dog on the urn had a halo and wings—"

"Nina! You're nuts. Just like your name," Marcia had said, and she'd hung up in frustration. She had driven to work thinking for the millionth time about the strange clause in Howie's settlement from the wrongful-death suit over Silvestro's demise. It had mystified her then, and still did: for Howie to receive the distributions from the trust, Marcia had had to agree that she and Howie would reside in Round Stone until he was twenty-one. He could take up temporary residence elsewhere (e.g., his fellowship on What Island). But his permanent residence, and hers, had to be in Round Stone. And so there was no escaping Nina, who had done a night-school MBA and come to Round Stone only a few years after Marcia arrived, having coincidentally applied for, and landed, an excellent job with Holliday College. She'd married Kirk, and they'd stayed, working their way up their respective career ladders and both surpassing Marcia, who had never found much use for her history BA/business minor and couldn't go to graduate school because she was stuck in Round Stone with Howie.

Later that morning, in between alarm blasts, flowers had arrived at Marcia's office from Nina with a greeting card showing a pouty-faced little girl that said, *I'm so sad that you're mad. Let's be friends again! i'm sorry!*

Ha, Marcia had thought. Never. We have never been that, and never will be.

And then the fire alarms started up again, and then she got the text and watched the video of the blue Focus bringing Orson's ashes closer by the minute.

The ashes arrived just as she was locking up. The ponytailed courier came bounding up the stairs with one of the grocery bags Marcia had seen in the live video. The top was folded over and heavily stapled. Written on the side in black marker were her name and office number.

The courier was a woman. Not young, but younger than the lines in her face made her appear. She looked Marcia in the eye and said, "I'm sorry about your dog. Be careful of the resin vessel. These things aren't very sturdy. You should probably get a real urn soon." She stood waiting for a second until Marcia caught on and tipped her. Then she loped away, and Marcia finished locking all the office doors and went slowly down the stairs and drove home with the paper bag on the passenger seat. She wished she could talk to Orson, as she had when he was in her freezer. She would tell him about Howie and how the ever-increasing death toll in Kanz-_ika, Limes's More-Tally, sometimes caused her to wake in a cold sweat, having dreamed of bodies in freezers and trunks and her son wandering somewhere, unreachable, with pockets of applesauce.

But something was different about Orson in his new state. She thought at first it was just that she couldn't see him—couldn't even see the resin vessel, because it was in the bag—but as she drove, a strange feeling came over her. And over the car, too. There was something new here. An aura. A whisper of newness and adventure that had not been characteristic of her relationship with Orson. And deep mourning at the same time. Maybe Orson was mourning the loss of his dog life but looking forward to the adventure of being a dog spirit. But she knew what Howie would say to that, and he would be right—it was pure sentimentality, and therefore pointless.

Yet the aura persisted. It was emanating from the bag full of ashes. Something strange was here. Something full of mysterious promise.

She was glad she'd called Nina and chewed her out this morning. She needed to do things like that more often. The bag of ashes seemed to be confirming this. Then suddenly she felt grief and longing pouring out of it. Then it was back to the positive. A bag of ashes could not talk to you, but this bag was planting words in her head. *You did the right thing by calling out Nina, it said. You did right by Orson and Howie. You were right to take the job at Homerun Donuts, and you were a good Donut-Dispensing Associate for two and a half years. You might have screwed up mildly when you hooked up with Silvestro. But look—you got Howie out of it, and you love him. You've always done the right thing, Marcia Farrar. You're Dale Farrar's daughter, and stoner-loser or not, he knew more about dog cartoons than anyone and was the kindest, friendliest soul on the planet. And he always did the right thing, too.*

There was never any doubt in my mind that I was destined for fame. Glory, even. But of what sort? That was the question. My father could have his airline holdings, and I'd gladly enjoy the fruits of his boring interests, but business was not for me. I wanted to amass something more original than a pile of money stacked on wings and fuselages. Something that would get me noticed. Leave a mark. Something that would live on, cement my name in history. Something extreme yet inevitable. Something that skated on the edge.

They say the children of the superrich are psychologically stunted. Experts report that we have low self-esteem. We're ten times more likely to be addicts. We're depressed. Delinquent. We're narcissists with the frustration levels of infants. Devoid of empathy. Full of entitlement. I can't deny any of this. I understand why, behind my back, the junior assistants called me names and then the whole set crew started doing it. But Dale Farrar did not. Blessed are the truly friendly souls. Blessed and rare. He was one.

"Decent." An unassuming little word. No one yearns desperately to have it said of them. No one fights with everything they've got to be decent. Or maybe they do, and I've missed the whole point. Anyway, Dale was decent, and he never called me anything but Socraties. Or "Soc" for short. Which is why, later, I decided to preserve that name. Sanctify it and retire it from use and take another. I thought it would help me stay true to both self and ambition. It's all about self and ambition, isn't it? Not decency (poor Dale). You can't contest that.

—MEMOIRS OF SOCRATIES LOVE

Chapter 8

On the afternoon of the day Marcia met Thomas Cook, she left things up in the air about a job at Homerun Donuts and trotted briskly back to the warehouse for her personal finance seminar. They were learning about health insurance, and the students had been given a set of worksheets detailing the assorted medical issues, some calamitous and some minor, plaguing a man named Cyrus Virus. Unhealthy and accident-prone, Cyrus, beginning at age thirty-one, had a comprehensive medical insurance policy with a $500 annual deductible and an 80/20 coinsurance clause. At thirty-two, he'd fallen off a boat and sustained a concussion. At thirty-three, he'd had his stomach pumped after eating tainted circus food. The next year, he'd undergone several cosmetic procedures, including a port-wine-stain removal and a nose job. He'd had a lung transplant at thirty-five and been diagnosed with pernicious chronic idiopathic gout that same year. He struggled to pay his bills because some of them were large, and they came on like a tidal wave, and his pay was middling; he worked as a box-office manager for a traveling circus (the source of the tainted food). He had not gone gently into debt, however. Cyrus was scrappy and indefatigable; he took pleasure in fighting the insurance companies.

Marcia listened to the class joke about Cyrus's name and job and misfortunes as they filled out the worksheet and figured out how much he owed in medical bills and what he could do about it. She was thinking of her mother's death from anesthesia during ankle surgery. On the inside of her wrist was Thomas's phone number, which he'd written in blue ink with a Bic.

"Why don't you just give me a business card?" she'd said.

He shook his head while she perused his rubble-strewn face, unable to decide whether he was handsome underneath the acne or whether he was homely but the acne created the illusion that he might not be.

"You could lose a business card. Or ignore it," Thomas said. "You can't ignore your arm. I am determined to have you as the next Homerun Donuts Donut-Dispensing Associate. Seriously. Determined."

"OK," she said noncommittally. She had to give it some thought. Heading back to the college, she ruminated on the question as the wind tossed her hair around and bit the back of her neck. She wondered what her parents would have thought of her working in a donut shop with a loaded gun under the old-fashioneds. Dale would probably have been cool with it; it was a job he would have enjoyed himself, and he definitely would have appreciated the menace of the gun, which would have reminded him of a cartoon, though never in a million years would he have shot anyone. Susan might have been ambivalent, wanting more for Marcia—along with safety, of course—and at the same time happy that she was earning money. Her mother had been back in school at the time of her death, working on a graphic design degree. Sad irony: she should have settled for premature mobility issues and/or less invasive treatments and not had the surgery for her ankle arthritis. Presumably, you could lay out brochures with a cane or a walker. You didn't need to be ambulatory to set type and create logos. Marcia wished her mother had not died and that she'd never had to live with the Noisetteses; it was the nadir of her life. She remembered Mrs. Noisettes's creepy-weird way of coming into her room in the night and just standing there, listening to her breathe, while Marcia pretended to be asleep. There was never any acknowledgment of this, and Marcia assumed she was afraid that her foster daughter might steal things in the night so was keeping an eye on her. Only much later did it cross her mind that Mrs. Noisettes might have seen something in her that she knew was missing in her own daughter. This would explain her persistent ambivalence about Marcia.

The class was filling out the part of the worksheet about Cyrus Virus's lung transplant.

"My mom died during ankle surgery," Marcia said out loud.

She felt grief swell inside her. The corners of her eyes got wet, but she was a stoic. Reading Cyrus Virus's case history—seeing how he'd sometimes been talked into unnecessary procedures not covered by insurance and how he'd negotiated the billing mess and fought back—she realized her mother had been snowed. Misled to the gain of some already rich orthopedic surgeon. She'd been persuaded to embark on an ill-advised procedure, then left dead on the table.

Grief turned to rage. Her incipient tears dried, and fury bloomed in her. Her mother hadn't needed to die! She saw this now—and she was mad. As a child, she'd accepted Susan's death and the subsequent legal arrangement by which she became ward of the Noisettes and had to wear the clearance dresses that Nina's mom bought for her and pretended were as expensive and pretty as Nina's (the humiliation of a steel-colored tent dress with puff sleeves haunted her). Dale had been dead even longer, of course, and experience had showed Marcia that she was the kind of girl this sort of thing happened to—a girl whose family of origin had been so impecuniously adrift that the only possible outcomes were disaster and/or death.

All these thoughts went on inside her, undetectable, in the seconds after her pronouncement. Then she said it again, much louder. "My mother died DURING ANKLE SURGERY."

It was a small class of mostly first-year students, still unsure of what they were doing. So no one reacted when Marcia spoke up. Except for her personal finance professor, a short-legged man who favored a Cubs cap that he took off when he entered the classroom and slapped back on his head every day when class ended.

He looked at her hard. After a second he said, "I'm sorry for your loss, Marcia," and went back to talking about Cyrus Virus.

"It didn't happen recently. It was a long time ago," she interrupted.

The professor said, "I'm sure ankle medicine has made great strides since—"

The unintentional pun was too much. Marcia slammed her hand down on her desk and shouted, "You don't understand. She didn't *have* to die!" She wanted to jump up and run out of the room.

Not even this emotional display could nudge the class out of its hesitance, though a few people looked nervously around.

"I'm very sorry," repeated the professor. "If it's troubling you, you should make an appointment with the counseling service." (Marcia had not been aware there was one.) "Now, where were we?"

"Cyrus Circus Guy. Poison corn dogs," muttered Marcia. "Port-wine stains. Collection agencies."

The professor looked her in the eye for a long moment. "Right."

She had the feeling, suddenly, that things weren't quite what she'd imagined.

That evening, back in her room, she plugged in her hot pot and listened to it clink gently, then roar to a violent boil. She sprinkled a packet of Lipton soup mix in a bowl. Lipton: tea bags, soup mix. A whole company was devoted to dried shreds of stuff you soaked in hot water and then ate or drank. It seemed ridiculous, suddenly. But not as ridiculous as all that had happened to her today: talking back to *two* different faculty members and being offered a job in a donut shop with a gun in the pastry case.

Soup was *reconstituted*, though. Tea was an infusion. There was a difference, and for just a second, this idea of reconstitution seemed like something she should take note of.

She was too hungry to think about it. She blew on her soup and considered calling Thomas. She applied the formulas they'd been learning in the investment part of her class to the money she might earn at Homerun Donuts. He hadn't said how much he'd pay her. She thought maybe five-fifty?

She drank the dregs of her soup and wiped the bowl and spoon with the baby wipes she kept for dishwashing and put the dishes back on her dorm-issue desk hutch. She went to the phone and consulted her wrist for Thomas's number.

It wasn't there.

She stared at her white skin and blue veins. No sign of a number having been written on her wrist. Not even the ghost of a shadow of blue ink. It had been there in class; she knew because she'd kept glancing at it. Now there was only a long, thin scratch. Not deep or bloody but red. Fresh.

She was out of soup, or she would have made some more. Stress had a way of making one hungry. Surely Homerun Donuts was in the Yellow Pages. She looked at her wrist again and fingered the scratch.

When she opened her door to go borrow a phone book from one of the girls down the hall, Thomas Cook was standing there. She had the impression he'd been out there a few minutes, listening. He'd taken a shower and didn't smell like donuts. He'd put some glistening topical ointment on his acne bumps, and they gleamed like decorative studs.

"Hi," he said. "Did you lose my phone number?"

"No," she lied. "I haven't made up my mind."

He grabbed her wrist before she could stop him. Turned it over. "Cat scratch you?"

"I don't have a cat. Pets aren't allowed in the dorm," she said. "I've never had a pet in my life. My dad was allergic. I only know about cartoon dogs."

"Shhhh!" he said urgently. "You're a liar."

He pushed his way into her room, dragging her along, and slammed the door. She should have been alarmed, but despite his sudden appearance and aggressiveness and her own earlier reservations, she had a palpable vibe now of *trustworthy*.

"I brought dinner." He had a bag of Greek food. The Noisetteses ate only baked meat and frozen vegetables. On Dale and Susan's tight budget, they'd eaten a lot of Spam and cornflakes. Marcia had grown up on this limited diet and had never had a gyro before. At college she mostly ate soup or noodles, with red apples for roughage.

"What's this sauce on it?"

"Cucumbers. Other stuff. I'm not sure."

"It's delicious," she said. She sat on her orange beanbag chair and began devouring the gyro Thomas handed her. He sat a foot away on the floor pillow that she liked to lie on to do homework; he ate his own food, which included a salad.

"What's that white stuff?"

"Feta." He extended his plastic fork, and she leaned forward and took a bite, and they looked into each other's eyes. She sensed that he was interested in her but could not tell in what way. She'd never had a boyfriend because men her age were scared of her height and put off by the aura of orphan she exuded.

But she was hungry more than anything and went back to reclining in the chair and finished the gyro, intermittently wiping her fingers on the orange vinyl.

Thomas shook his head. "You eat like an animal."

"So?"

"It's not very polite."

"Nina Noisettes can be polite. I'm just the poor stepkid."

He laughed at this. "Yeah," he said. "I can see how you might feel that way." Then he said, seriously, "Look. You don't have a choice about this, Marcia. There are a few things in life that aren't yours to decide. And this is one. You're coming to work for me. You can't ask me why. You can't say no. You can't quit once you start. You WILL do this. It's one of the most important choices you'll ever make. But it's not really a choice. To say no would be a mistake."

He got up and got a baby wipe and wiped off her chair where she'd rubbed cucumber sauce on it. "Look at your wrist," he commanded gently.

She turned over her left hand, the one farthest from him.

"*Other* wrist."

She turned it over. There was no sign of a scratch. And there was his number, in bold blue ink.

"How—?" she said.

"Don't worry about it. It's complicated," he said. "It will be complicated. Right now, it's simple: I'll pay you five-fifty and all the coffee, milk, and soft drinks you want. And donuts, but I don't advise it; they're not good for you. You start tomorrow. Right after your last class. You'll need to wear this." He tossed her a White Sox cap that had been tucked in his jacket. It made her think of her personal finance teacher and his Cubs hat.

"Do I have health insurance?"

"Are you kidding? You're just part-time," he said. "And you've got student insurance or something, right?"

"The Noisetteses pay for my insurance," she said. "I'd like to cut that cord."

"You will," he said. "But it's going to be quite a while yet. Although technically, it's possible that you already have." He moved toward the door to leave.

Then he was gone.

"I have a job," Marcia said aloud. "I'm a Homerun Donuts Donut-Dispensing Associate." She checked the hot pot to make sure it was unplugged. She looked at the floor pillow with Thomas's dent in it. She lay down in the dent, which was still warm, and put the cap on. It was tight, so she took it off and moved the snapback adjuster two bumps. Then it fit perfectly.

Chapter 9

As SHE WAS driving home with the grocery bag of Orson's ashes on the passenger front seat, feeling comforted by the wonderful new aura that emanated from the bag, Marcia thought about Thomas Cook. In a back room of her mind, she still thought about him, though she would probably never see him again. She had not been sure then, and she still wasn't sure, how she'd felt about him. The terms of Howie's financial settlement had forced her to move hastily to Round Stone and prohibited her from having any contact with the management or employees of Homerun Donuts. So she'd never know how Thomas had found her at her warehouse dorm when he'd had no idea where she lived. Or how he knew she liked gyros when she hadn't known it herself, or how he could claim that she'd one day be unyoked from the Noisetteses (but that *still* hadn't happened). She'd wanted to ask him all these things during the time she worked for Homerun, but every time she worked up her nerve, he headed her off by reminding her—before she even could ask—that it was not her job to ask questions; it was her job to dispense donuts.

She'd never forget the first time she'd seen him, mixing lavender-colored batter in the Homerun kitchen. So upright and deliberate, so controlled and expert with the mixer. Or the second time, when she opened the door of her dorm room, and there he was, gyros in hand. She still had the White Sox cap he'd given her. She'd worn it the whole while she worked for him. And kept it, and sometimes, when Howie was little, put it on Orson to make him laugh. Later, Howie used it one year as part of a Halloween costume. She knew exactly where it was, on a peg at the back of her closet. If she looked at the cap, it would make her melancholy.

She was stopped at a red light when her cell rang.

It was *Nina Nuts.*

"Marsh. Are you driving?" Nina said. Then, without waiting for a reply, "So they *delivered* the ashes? Right to your office?"

"How do you know about that?" Marcia asked suspiciously.

"That gossip Jerome in IT." Nina giggled. "I ran into him in the parking garage. I think he likes me."

"You're forty-four and married. Jerome is twenty-eight," Marcia said in her head to Nina.

"Marsh? Marsh? What are you thinking?" said Nina. "You're thinking about *him*, aren't you?"

Him who? Jerome? Nina couldn't possibly know about Thomas.

"Have you looked at him?"

"Looked at who?" Marcia was confused.

"The dog. Orson."

"There's nothing to look at. It's just a box, Nina."

"I know, I know," Nina murmured sympathetically. "If you like, I could come over and we could drink some wine and shop on the Internet for an urn."

"I would not like that," said Marcia. "Plus, he's in a drawing for a permanent brass urn."

"No one ever wins those drawings. I don't think they're even real."

"I might sprinkle him, then. Or I can get the ashes made into jewelry. For Christmas presents."

"Ewww!"

"Oh. Ha-ha, right," Marcia agreed. "Who would wear dog-ash jewelry? Guess we're back to that brass-urn drawing, then. Cross your fingers for me."

"*Can* I stop by tonight? To make sure you're OK and all?"

"No," said Marcia. "Nina, I really need to commune with Orson's flaky bits for a while and get comfortable with his new condition before I can have guests. Otherwise, I can't guarantee anything."

Having made this pronouncement, she hung up.

At home, she put the bag with Orson's vessel on the couch. The aura surrounding the grocery bag had changed from the initial wonderful optimism and reassurance it conveyed to a mildly supercilious disdain.

Marcia rolled her stability ball and tried to pretend her abs were sculpted marble. This was patently not the case, and it also didn't sit well with the bag, which did not like her exercising, she could tell. She put the ball away and turned on some music to (hopefully) placate it and got a bagel out of the freezer and walked around the house, nervously breaking off frozen chunks of bagel and sucking on them. She liked how the bagel thawed and got gummy in her mouth.

From the front of the house, the ashes began to throw off a very strong negative tone.

Marcia went into the living room and stood staring at the bag. WHAT DO YOU WANT? WHAT DO YOU WANT? she thought at it. She concentrated on this communication hard, and harder, and wondered if it was going anywhere.

FISH, came the answer—a dart shot directly into her brain.

She didn't understand this. Orson had not been allowed fish because of the dangerous bones. I NEVER FED YOU FISH, she thought at the bag.

YOU NEVER FED ME ANYTHING, the bag exuded.

Marcia was not going to get into a dispute with a grocery bag of Orson's ashes by calling it a liar; this was only a few steps from the psych ward. Yet she didn't feel delusional. She felt frustrated. Of course she had fed Orson. She'd fed him grain-free kibble and more table scraps than she should have and jerky-like treats and, on the most special occasions, steak. She might never have guessed how much he liked steak but for Kirk sending her home from one of their barbecues with a literal "doggy bag" of grilled beef for Orson. Nina had been so pissed about the doggy bag that

Marcia had rushed right home and fed it all to Orson on the spot to spite her.

She swallowed the bite of bagel lingering in her mouth and put the remainder of the frozen bagel on the coffee table while she carefully unfastened the dozen staples and opened the bag.

There was the resin vessel. Pasty white, eight inches tall. So clearly temporary—but then, so had been Orson, furry and warm though he was.

Now that the vessel was directly in front of her, there was suddenly no more aura—the essence of Orson, with his strange new moods, had gone dark. There was a cast paw print in the bag, too. Marcia got it out and looked at it quickly, then put paw print and vessel on one of the built-in living room shelves that had been a selling feature of the house, along with the hardwood floors (scuffed now from years of Howie and Orson). She'd thought Orson's paws were bigger than that—but so much of him had been fur, obscuring what he really was: a compact mutt in a big-dog coat.

She set the vessel so the gold sticker that said *Orson Farrar* faced outward.

What if Silvestro had lived? She would have had child support, even if they'd never married. Together with her income, it would have been enough. There would have been no wrongful-death settlement and thus no relocation to Round Stone. No forced continuation of her relationship with Nina. Maybe—it was too much to imagine—a chance to choose her own future.

Marcia looked at the vessel on the shelf. "I miss you," she said aloud. Not knowing if she meant Orson or Howie, whose disquieting situation on What Island was never far from her worries, or maybe even her father, with his cartoon humor and goodwill at every juncture.

For just a second, there was a hint of empathy from the vessel.

It had been a long, stressful day, and she decided to take a bath. She ran the tub. She had always preferred baths to showers. Her mind drifted but inevitably circled back to Howie and the unlikely fact of his being recruited for a linguistic fellowship and then sent to a different place, not Kanz-_ika but an island where there was no use for his skills. She remembered that he still hadn't told her about the islanders' scavenging. She would ask him when they talked again. She'd been doing more reading online, and none of it made her feel any better about him being where he was. The Cor-Spamkeer More-Tally, which just a few weeks ago had been half a million, had risen to 621,502 the last time she'd seen a headline about it.

The water cooled more, and she ran more hot. Again. And soon she was entirely submerged. Only her head, on the spa pillow, and her toes poked out.

She was very tired. Her eyes started to close. . . .

Moments later, she was alert again. The bathroom door was rattling, and there was a mild swaying, and then the sound of breakage from the front of the house.

Round Stone was a center of seismic activity; it sat on a geological lazy Susan (this was how it had been explained to Marcia, though it might not have been accurate). Lately there'd been hints that a new quake was coming, and Nina kept reminding Marcia to batten down the glassware. But Marcia ignored her because most of her dishes were unbreakable ware she'd bought when Howie was young and had never replaced.

Then she remembered the resin vessel, whose fragility the delivery woman had warned her about.

She leaped out of the tub and ran to the living room, cold bathwater streaming off her. A few feet from the coffee table, she halted and stood, naked and aghast. Most of Orson's ashes were in a pile at the foot of the shelf, with chunks of white resin strewn among them; but in the crash, a spray of ash had flown everywhere. Afraid to take another step, she shivered and dripped tepid bathwater in the fine dust, a grit of ash under her feet.

Far, far away, in the bathroom, her cell rang: Nina, checking up on Marcia and her breakables. She ignored it and looked at the mess, dismayed. There was the cast paw print, chipped but intact. A shard of the vessel lay at her feet. It was the piece with the label on it. She picked it up and saw that the gold label had been pasted over another.

She pulled. Off it came, and underneath, she found another label that said, *Mr. Whiskey Martin.*

"They couldn't even put you in a new vessel. No wonder it broke," she said angrily to the now dispersed Orson. "You got a *used* one." She should have collapsed in tears, but her feelings were frozen.

She certainly had no heart to sweep Orson up now. She set the chip of resin on the coffee table, then went for a towel. It was all she could do to dry the floor where she'd dripped, and some ashes got on the towel, and she threw it down, shaking. What could she do with an ashy towel? Run it through the washer and send a part of Orson into the Round Stone sewer system?

What could anyone do in this situation except try to escape? So she put on some sweats and went to bed. Before she did, though, she found the White Sox cap at the back of her closet.

She wore it all night.

In the hazy early morning came an urgent need to pee, accompanied by a roaring sound. A motor. A train engine. Regular and soothing though intermittent. Yet persistent. Someone, somewhere, was sawing or drilling or mowing or doing something else inconsiderate at this hour of the morning. Before Marcia could come fully awake to look around for the source of the motor noise, it stopped. A light thump. Pattering.

Orson's ghost?

Her grief, making her crazy.

She rolled out of bed and went to pee. Washing her hands, she looked in the mirror. She was ragged but there. She'd survived the night, and there had not been any more earthquakes, at least.

She still had the cap on. Once Thomas had told her that she had a way of making even a ball cap look unorthodox. She wanted to know if that was an insult, but he said amiably, "It's not your job to ask questions; it's your job to dispense donuts, Marcia."

Before work, she'd have to sweep up Orson and put him in something. She couldn't leave him spread all over the place all day. What if ants got in him?

She put a robe on over her sweats. In the kitchen, she started a cup of dark roast brewing and rallied herself as she went to the cleaning closet for the broom and dustpan. She wiped off the dustpan so Orson's ash might remain pure. Which was silly because it would get mixed with floor dirt, but one had to try, at least.

It was weird, but she had a feeling that someone else was in the house.

She found a funnel to pour the ashes into a vase she'd always liked and carried broom, dustpan, funnel, and vase into the living room.

And stopped dead, because the floor was now entirely clear of ash, although crumbly pieces of the vessel were still there, randomly scattered, where the earthquake had sent them flying.

Crouched on the coffee table was a cat. It was chomping on the last bite of bagel she'd left there the night before and making the noise she'd heard in the bedroom on awakening. *Purring.* A gray cat with white paws and a gray tail that lashed wildly as it ate.

Then it heard her and stopped. Turned and looked, licking around its mouth. The whiskers were very long. The word *infinity* came to mind—but they weren't infinite. They ended in the usual place, even while they gave the impression of something much, much longer than the usual whisker.

The cat stared at her. Its vertical pupils, two black-pointed ovals, bisected two rounds of green. It was speaking to her in a thought-voice like the grocery sack's, but not quite the same. This was more like actual speaking, even though the cat's mouth didn't move.

"This stuff is better than I thought it would be. But it's *not* salmon," the cat said.

"What are you?"

"A cat," the cat said. "Mr. Whiskers to you."

"The label on the resin vessel said Mr. Whiskey," Marcia recalled.

"Mr. Whiskey, then. Whatever."

"What is going on?" Marcia said, increasingly distressed. "Where are Orson's ashes?"

"No clue," the cat responded. "Who's Orson?"

"My dog."

"Are you sure he was cremated?"

"Of course. His ashes were in the resin vessel."

"Those were my ashes, not a dog's. Did you actually see him incinerated?"

"Of course not!" Marcia shouted, quite upset now. "Why are you talking when you're a cat? How are they your ashes?"

"I'm talking because you're asking me questions. Though I'm pretty sure you've been told that asking questions is not your job." The cat's tone was overweening. "And they're not my ashes anymore. They *were* my ashes. But for some reason, I seem to have been reconstituted."

The speed and precision of executions at Cor-Spamkeer have elevated it in the cultural vocabulary to the status of a collective nightmare. Originally intended to house a maximum of 3,000, Cor-Spamkeer now has a maintenance population of over triple that number. Inside sources report that the daily "More-Tally" from executions, some by simple deprivation, most by mechanical means, totals in the hundreds and sometimes reaches a thousand or more. This confirms that there is a steady influx of new prisoners.

Unlike other famous genocidal strongmen, Limes doesn't necessarily target political rivals or dissidents, though he's quite happy to kill them. His famous mantra, "I'm in the numbers game," appears to be true. To be arrested and killed in Cor-Spamkeer, all one has to do is be alive and in the wrong place at the wrong time. In this way, his regime is exceedingly just: death under Limes is doled out equally to all ages, races, occupations, social classes, orientations, and sexes. Guards and administrators keep meticulous "More-Tally" stats, since he wants to know exactly how many have died and how efficiently. Once a week, an aide reads the names of the week's dead to him while he has his calluses buffed. On holidays, he celebrates by ordering spontaneous random executions of his own prison staff, just for ironic fun.

—THE INFORMATION HATCH

Chapter 10

Marcia was casting about for sense amid this bizarre turn—Orson's ashes were not Orson's and apparently belonged to an opinionated fish-loving cat that had risen from them, phoenix-like, and was talking to her—thought-speaking—when her phone made the squishy bloop-blopp sound that signaled a FaceTime call. Only one person would be FaceTiming her. She dug around frantically in her sweats and found her phone. Once again, it was the unknown number, but she knew who it was and accepted.

Howie appeared at the same sketchy-looking temple as before. He looked upset, which made her heart lunge from the gate and start pounding the track. She sat down abruptly on the couch.

"Mom. Mom," he said. "Mom."

"Howie? Are you OK?"

"Mom." He was sooty, which was also worrisome.

"What's wrong? What's that black stuff on you?"

"Mom," he said. "They're What Island nets. *Gnats*, sorry. They're thick around here. Totally harmless." He waved his hand, and the soot rose off his cheeks and neck to shuffle itself in midair and settle again. His skin was gently tanned, she saw when they lifted.

"Promise you won't try to come here if I ask you something."

Marcia's heart sank. She was still thinking about Cor-Spamkeer and the latest tally. She started to say that if he was in trouble, she couldn't promise anything. But a voice cut in like interference. "Promise. The kid knows what he's talking about."

It was the cat, speaking—or thought-speaking—again.

"You stay out of this, Mr. Whiskers," said Marcia.

"Mr. Whiskey."

"I thought it was Whiskers."

"A new incarnation requires a new name," said the cat. "I am the same, yet not the same."

"*Mom*," said Howie urgently.

"OK. I won't try to come there."

Howie lowered his voice to a whisper. He had the worried look he used to get when he'd done something he later realized he was going to have to tell her about. The look he'd had when he notched Orson's ear with scissors to see if it would bleed. The look he'd had when she discovered condoms and a bottle of spiced Captain Morgan in his chest of drawers.

It was that look, amplified.

This occasional fear Howie betrayed was, in her opinion, a legacy of the Marco side of the family. It did not come from her people. Susan, her mother, had been admirably resolute in the face of everything: her out-of-wedlock pregnancy, their straitened finances, even the discovery of Dale's body in the woods on New Year's Day, leaving her a single mother with nothing but a mediocre eye for color and line to make her way in the world. And Dale, Howie's grandfather? What could *he* have feared? He'd lived in his own fantasy world, full of cartoon characters that bounced back from anvils falling on them and villains bisecting them in sawmills. Her parents had both been fearless, to travel across the world on impulse to work on the space film.

Howie's fear, then, was not from her genes.

"Mom. I'm not sure what's going on," said Howie, his face flecked with "nets." The temple walls in the background were the crumbly texture of an old cookie. "Do you remember me showing you my invitation letter for the fellowship?"

"A lot's happened in the past couple of days," she said absently, thinking of the reconstituted cat.

"Mom! The letter inviting me to apply for the fellowship! Do you know where it is?"

"Oh, that. I looked for it a few days ago, but I couldn't find it. What's wrong?"

"It's just—I wanted to maybe call the person who sent it. I started thinking. Why would they send me to an island where everyone speaks English? Even if it's *shifted* English. And Shyl watches my every move, and I can't ever be alone with the islanders. She's not creepy, and she doesn't keep me locked up or anything. She's perfectly helpful, and she can be funny, though it's unintentional, I think. She makes sure I have whatever I need— but she's always *there*. And she insists on me using her phone instead of mine. And we have to go to these out-of-the-way places to call you."

"Howie? Do you want to come home?"

"Mom, no. Not that. I'm just concerned that there's something going on. I haven't heard anything from the fellowship coordinators. They said I'd be on my own, but it seems funny that *no one* has been in touch."

She could hear the doubt in his voice. "Are you sure you don't want to come home?"

"No, not yet. The lore is so absorbing. Shyl let me start researching it because they had to give me something to do, and I couldn't study the language. And then she and Crumb got excited about these interviews I'm doing. Crumb—she's Shyl's boss, I think—is an absolute gem."

"Wait—who?"

"Crumb's the one actually working with me on the research. She's *amazing*. She's a ninety-two-year-old soup maker and a folklorist savant. A taproot drawing from the deep reservoir of the island's collective unconscious. She knows *everything*. Her name is Me in What Islander, but I call her Crumb, like the French word."

Marcia wasn't sure she understood. "Your guide is an old woman who makes soup?" she asked stupidly.

"Soap. Soup is sape. Soap is soup."

Marcia felt her impatience flare. "Howie? I think it's gotten too dangerous there. Since you're not able to do the linguistic field-work, wouldn't it just be better to—?"

"Mom, what's that gray thing?" he interrupted.

It was the cat's tail. He'd climbed on the couch with his haunches in her lap, and his agile tail was flicking back and forth in front of her face, which was lowered, the better to examine Howie's facial expressions for signs that he was being held hostage and trying to blink out messages in code.

"You're being ridiculous. Do you even know Morse?" said the cat.

"How do you know what I'm thinking?" said Marcia.

"I'm reconstituted," said the cat. "I'm the same yet not the same. It seems to have given me some additional abilities."

"Mom, who are you talking to? What's that gray snaky thing?"

"A tail," said Marcia. "I got a cat."

For just a second, Howie's face lost its adult-male geometry and grew soft as a boy's. "A cat," he said, his voice musical with surprise. "That will be very nice for you, Mom. To help you move beyond Orson. Did you get his ashes?"

Marcia didn't want to stress him out further by telling him she had gotten them but they were the wrong ones. "Yes, I got them yesterday," she said simply.

The cat looked away and pretended not to hear this.

"Howie, are you sure everything's OK? I'll keep trying to find that letter," Marcia promised.

But Howie had turned jerkily, sending the gnats away in a cloud. "Mom," he said, "it's all right. Don't worry about it. I have to hang up now." He seemed to be talking or signaling to some-one. Shyl, she supposed. "Mom. Mom. Loveyougoodbye."

The call ended.

Marcia sat staring at the last frozen image of Howie, and then the screen went blank. She'd known intellectually that she would miss him, but that was before. Now it seemed unbearable. What if she never saw him again? She put her head down on her knees, but something was in the way. It was the bill of the ball cap. She realized she still had it on. Also that it was a workday, and she was going to be late.

"Don't forget to feed me," said the cat.

She sat up and looked at him. "I'm late for work, and I don't have any cat food," she said.

Mr. Whiskey replied, "I am the same yet not . . ."

"And you don't eat cat food," Marcia concluded. "OK. But I don't have any fish."

"Scrambled eggs?"

"Cage free," said Marcia and expected a pat on the back for her humaneness, but the cat did not give her one.

She went to the kitchen and scrambled four eggs. She put two of them on a plate for herself and two on a plate on the floor with a saucer of water. But Mr. Whiskey made her understand that this would not do. So she put his plate on the butcher block by the window, from where he could look out at the bird feeders in the backyard and the hibiscus and the squirrels and the busyness of the school bus stop on the street behind her. Then she lifted him to the butcher block. He was sleek and warm in his cat armpits, and rounded in the middle, but not too heavy. She had lifted only Orson and baby Howie in the past, and he felt different. Limp and loose, yet magisterial, like she was lifting a fur-covered bundle of the assorted royal possessions of a prince disguised as a tramp.

He ate the eggs and every now and then paused to look out the window at the birds and the bus stop. He said nothing. Maybe she had imagined it all.

She got dressed and went to work. Her email was blowing up with reply-alls about some snafu in the future application of Tuition Redefinition to the students in the Department of High Cultural Endeavors. In the midst of her skimming and deleting these and answering questions from the perennially confused department faculty, Nina texted, *Did you feel the earth move last night?* It was Nina at her annoying worst.

I don't know what you're talking about, Marcia texted back. She would not give Nina the pleasure of engaging in a dialogue about whether her breakables had survived the earthquake.

AT LUNCH, TO take her mind off Howie and Nina and everything else, she did a quick search on her phone for "cat care." Would Orson have liked Mr. Whiskey? She decided they probably would have learned to get along. Orson had been anxious at times but seldom aggressive and had shown little interest in chasing cats on their walks.

One of the sites she looked at said to introduce pets slowly. First you had them eat on opposite sides of a door, and then you put them in the same room and moved their food dishes closer together, little by little. How would she have explained to Orson that while he was required to listen to her, *she* sometimes had to listen to Mr. Whiskey? How to make him understand why Mr. Whiskey ate human food? And not on the floor? Would he have understood the cat's thought-speech? Would it have sounded like meowing to him? Maybe it was inaudible to dogs. How would she even have been able to figure that out? Interspersed with this train of thought were moments of sudden, sharp worry about What Island and Howie and his hovering bodyguard, Shyl.

The day went on. She got through it without having to redo any spreadsheets and even managed to update the HCA website without incident. She was just pulling out of the parking lot at five fifteen when two portentous words resounded in her brain like the knell of a gong struck twice.

Litter.

Box.

Old Mrs. Stowe was at the Stowes register when she went in. It was almost always Old Mrs. Stowe. Young Mrs. Stowe was there weekends, or evenings when Old Mrs. Stowe was under the weather or they were otherwise shorthanded. During fireworks season, Young Mrs. Stowe worked long hours under the tent in her low-rise short shorts and cropped athletic tanks that showed off the I ♥ STOWES tattooed on her lumbar region. Old Mrs. Stowe couldn't take the heat and, besides, was convinced that the stand would blow up someday from one of the bottle rockets fired at them by rival Floods. Young Mrs. Stowe was Diana. She worked days in Payroll at Holliday College and was the sole person responsible for everyone's withholding.

But today it was Old Mrs. Stowe. She came in at ten every day to make sandwiches for the working people who got lunch there. Stowes' sandwiches were legendary: a half-inch slab of your preferred meat or cheese on bread so soft and fresh it was like eating a delicious pillow. With the condiment of your choice, slathered or squirted to order. Old Mrs. Stowe sliced the meat herself; her gloved hands were gnarled but manned the blade of the slicer like one of Robespierre's own. Stowes had smoked turkey as sweet and tender as foie gras. They had olive loaf. Not presliced in packages: a whole loaf in the deli case, riddled with green bullets of manzanillas. Stowes had loaves of things no one ate except in Round Stone, proving that if you sliced it and put it in a Stowes sandwich, people *would* come and get it. Stowes had salmon loaf, and Marcia asked for a pound and then went to do the rest of her shopping.

Stowes also had everything else. Kayaks. Tampons. Foil roasters. Amish eggs. Propane heaters. Barbies. Pipe cleaners. Light switch plates. Stuffed animals. Fake press-on tattoos that said I ♥ STOWES (but Diana Stowe's tat was real). The only frozen noodles anyone in Round Stone would eat. Housecoats. Deadbolts. Any brand of chew you might fancy. Udder balm, butter mints, peach pie and Yoo-hoo, and the best prices on beer and ice. Stowes was Your Party Center and More.

Stowes had litter boxes in two sizes. Marcia went back and forth. Mr. Whiskey was a full-sized male, but there was just one of him. How large a toilet did a single cat need?

She took the small-sized box in burgundy and got some Amish eggs and then went back and switched the small box for a large green one, which would pick up his eye color. In her head, she could hear Mr. Whiskey deriding her—by this logic, shouldn't she have blue commodes?

"How's that Howie?" said Old Mrs. Stowe at the counter, after she'd wrapped the salmon loaf in white butcher paper.

Marcia couldn't bring herself to discuss their most recent conversation and Howie's proximity to the bloodshed in Kanz-_ika, so she said simply that he was doing folklore research on an island. "He's made a couple of friends," she said.

Mrs. Stowe smiled. "That's nice. Other college boys?"

"He graduated," said Marcia. "His friends are women. He has a guide who's kind of a bodyguard. And an older woman he's really connected with. She makes soap."

Mrs. Stowe got a funny expression. Marcia realized she was envisioning a soap-making island cougar in a bikini top and leopard-print sarong.

"She's ninety-two," Marcia said quickly.

This made Mrs. Stowe's eyebrows go up almost to her scalp.

Fortunately, Mrs. Stowe then changed the subject. "Got a new cat? What happened to Orson?"

"He died," said Marcia. "So I got this cat. He's gray. He won't eat cat food. I thought he'd like the salmon loaf."

"Sounds like an awful finicky cat. Maybe you oughta take him back where you got him."

Marcia tried to imagine how that would be possible.

"I always liked your Howie. He used to say, 'Old Mrs. Stowe, you're not so old. How come you don't ever work in the fireworks stand?' And I'd tell him, "Cause I don't want to get my ass blown to Timbuktu when Floods finally hits us.'

"Where's that island he's at?" Old Mrs. Stowe asked.

"Near Kanz-_ika," admitted Marcia.

Old Mrs. Stowe frowned deeply. "I been reading about that More-Tally," she said, grabbing a *Post* from the small stack behind her. "You ought to look at this." She added it to Marcia's order and rang it up, and Marcia said she'd tell Howie that Old Mrs. Stowe said "Hi."

At home, Mr. Whiskey was asleep when she walked in. She sniffed to see if she could detect any pet toileting odor, but her house smelled like the morning's scrambled eggs and the mixture of smells that was Marcia's furniture and rugs, and now a slight deep gray smell. The cat woke and looked up and saw the litter box. He glared at her. "I won't be needing that," he said. "I'm—"

"Oh, right," said Marcia. "I should have figured. So you don't make waste anymore?"

"Thank you for not saying 'poop,'" said the cat. "I do not do that. I make what pleases me, and waste does not please me."

She set the litter pan on the couch, thinking she'd take it back to Stowes later. She'd forgotten the litter anyway. She'd tell Old Mrs. Stowe that she'd taken her advice and returned the cat.

"Salmon loaf?" she said to Mr. Whiskey.

"Sounds delicious. What are you having?"

Marcia shrugged. "I'm not really hungry," she said.

And she wasn't. Before leaving Stowes, she'd unfolded the *Post* and read the two headlines on the World News main page:

UN PROPOSES SANCTIONS FOR DEATH PRISON NATION

AS "MORE-TALLY" CLIMBS

and

LEAKED VIDEO SHOWS MASS GRAVES ON KANZ-_IKAN SOIL

Our time in North Africa was short. The crew hated the
heat and the dirt. They hated the movie itself. Cheesy space
flick—who could blame them? The place reminded me of the
desert back home, which had frightened me from childhood.
Into even the most privileged lives of luxury, fear must crawl.
There was nothing for me to fear. I was fed, clothed, protected,
pampered, pandered to. An occasional light fray with my father
convinced me that I was the stronger, smarter man.

But then there was the desert, with its reverberations of
eternity and all the lore of its mysterious people. Sorcerers or
ghosts or necromancers—people called them all these things.
They were people who had tasted death and come back from it;
they could twist time; they could fly. It was terrifying to think
about: I dreamed of them coming for me, and when my mother,
with her stupid, sadistic bent, discerned this, she deliberately
tried to frighten me more and then laughed at my fear.

But I was curious, too: I often asked to be driven out to
the edge of that desert expanse as dusk was falling so I could
shudder. There was something there—for me. It felt like destiny,
and when I finally was old enough to choose for myself, I chose
to go there: to see what it was. To test myself.

I would have left Africa when the film crew did if Dale
hadn't asked me to stay. The filming would move now
to Europe. The junior assistants weren't needed; their
replacements were in Berlin or Paris, wherever the crew was
bound. Most of the young Americans were homebound. Dale
and his girlfriend wanted to see some ancient wind sculptures,
so they were staying a few extra days. I was touched by the
invitation. He said I was "his dear friend."

Dear friend. No one had called me that before. Not once in
my life.

Dale and Susan had kept up their round-the-clock
screwing. I found it alternately funny and painful, as it took

him away from me. On our last night at the hotel, they must have been at it again, and around two A.M., Susan, stumbling back from the bathroom, wandered into my room by mistake, holding a diaphragm that looked like a miniature domed tent. "Whoops, wrong room," she said. Her fingers played with the diaphragm nervously as she backed out of the room, and then her expression clouded with worry. She drew the device up to her face and looked at it closely. "There's a hole in it," she said.

—MEMOIRS OF SOCRATIES LOVE

Chapter 11

For the second night in a row, Marcia put on sweats and the old ball cap from her closet and went to bed early because things were too much to deal with. The evening news had reported the same information she'd read in the *Post*: a rising More-Tally and chilling drone footage of soldiers dumping inert bodies, some naked, into a vast rectangular pit.

She lay awake for a while trying to beam her thoughts to Howie or make her mind into a receiver that could decode messages directly from him. It did not work.

In a frenzy, she tried FaceTiming the number from which Howie had last called her, but no one picked up. Much later, just as she got into bed, an iMessage arrived with a row of bowling-pin emojis. She stared at it and tried to translate. "Bowling pins" in What Islander gave her *bulong pons*. Which told her nothing and made the hollow pit in her stomach expand.

She tossed until she fell asleep, but even then, she was restless and kept waking. The last time she woke, her face was wet, and she knew, groggily, that she had been crying. Her pillow was plush and had acquired a vibrating feature that soothed her into sleep again. Just as she was falling into oblivion, she felt someone wiping her wet cheeks with a sliver of rough sponge.

When the alarm woke her at six o'clock, she understood that Mr. Whiskey had heard her crying and come to comfort her: the plush, purring pillow; his raspy tongue licking her salt water. But now he was nowhere.

She got up, hung the cap on a peg, started coffee, and walked around looking for him. She found him on a stack of old towels in the linens nook, lying in a way that implied he had been there all night, though they both knew he had not.

"What's for breakfast?" he said.

"If you don't make waste, where is all this food going?"

"It just gets absorbed into my essence and fuels my new abilities," he replied and yawned, showing the white barbs of his teeth against his carnation-and-charcoal-colored mouth.

"What abilities?" So far, except for whipping himself together from spilled ashes and claiming not to poop (and talking and reading her mind), he had mostly behaved like a normal cat.

"I need to do a skills-and-interests inventory while you're at work today," said Mr. Whiskey. "I used to enjoy chasing bottlecaps on the floor and trying to get into the cupboard under the kitchen sink. Those activities no longer enthrall me. I have not just been reconstituted; I have been retooled, regeared, reappointed, *enhanced*."

Marcia was listening but simultaneously thinking of Howie. Why had she let him go off to such a dangerous region? She would not for all the world have put him in a bubble, but if someone else had? If Silvestro had lived and turned out to be a controlling, heavy-handed father? She might have gone along with him sheltering their son until Howie was grown-up enough to practice caution. And if that had been the case, Silvestro would have vetted the unexpected fellowship invitation much more carefully than Marcia or Howie had thought to do.

It was not the first time recently that she'd *almost* wished Silvestro had lived.

"Can you see across the ocean?" she asked the cat wishfully. "Can you see if my son is safe?"

"I can't even see in the dark anymore. Not like I used to, anyway."

"I thought you were enhanced."

"Enhanced through loss," Mr. Whiskey said.

The word "loss" made her think of something. "Do you still shed?"

In answer, he rolled around on the towels he was lying on, really getting into it for a minute; then he got up, and they could both see the coating of gray hair.

"Yeah, looks like it."

"Can you predict the future?"

"Absolutely: you're going to work today. *After* you feed me."

"Ha!" said Marcia.

"Trust me on this," said Mr. Whiskey. "I've been changed quite substantially, but I need some time to figure it out. It could work to both our advantage."

She did not see how, if he couldn't tell her anything about Howie, but she didn't argue. She fed him on the butcher block again and went off to Holliday College.

It was a day of fillable calculating forms that did their own wizardry, so all she had to do was type in numbers and watch the chain reaction as each numeral she typed made more, new numbers appear in boxes down the page. If she typed in the wrong first number, there would be a whole chain of errors, but whose fault was that? The form's, not hers. Mr. Whiskey and Howie padded across her work thoughts and into the mist of her sidelined better mind and then back through again. Son and cat. Cat and son. And somewhere in the middle of it all, Dale joined them, with his happy cheer and cartoon plots and gentle lectures about death and laughter.

At lunch, she tried FaceTiming her son; it was around nine P.M. in Kanz _ika. Nothing. She wondered if the stress about Howie had made her start imagining a talking cat. Maybe she'd go home and find the resin vessel where she'd originally left it.

Later, she did a search for *hallucinations*, but though she discovered some basic facts about drugs and psychosis, nothing explained how one might start seeing a fictive talking cat that shed real hair. The hair *was* real. It was confirmed when the work-study students came in and noticed some hair on her sweater. One of them dug around in her pack and pulled out an eco-friendly lint roller that she offered to Marcia. "Did you get a new puppy?" she asked. "Wait. Is that *cat* hair?"

Driving home that evening, Marcia did not want to think about the talking cat or Kanz-_ikan death prisons. Or Howie's safety. Or his old soap maker. She turned on the radio to a pop station. It was sad love-and-heartwreck music tonight, and this led her to musing on the men in her past and how they were all odd ducks and mostly unable to hold the kinds of jobs that made comfortable livings. There was her father. Enough said. And Thomas— genius at making donuts, but she hadn't been sure, even as a naive twenty-something, that the donut shop was exactly what he'd said it was. Silvestro was the most conventional of the lot and the most determined, launching a romantic onslaught that she could not stand against. Their first night together, in the bedroom of his bachelor apartment, he led her to his bed and stood stiffly a few paces away and very seriously removed his clothes, watching her closely all the while, like a museum guard doing a striptease. Marcia was a virgin, and she wondered if it was always like this. Off, very slowly and silently, with the bottom things, down to the briefs. Eyes never leaving her. Then off, equally deliberately, with the silky shirt. There was a lot of hair. He thumped his chest in a show of masculinity that seemed a little out of character, goofy as he was, and gazed down at her and exclaimed, "Mar-see-a, *this* is what I offer you. Every *musculo* and every drop of my *affamato sangue!*"

She did not have a chance to reject the offer of his "famished blood" because he leaped over and began kissing her everywhere, quite sweetly, and, when she didn't object, peeling her out of her clothes. She discovered that her blood, too, had an appetite. He climbed on her. Off came the briefs. He was fully prepared in everything but a condom. He tumbled her onto her back and went to great lengths to please her. Much later, she would wonder at her oversight, and his, in never using birth control—though it had led to the happy outcome of Howie. After, there was interminable pillow talk. He wanted to know *tutto* about her. He plied her with Lorna Doones and wine and demanded to hear about her girlhood and family, her life with the Noisetteses, her school, her favorite foods and colors, her dreams for the future. Eventually, he wound down, and they slept, and they woke and went to work and school, and after that were a couple until he died, just months later.

She swiped the turn signal up, turned onto Funnel Street. Something was bothering her. Something missed. Did it have to do with the cat? She drove on down to her house, at the far end, where the street narrowed and the houses stopped having stamped concrete patios and started having driveways that heaved. Her driveway was all right, though. Perhaps if Silvestro had lived, he would have built her a patio. He'd spared nothing to make her happy, even though that had sometimes annoyed her.

Nina was parked at the curb in front of her house. *That* was what she'd missed. Marcia had not heard a peep out of Nina all day. Now Nina was standing, leaning against her SUV, in a pair of power/performance leggings and a black stretch athletic jacket. Her blond hair lifted in the wind, and her shoes were the white of a scrubbed bathtub.

From a distance, Nina waved at her. When Marcia pulled into the driveway and got out, she called, "Marsh, it's a *gorgeous* evening. Come walk with me!"

So she did. Navigating the trail through the park nearby in khakis and clogs (she'd refused to go in and change, wanting to keep Nina away from the cat), Marcia wondered what she could feed Mr. Whiskey tonight. He liked eggs and salmon loaf. Maybe a salmon-loaf omelet?

Nina was uncharacteristically quiet. As they walked, she breathed with squeaky sounds and every now and then pointed to a toadstool or a blue jay and said something inane. Then, abruptly, she brought up Kanz-_ika. She, too, had seen the news.

"Is Howie safe?" she asked. "My God, you must be kicking yourself for letting him go. If I were you—not that I ever wanted to slog along on the mommy track—I'd be frantic with worry."

"I'm not too worried," Marcia lied. "We talked yesterday, and he's having the time of his life. He's doing great research, and he's met a woman he says is amazing. It's a carefree place: simple food, simple pleasures, and the quaintest dialect. They don't have much interaction with the mainland. And he has a very diligent guide."

Nina continued on the path and said nothing for a while. Finally she sighed. "Always the 'I'm-a-tough-little-thing' act with you, Marsh. I admire that. But if it gets to be too much, I'm just a phone call away."

Marcia assured Nina that she would call, day or night. In her mind she said to Nina, "I would not call you if my head fell off and you were the only person in the universe who could put it back on." Her clogs were muddy and had leaves stuck to the bottoms. The khakis were stiff and made a rustling sound. "I need to get back now," Marcia said abruptly. "It's about time to feed my—" she'd been about to say "cat" but caught herself and said, "family of backyard foxes."

"You have a fox family?" exclaimed Nina.

"Five, I think. They're clever. And funny."

"Five funny foxes? What do you feed them?"

"Chow," said Marcia and quickly changed the subject before she dug herself into a lie too elaborate to remember.

Back at the house, Nina insisted on coming inside to pee. Marcia tried to stop her on the grounds that the house was a wreck. She did not want Nina to find out about Mr. Whiskey. But Nina danced up and down and said she was going to wet herself, and when Marcia relented and unlocked the door to let her in, the cat was, happily, absent. Marcia took off her clogs and was cleaning mud out of the treads with a nail file when Nina reappeared from the bathroom.

"Did you feed the foxes already?"

Marcia averred that she had.

Nina watched Marcia flick mud on the floor. "You were right about your housekeeping. I'm very sensitive to mess. But I was wondering, where are Orson's ashes?" she said.

Marcia flushed red; the question had come so unexpectedly. Then she recovered. "Nina, he's still in his resin vessel. Put away in a safe place. I just can't . . . look at it now. I need some space, you know?"

Nina nodded and gave a tight smile. She was still smiling like that when Mr. Whiskey strolled in.

He stared at Nina, and she stared back. Her eyes narrowed. His were wide and unreadable. He sat on his haunches and started licking his chest nonchalantly.

"Marsh?" said Nina. "When did you get . . . that?"

"The cat? Friday," said Marcia. "I got him last Friday. His name . . . his name is Friday. He was nosing around in the trash at the college and looked desperate, so I brought him home. You could tell he'd been traumatized. Weren't you, *Friday*?" she finished in a cooing voice.

Mr. Whiskey shot her an annoyed look.

Nina watched the cat with an expression that could only be described as "black." Marcia was surprised she felt this deeply about it. She wasn't jealous, was she? But she had never liked animals.

Mr. Whiskey began an elaborate slo-mo walk in Nina's direction. He pretended not to see her, even as he moved unswervingly toward her. "Mew!" he said. "Mew! Mew!" His tail snaked, and his eyes were bright with wicked intent.

"I don't know why—" Nina started and then stopped and said, "You know I don't like house pets."

Mr. Whiskey was rubbing against her now. His tail did a dance. He wove around and between her legs as she tried to edge away.

"Mew! MEW!" he cried. Then he nipped her sharply on the ankle.

"Ow!" sputtered Nina. In no time, she was at the door, casting a few choice words at Marcia about her callous "replacement" of Orson before he was even inurned.

"What was that about?" Marcia asked Mr. Whiskey after Nina had left. He had jumped up on the back of the couch to watch as Nina hurried to her car and pulled away from the curb. His hackles were up, and he growled.

"Bitch," he said. "My dinner is late because of her."

Then he spun around. "Wait!" he said. "I don't have to be hungry. That's bullshit. I'm going to *do* something!"

He leaped from the couch to Marcia's shoulder and dug all four sets of claws in. His tail twitched. Fast, faster. And even faster, and she was flying, and then she was turning into a long thread of herself being sucked through a wind-filled straw with the cat on her back, and all the way down and through and out into—

Chapter 12

—HER CAR. SHE was driving home, and all her worries about Howie and the shady fellowship situation and porridge-roll-eating scavengers and mass graves and death prisons were like a small but heavy and persistent weight on her shoulders.

And Orson's missing ashes—she couldn't let that slide. She wanted to confront the people at the megachurch, the Pious Body of Formally Doomed Souls. But what would she say to them? "You delivered the wrong ashes to me"? What proof did she have, except the gray cat that had sprung from them and was bossing her around? Who would believe that? And if she took the cat evidence out of the equation, how could she claim to be able to tell one incinerated pet from another?

A pain, like needles piercing her back. It must be the stress, though she was not one to feel phantom pains or vomit from anxiety, like the high-strung academics she had to deal with in High Cultural Endeavors. Even Nina could be like that. For example, when she'd barged into Marcia's house this afternoon and said haughtily that she was "sensitive to mess."

But wait—how could it have been this afternoon if Marcia was still in her car now, driving home? It must have been yesterday.

Yesterday. Was the earthquake. The reconstitution of the cat. Or not. She couldn't remember.

Marcia frowned, wondering how the days had gotten so jumbled in her head.

She turned on the radio and started to push the button for NPR, then changed her mind and went to a pop station. Tonight it was sad love-and-heartwreck music, and she started to muse on the men in her past: on Thomas, with his face like a botched mosaic; and on her first night with Silvestro, who'd also been sort of high-strung, come to think of it. He was always worrying about losing her—until he did, because he died.

But.

But.

She'd already had these thoughts before. *Every single one.* It was like she'd suddenly turned hypermnesic, remembering each minute detail down to the rub of her khakis against the seat fabric (it had to be the same afternoon, or else she'd worn the same clothes and necklace two days in a row). It was like a video replay, the most precisely replicated moment she'd ever experienced. So déjà that she knew it was no déjà vu. Something was up.

And there was still that pain, which felt like *real* needles.

At that same moment, Mr. Whiskey's tail brushed her cheek, and she looked in her rearview mirror and screamed, "Aarghgetoffmeyou!"

It was not needles of pain in her back. It was cat claws, and the weight she'd felt was real; it was the gray bundle of reconstituted cat, balanced daintily on her shoulders.

"What are you doing here?" said Marcia.

"Time-traveling with you," said Mr. Whiskey calmly. He retracted his front claws, turned around, and stood on his hind legs to set his front paws on the headrest behind her. He hopped his hindquarters up so he was perched quite precariously on all four paws on the headrest. From the headrest he leaped gracefully down to the passenger seat and curled up next to her purse. He began kneading the purse. It was an old fabric bag from Stowes that had cost a mere twelve dollars, but she was fond of it.

"Hey!" she said. "Stop that!"

The cat stared at her. He kept kneading. After a minute he stopped, but then his tail twitched. It switched up, slapped down. Up. Down. Each time he slapped the seat, the tail made a light thwack.

"What do you mean, 'time-traveling'?" said Marcia. "When is this?"

"I'd say late afternoon, by my stomach," said the cat.

Marcia could see this by the way the sun had trundled along and was starting to flare and dip at once. It blazed above the town's western rooftops and would ultimately "plunge into the Sawgash River like a slice of raw potato into a vat of hot oil, where it would cook to a crisp, in order to rise in the eastern sky the next morning as a perfect golden round disc like a Pringle." This absurd and multiply problematic image came into Marcia's brain in quotation marks—something overheard long ago in a forgotten conversation—and she could not for the life of her think where it came from.

"I can see that it's afternoon," said Marcia. The events of earlier were coming back to her: Mr. Whiskey's rage at having his dinner delayed and his pronouncement that Nina's intrusion was "bullshit." Then him leaping on her back, saying he didn't have to be hungry and was going to do something, and the extraordinary feeling of being sucked through a straw.

"Did we go back in time? Is it earlier the same day? We didn't go forward, into the future, did we?"

"I don't think so. No, I'd say not. I'm not quite sure. This is a trial run, you know."

Marcia's thoughts were spinning, but she kept driving. Fortunately, she knew Round Stone like the back of her hand, so being unexpectedly transported to her car in transit on her own city's street with no advance warning didn't affect her sense of direction. She knew exactly where she was.

She swiped the turn signal up to turn onto Funnel Street. "Is this just a redo?" she said to Mr. Whiskey. "Am I supposed to get rid of Nina this time around so I can feed you on schedule?"

"Silly!" said Mr. Whiskey. "Don't turn here. Go on up to Loose Street. You can park there and cut through the neighbors' backyard and go in the back door. You'll avoid Nina entirely."

"How do you know the name of the next street? You've never been out of my house. And how do you know she's there? And are you sure it's the same day? And even if it's the same day, couldn't things be different because it's a replay?"

Marcia gripped the wheel hard. She drew a deep, frustrated breath. This was ridiculous. She was talking to an ash-cat about the fact that they'd just time-tripped back to the past. An hour and a half in the past. Who went back in time just an hour and a half, to a place like Round Stone in 2018? She'd read enough time-travel stories. You went back to the New England whaling days and had a fling with a nicely built captain who smelled like blubber and waterlogged wood, or to the French court in the eighteenth century and showed off your snowy-white cleavage in a ball gown, or joined an antique Arctic expedition led by men with mustaches, pleated wool pants, and fur parkas, and you taught them about the future—that holes in the ozone layer were going to devastate both polar caps, and they set you adrift on an iceberg because the expedition was a boys' club, and they didn't like a woman telling them scientific stuff they didn't know.

She wished fervently for things to go back the way they were before the cat showed up. Maybe they could time-travel back farther and . . .

"Sorry. You can't do that," said Mr. Whiskey. "Once I've reconstituted, I'm here to stay. I can't be undone. I'm eternal."

"I still don't understand why you reconstituted."

"Neither do I. I'm trying to figure it out. Here's Loose Street. You can turn now," he insisted, more gently, and then he told her where to park. When she got out of the car, he jumped out after her, a gray slip of shadow. "Pick me up," he said, rubbing against her ankle so seductively that she automatically did it without thinking and carried him across the neighbors' backyard and through a gap in the fence into her own. The door to the porch was already unlocked.

"Did you do that—unlock it?" she asked him.

"I'm not always sure what I can and can't do," he said and commenced purring, and she carried him past the recycling containers and into the house, where she set him on the butcher block and fed him an hors d'oeuvre of cheese shreds and a Ritz cracker.

"Can you wait a few minutes for dinner? I want to see if it really is the same day and if Nina is out there," she said.

"Just look at your phone if you want to know what day it is," said Mr. Whiskey. Neither of them had thought of this before.

It was the same day. Same attempted FaceTime calls to Howie. Same phone silence from Nina.

"Now, follow me," said Mr. Whiskey. He jumped down to the floor and strolled out of the kitchen. Marcia trailed behind him.

"Get down!" he said urgently. "Or she'll see you."

So against dignity and reason, she got down on hands and knees and crawled after the cat, along the wall, out of view of the front windows. When she reached the front door, she crawled along that wall until she got to the edge of the window. Mr. Whiskey jumped onto the couch and looked out. "Take a peek," he said. "Be careful, though."

Cautiously, Marcia raised herself into a kneeling position at the side of the window and pulled the edge of the drape away from the trim just enough to make a crack to look through. Nina was parked at the curb in front of her house. She was standing, leaning against her SUV, in a pair of power/performance leggings and a black stretch athletic jacket. Her blond hair lifted in the wind, and her shoes were the white of a scrubbed bathtub. She was checking the time on her phone impatiently.

"Nailed it. Down to the minute!" gloated Mr. Whiskey, and then, as an afterthought, he added, "Bitch!"

He trotted back to the kitchen, and Marcia crawled after him, still edging along the wall, though because of the drapes being drawn, Nina wouldn't have seen her if she'd stood up and walked, so why was she doing all this crawling? She wondered if Nina might go around the house and look in the windows where there were curtains open, but that was not her style. And indeed, a few minutes later, they heard Nina's car engine start and the car pull away.

Marcia fixed dinner for the cat and an impromptu quesadilla for herself. As she was loading the dishwasher, Nina called.

"Where were you, Marsh?" she said with no preliminaries. "I came by earlier. I thought we might take a walk—it was such a gorgeous afternoon. And I wanted to ask you about Howie. You must be so worried—"

"Nina, I'm not really worried about Howie," she lied. "The islanders don't have much interaction with the mainland. And he has a protective guide.

"But to tell you the truth, I'm not feeling well; I seem to have a bit of a GI bug. I've been vomiting all day, so after work I went to Stowes for stomach medicine, and when I came back I lay down and fell asleep for a while. I'm still throwing up. It's worse than morning sickness."

"I wouldn't know anything about that," said Nina.

"No, I guess you wouldn't," said Marcia and laughed delicately and then added, "Imagine that every time you sit down to eat, no matter what's on your plate, there's a smell in your nose like a dead, raw, plucked baby chick with its eyes gouged out."

"Ugh," said Nina. "No wonder people aren't having babies anymore."

"It's just one of those things mothers go through."

"I have to go," said Nina abruptly. "I'll give you a call soon."

"OK."

"But Marsh?" she said. "Did I see a puppy in your window, looking out?"

"A cat," Marcia said reluctantly. "I couldn't bear to get another dog, not after losing Orson."

"A kitty-cat! What's its name?"

Again Marcia cast about for a name. She couldn't remember what she'd said in the other version of this afternoon. She'd said something, but only parts of that other version were at her fingertips. "Cinders," she announced after a long pause.

Mr. Whiskey, lounging by the kitchen door, glanced over, and from his expression, she could tell she'd screwed up.

"I thought you said it was 'Friday'?"

"When?"

"Friday."

"I mean, when did I say that? You just asked me about the cat a second ago."

"Oh." Nina sounded confused. "But I thought . . . I mean, didn't you tell me?"

"No, I don't think so, but you're right. His name is actually Cinders Friday because I found him on Friday, and when I first saw him, he looked like cinders."

Mr. Whiskey growled low in his chest and glared at her. Marcia looked away.

"All right, then," said Nina. "Call me if you need anything. Promise?"

WHEN SHE WAS done cleaning up dinner, Marcia put on her sweats and walked around and down into the basement for privacy so she could try Howie again. But her FaceTime summons went nowhere. The freezer was still gone.

She went upstairs to the living room and sat on the couch and tried to read a book. She liked sweeping historical novels about poor children who grew up to be wily entrepreneurs in small-agriculture endeavors that ultimately went global. Mr. Whiskey came and curled up on her lap. "I can't believe I feel compelled to sit on top of you like this," he muttered. "You'd think I would be past that. And I can't believe what you told Nina. 'Cinders Friday'?"

"I know, I know. But I couldn't remember what I said . . . in the *other* version of this afternoon."

"It's fine," said Mr. Whiskey. "I can hold two versions of the same time in my head at once, but I guess you can't always do that."

"Why did Nina remember part of what originally happened but not all of it?"

"I've no idea. You and she have known each other a long time— maybe she's got a line to your brain. I'm not sure how any of this works," said Mr. Whiskey. "But I'm taking notes," he added.

"So have you figured out why you reconstituted?"

He didn't answer. Instead he asked, "You've worn that ball cap a number of times lately, but as a rule, you don't wear it, do you?"

"No," she said.

"But you wore it the night the resin vessel broke."

"You're reconstituted because I wore a ball cap to bed?"

"Because you lost something precious to you. And *I* lost something precious to me. And your deep feelings and my deep feelings together created a vortex of intense grief. And *that* was what did it."

"What did you lose?" said Marcia.

"A friend. The man who rescued me. I can't remember his name," said Mr. Whiskey mournfully. "There are only fragments of fragments of memories. He was not your usual human; he was no intellectual."

"Most of us aren't," said Marcia.

"He used to pick me up. It was different than when you pick me up. His hands were rough, but I could feel how much he loved me."

"So you think maybe I could help you get back to him, and you could help me get Orson and Howie back?"

"Not Orson. He's dead for good. Sorry. And Howie—I'm not sure what's going on with that, but he's obviously all right for the moment. But I could help you get your life back. The life you started on in Chicago. The life you might have had if you'd stayed there and let things unfold. If you hadn't been forced to take the settlement and move to Round Stone."

"Oh," said Marcia. "*Oh.*"

She closed her eyes and felt the fullness of her heart. It was always there, though never acknowledged. Years of being an unloved orphan and poor ward of the Noisetteses had given her a lot of practice: she neither expected to have the life she wanted nor even allowed herself to want it. She had Howie. She'd had a spotted dog. For a long time, she'd told herself that was enough.

Mr. Whiskey said, "I've been thinking. And picking your brain when you didn't know it. That's how I know about Chicago and Thomas and the donut shop and Silvestro and everything else. It seems to me that to change things, have the life you were meant to have, where you *didn't* come here and work at Holliday College and you *weren't* bound to Nina—you'd have to avoid Round Stone like the plague."

"Howie would be safer somewhere else." Marcia was thinking out loud. "No Holliday, no fellowship, no danger. But we might be poorer if there wasn't a settlement for Silvestro's death. Which means . . ."

"Exactly what you've been thinking about lately. What would happen if Silvestro didn't die? There would be no wrongful-death settlement, and you wouldn't be forced to live here, and you could have stayed in Chicago and—"

"It would be a good thing for Howie's sake to have that urban experience."

"What about for your sake?"

"The thing is—" Marcia began. Then she stopped and said simply, "It seems like it's worth trying. At least I wouldn't be stuck in Round Stone and stuck to Nina. Do you have any idea how we could prevent Silvestro's death?"

"Not yet. But I'm a smart cat. You're a resourceful woman. I think maybe we could pull it off."

"I bet we could," said Marcia. She tried to picture what life would be like, cut free from Round Stone and Nina and High Cultural Endeavors, but it was like trying to imagine how it would feel to be a tumbleweed, or a rainbow.

"Of course, I could always be wrong about all of this," said Mr. Whiskey. "Let's revisit it in the morning."

He snuggled his head down tighter against her leg and purred and purred.

A Dialogue between Dad and Daughter

———————

"Quiz time, Marsh. That 'I'm so happy' canine, Droopy Dog: 'The Shooting of Dan McGoo.' Name one of the animation artists. Just one."

"Dad! You know I can't remember all that. But I know that cartoon is a spoof of a real poem."

"And what's that called?"

"'The Shooting of Dan McGrew.' By Robert Service."

"Good, good. And what about where the cartoon is set? 'Coldernell, Alaska.' What's funny about it?"

"Colder than Hell, Dad. It's a pretty weak pun."

"Did you smile the first time you got it?"

"Maybe. A little."

"Then it's funny enough. Now, why is the population of Coldernell rapidly declining?"

"Daily hangings. There's a sign that says, 'Double Header Today' and two gallows. And a baby gallows next to them."

"Literal gallows humor. Even junior gallows for the little kids. Do you think that's funny?"

"Sort of. It's meant to be funny. In cartoons, death isn't that serious."

"Because? Why not? Think hard."

"Mom says you patronize me."

"I don't. I'm trying to teach you something important. Why isn't death that serious?"

"Because cartoons are a distortion of real life. The animals in them act like people. The people in them act a lot like animals. They're all id, no filter. Time gets accordioned, so a year's events take a second. Motivations are basic. Primal, sometimes. Sometimes they're not even there. It doesn't matter because the point is the antics. Death is just another comic consequence. It's not even necessarily final. Or real.

"But is that OK, Dad? Turning death into a plot device? Acting like death doesn't matter when it *is* real, and it matters a lot? Do you think that's OK, Dad?"

"Hmmm."

"Sorry, I didn't really answer your question."

"Close enough, Marsh. You've got a good head for this stuff, you know?"

HOWIE MARCO'S INTERVIEW NOTES 9/5/18

Informant 12

"I remembered something else. The desert. They come from the desert. That's why they're Desert People. No one knows if they're real. If they're alive. They might have been dead once. They know the secrets of life and death. They know if there's even any difference."

Chapter 13

THE NEXT MORNING when she woke, there was an iMessage from an unknown number: *Ho, Mum. Ots Who I. Om phone. Kent see ani mur. Thirz e lut uv 🛻 rot nu end—*

It took Marcia a minute to translate: Hi, Mom. It's Howie. I'm fine. Can't say any more. There's a lot of 🛻 right now and—

The pickup emoji confirmed that it was really from Howie, but it frightened her. Growing up, Howie had played constantly with a toy plastic pickup, but later, he developed a terror of it when he saw a dump truck at a worksite dumping a load of rock that buried a groundhog which had been scurrying across the lot. "How long will it take the pup-pup to dig out, Mom?" asked three-and-a-half-year-old Howie. And Marcia, who did not believe in lying to children to shelter them, told him it was not a pup-pup but a groundhog, whose life was considered expendable, and that it would never dig itself out because the rock had crushed it quite painfully and it was now a flattened pile of bloody fur and gore. From then on, the sight of any truck, even his own toy, made him dissolve, screaming, so Marcia gave it to the Goodwill shortly thereafter. Now she had to ask, what was he trying to say to her with that emoji?

She started to check the news to see if there was anything more about Kanz-_ika or the More-Tally or Cor-Spamkeer, but at that instant, she was distracted by a thump-swoosh in the hall.

It was Mr. Whiskey, who, in jumping out of the linens nook, had unintentionally pulled a stack of sheets after him.

"I'll pick those up," said Marcia and immediately realized it was a stupid thing to say because Mr. Whiskey wasn't going to do it, not with paws for hands and a total height of eleven inches.

She balled up the sheets and stuffed them on the top shelf.

"You're quite the domestic virtuoso," said Mr. Whiskey.

"Ha," said Marcia.

"So how far back in time do we have to go to save Silvestro?" said the cat.

"And protect Howie."

"That, too," said the cat.

"Late '90s," said Marcia.

"I need more exact dates."

"We met in 1997. He died later that year. When are we going? This weekend?"

"This weekend!" cried Mr. Whiskey. "Time is of the essence. The more forward you go, the harder it is to redo the back without messing things up. We're going *today*. After you feed me breakfast."

Marcia did not point out that she'd already gone quite a bit forward—twenty-one years—and that a couple more days could hardly make much difference. She just said, "I have to go to work."

"You will," said Mr. Whiskey, "when you get back to now. If you're even working. Maybe you'll have married into money and you'll be taking jewelry classes and volunteering at a raptor rescue. You won't be living in Round Stone or working at Holliday College, at any rate."

"What about this?" said Marcia, waving her arm to indicate the house and everything in it. "What will happen to all this? What about Orson? If I go back and save Silvestro, will Orson even exist?"

"Surely you're not so naive as to think Orson's existence was predicated on yours," said Mr. Whiskey.

"Howie's was," said Marcia quite logically. "I meant, what will happen to Orson if I'm not here to adopt him?"

Mr. Whiskey looked irritated. "Lost dogs find families or get put out of their misery and 'cross the rainbow bridge,' whatever that means. Bliss awaits them either way. You're throwing up roadblocks to your liberation from Nina and a shot at reclaiming your life. Do you want to do this or not?"

"How can you be sure we'll end up in the right time and place?"

"*Place* is easy. We can only go where you've been: where you were at the time we go back to. So—Chicago. Time is harder. The longer ago, the harder to hit. Yesterday was easy. But twenty years? It's like when you zoom out on a map—the point you were looking at gets smaller and smaller. Zoom out enough, and it disappears. In other words, it won't be as exact as yesterday."

"Where will you be?"

"Then. There. With you. You can't go without me."

"Will people be able to see you?"

"I don't think so. Not if it's not now."

"Great," sighed Marcia. She'd have to think of a creative explanation for why she was talking to the air.

"And what about Howie? Are we sure this will keep him out of danger?" she asked, thinking of the truncated message with the pickup trucks.

Mr. Whiskey avoided answering this and stalked to the kitchen. He sat on his haunches in front of the refrigerator and yowled aggressively until she got out the kipper cake she'd concocted the night before. It smelled like a hatchery, and the kitchen was instantly permeated with fish-stink. She sliced off a wedge of oily cake and put it on a fresh plate on the butcher block. Mr. Whiskey jumped up, gobbled it, and said, "More," so she gave him another, larger wedge and a saucer of cream and made herself a three-minute egg.

"That's all you're eating? You might get hungry," he said. "We're traveling quite a long stretch."

Fear whacked her like a club. Was she really going to do this? Jump into a time-tunnel/wormhole with a talking cat she'd just met? What if she was atomized and obliterated? Or sent to ancient

Gaul? She tried to reassure herself with the thought that the desired goals—her freedom, Howie's safety—were worth the risk.

"I do know what I'm doing, you know," said the cat.

"Will I be young again?"

"You'll be this Marcia and that Marcia," he said vaguely.

"You never answered me about Howie."

Mr. Whiskey polished off his cream and looked up and said, "Yes. He's in danger. Everyone is in danger. You. Howie. Even your frenemy Nina, I suppose.

"Going back to the topic you raised: you're all in danger because you're all going to die," said the cat. "I'm the only one who won't because I'm already dead. Take it from me: death is no picnic. I don't remember a lot, but I remember being sick. And hurting. The man I loved cried. The next thing I knew, I was ashes. And the *next* thing I knew, I was in your living room, with no memory of who he was or how to get to him." Having said this, Mr. Whiskey grew silent and started to groom in earnest: the signal that this subject was closed. "Eat your egg," he commanded. "So we can get out of here."

It had gone more than three minutes, and the yolk was dry and chalky. Marcia chopped it in two, shell and all, scooped out both halves, salted and peppered them and mashed them together, and poured salsa on the whole thing. The cat watched without comment.

Back on the subject of Nina, Marcia asked, "Did *you* ever have a frenemy?"

Mr. Whiskey hesitated. "Yes."

"Who?"

"Blackie Bad-Cat," admitted Mr. Whiskey.

Marcia couldn't help it. She laughed out loud.

"Blackie Bad-Cat was *not* funny," said Mr. Whiskey. "He bit me and caused a painful abscess. Stole my food. Puffed his tail at me. Made threatening sounds in my direction. Peed in the water dish. But we did sometimes sleep together for warmth, in winter."

"How come you remember him and not the man you loved?"

"I guess because he hurt me. Pain is a great mnemonic device," said Mr. Whiskey sadly. "You need to quit asking questions and go change. You look terrible. You're still in those sweats you've worn for God knows how many nights, and there's toothpaste in your hair and salsa on your chin. Don't you want to put on something nice?"

"I thought when we got there, I'd be in the clothes I was wearing in 1997. Like yesterday, I was in my same khakis."

"That was just a short hop. If you went back twenty years and ended up in the clothes you were wearing then, some other version of Marcia in the next time slot over would be running around Chicago naked."

Marcia stared at him and then announced, "I'm going to change."

In her bedroom, she put on matching underwear, something she hadn't done since she'd gone to the hospital to have Howie. She tried to choose clothes that were nice but weren't so stylish that they'd look weird in the late '90s. This was easier than she might have predicted because she was not a fashionista like Nina and favored jeans or other dark pants and sweaters or T-shirts and clogs. She'd dressed much the same way in 1997; it had never occurred to her to change her look.

Mr. Whiskey had come in and hopped up on the bed and was watching her. "I like that top," he said. It was azure and had a notched neckline and white piping and just a faint flavor of nautical.

"Thanks," she said and put it on and stepped into her best clogs with the silver buckles. She put on her jean jacket and, as an afterthought, stuck extra Kleenex in the pocket.

"I'm ready," she said. "Let's go."

"Pee first."

She followed these instructions. When she came out of the bathroom, she asked, "Should I call in to work?"

"And tell them what?"

"That I'm not going to be there."

"It won't matter. It won't be now yet, where we're going. And they wouldn't know who you were, even if then *was* now," said Mr. Whiskey. "If we get it right, you'll never have been an employee of Holliday College. You'll have done something else."

Marcia felt increasingly confused and nervous.

"Trust me," said Mr. Whiskey. His voice was halfway between a wild yodel and a dark bass command: "TRUST. ME."

Then he was on her shoulder, and strangely, she did trust him. She should have been more scared, but she felt a peaceful nervousness that was entirely agreeable. The tail was whipping around. It wasn't like a propeller; it was more like a very actively wielded baton or staff, parting the wall-like waters of time, opening a passage—passages—for them to go through and at the same time stirring time around and peeping, prodding into one tunnel-like passage and then another until it discerned the *when* they were going to. Because she'd been through this previously, Marcia had time to observe it all before she was once again flying, turning into the long thread, feeling herself sucked through the straw into a deep, windy space with the cat. His claws were in her shoulders, and she and the cat went down and down and down and through and through and through, much longer this time, and on and on, until she felt herself reshaping into her normal shape, not a string anymore, but Marcia, slipping out. Mr. Whiskey was still there, but differently. He was with her in a new way, not so tangibly, and she was out of the straw and here in . . .

The donut shop. She was behind the counter, working. The Beretta was under the old-fashioneds tray in the glass counter case in front of her; she could see how the edge of the tray was pushed up by the gun underneath. There was a hollowed-out space for the gun in the wood shelf, but it wasn't quite deep enough, and the Beretta pushed the tray up. She heard Thomas's voice in the back, his lilting tenor, and conjured that pockmarked face. It was Pavlovian: just his voice, and she felt instantly young and like she'd been mummified for a long while in worry windings, but someone had just undone all the linen strips, and she was free. She was firmer and a little fatter.

A customer stepped up and ordered a blueberry cake donut to eat here, and she remembered how the cash register worked. It wasn't all debit cards, and the price was surprisingly low. She could make change. "I remember how to make change!" she exulted to Mr. Whiskey and discovered that their conversation was in another compartment of experience, on another plane, so to speak, and she could talk to him without it being noticed on the main plane of *now* in the donut shop.

"Bully for you," said Mr. Whiskey sardonically. He was sort of visible, but she remembered what he'd said and knew that he was likely invisible to others.

She waited on another customer and wished Thomas would come out of the back, but he was apparently busy. Somehow, she knew the shop was short-staffed today.

Mr. Whiskey retreated to a conveniently empty donut tray on the bottom shelf of the glass case, where he curled up but stayed alert, watching the customers at the tables. He took in the pennants and other decor. He sniffed the tray he was lying on, and then the aroma-laden air. His eyes darted to the plate-glass front of the store, and he watched people strolling by. His ear twitched and his fur went up when a Dalmatian trotted past on a leash. He sniffed again, and Marcia knew he was trying to sniff past the donut-shop smell and take in the scent of urban Chicago, a smell made of concrete, exhaust, shoe leather, tire rubber, pizza sauce, office furniture, trash, and the indefinable odor made by the friction of revolving hotel doors.

"I'm in my *then* clothes. My '90s clothes," said Marcia, noticing with some surprise that the azure shirt and buckle clogs were gone.

"I lied," said Mr. Whiskey. "I wasn't going to get in that tube with you in smelly sweats covered with food. There's a certain travel etiquette, you know. But just remember: *then* is now. This is as real as it gets."

"You sound like Howie: 'Ugh is ag. Ag is egg.'"

"Shh. Listen!"

The bell jingled on the door, which was just opening.

"Is that him?" said the cat.

Marcia looked. It might almost have been Howie, and for a second, her heart rejoiced to have him safe and home before she realized that this wasn't home, that Howie hadn't been born yet, and that it was Silvestro—how young and muscular he was, and eerily like vintage Leonardo DiCaprio. A look of passionate triumph was in his eyes. They were shining at her. "I found you!" he cried. "I have searched every donut shop in this city. For days and days, I searched. I thought it might never be. But today I have found the love of my life!"

Chapter 14

Marcia was surprised at how fully this moment came back to her in memory: unexpurgated, unabbreviated, and identical to what was unfolding around her at this very second. She had not forgotten a thing. She was *that* Marcia, twenty-two-year-old history student and donut slinger. But also *this* Marcia, mother of Howie, whom she was helpless to help because he was far, far away, in another place and time, amid a strange culture of impoverished scavengers, a short boat ride away from a death prison. Her memory of both pieces of her life, the '90s piece and the 2018 piece, was not just intact; it was sharp as a shaved stick. Her confusion during the "trial run" the day before in Round Stone must have been due to it being such a short time-hop.

She certainly was not confused now. She knew everything that was about to happen at this moment and everything that would happen in twenty-one years. She knew exactly *when* now was: four days after Silvestro had run up to her on the street and pursued her and she'd made a fast exit and trotted back to the Warehouse College, expecting never to see him again. She'd told no one but Nina about the encounter, and though she was sure she'd gotten rid of the seemingly benign but annoying Italian—What chance did he have of finding her? He didn't know her name, and Chicago was a big city—she breathed a sigh of relief all the same when he didn't show up at her dorm or one of her classes.

One thing she hadn't bargained for, however: she hadn't imagined *smell* could give her away. She'd so quickly gotten used to the aroma of freshly made, really good donuts filling the shop that she didn't think about it anymore. Every day, she inhaled chocolate, exhaled cinnamon. Inhaled blueberry, exhaled lemon crème. Inhaled the raspberry-essence jam that was the signature of

Homerun Donuts' Glazed Grand Slam, exhaled the sweet, plain, cakey-fried scent of the old-fashioneds. Under which lurked the gun.

This Marcia, Marcia the elder, knew what would happen next. Silvestro would enter the shop and stride up to the counter, eyes glowing, ecstatic, and say again . . .

"I have found you! The love of my life."

Marcia appraised him and then glanced down at the tray on the bottom shelf. Mr. Whiskey was listening but lying low.

"I'm not the love of your life," she told Silvestro. "I don't know what you're doing here. All I know about you is that you're a celibate software engineer."

Thomas emerged from the back. He'd heard the ruckus. *This* Marcia's heart flipped and somersaulted when he walked in. *That* Marcia was younger and more apprentice than master of her emotions, less sure of what she was feeling, but she felt a tug and had a sexy thought about Thomas's nice hands and fine posture.

"Sir?" said Thomas to Silvestro. "Are you pestering my employee?"

"*Non chiamarmi* 'sir,'" objected Silvestro. "Do not call me 'sir.' I am a man in love, not a *sir*. My heart is hot as a bubbling kettle. A person with a kettle for a heart is not a *sir*. Sir is *cold*, like the icicle. Or the shivering little bird."

Thomas ignored this strange pair of similes and said, "Are you here to buy a donut?"

"A donut!" cried Silvestro. "Of course I have come to buy a donut from this beautiful lady." He scanned the choices in the case. His eyes skimmed right past Mr. Whiskey without seeing that there was a large gray cat sleeping on one of the empty donut trays. He looked up and spoke to Marcia. "For days I have searched for you. All my soul has been exploding with desire to see you again. I am a man in tiny bits. Like a circus clown torn to pieces by the lion. My finger, sick with love, is there"—he pointed out the window to the sidewalk—"and my nostril, also sick with love . . . it is here." He pointed at the floor by his foot and then stamped hard, obliterating the nostril. "My feet—"

"Marcia, do you want me to escort this character out?" interrupted Thomas. She remembered this about Thomas: his lovely tenor voice, which was always level and calm at the craziest times and made her think he really could deal with the worst of the worst, though in fact she'd never seen him required to handle anything more serious than incompetent counter help and a malfunctioning deep fryer, or the city health inspector. (She wouldn't actually *see* him handle the cleanup of a corpse, and anyway, that hadn't happened yet.)

"I told you. I am not a *character*. Or a *sir*! I am a lion-shredded clown dying from desire. I am a bubbly black kettle simmering with love. I said to myself when you ran away from me, this girl smells like sweet dough. Like a Dunkin' donut. Possibly she cooks donuts. Possibly she eats too many donuts and needs to eat more fruit so she does not blow up like *un dirigibile gigante*. To smell like a donut, she must spend time where donuts are occurring. I will find this woman who slays my soul when I find the place that has made her smell."

Thomas stared hard at Silvestro with a look that said, "Is this guy for real?" Finally, he reached a judgment. "I don't like the way you talk to her. But," he said, turning to Marcia, "he appears to be harmless. If he wants a donut, sell him one."

"Harmless! What monster would harm this perfect woman?" snorted Silvestro. "I have come here to beg her to marry me, so I can take care of her and please her forever."

Marcia said, "I don't really like being taken care of or pleased. If that was your proposal, I'm not interested."

"OK, then I will *win* you like tenpins," said Silvestro with delighted conviction.

Thomas shook his head and went back to the kitchen, and Marcia, who'd felt secure and happy in his presence, now felt vacant. But she hid it as she waited on Silvestro. He ate two crullers at one of the tables, then carefully folded the napkin she had touched, kissed it, and put it in his pants pocket. He left, promising to the air on his way out that he'd be back the next day.

The bell on the door dinged as he headed across the street. Marcia's eyes went to the old-fashioneds. She felt an impulse to seize the gun and shoot something, *bang*. But the feeling quickly passed.

She looked at her watch and saw that she'd miss her three-thirty class if she didn't leave soon. "Hey!" she shouted to Thomas in the back. "I have to go to class!"

One of the fry cooks stuck his head through the kitchen door. "Mae's on her way. Hang on." And indeed, a minute later, there was Mae, short for Nelrethamae, darting in out of breath, hunched and wiry, a batik scarf covering her small bald head, which was shaved to a sheen in sympathy with someone important—a celebrity cancer patient or a political prisoner, Marcia could not remember which. Mae was the lady who replaced Marcia as counter attendant on Monday, Wednesday, and Friday afternoons. She was ageless—perhaps forty-eight, or sixty, or even seventy-five—and she was every bit the straight shooter, like Thomas. She was also ultrapolitical. At first Marcia had thought she and Thomas were mother and son.

"How are you, dear? Sorry I'm late," said Mae. "I had an appointment about one of my causes at a remote location, and time got away from me."

"That's OK," said Marcia. She suspected she was supposed to ask which cause, and where the remote location was, but she was rushing to get her things and leave.

Mae took off her headscarf, wiped her shiny head with a napkin, put on her ball cap and apron and gloves, and called back to Thomas, "I'm here, Tommy!" She always said "Tommy."

Marcia envied what seemed to be a close, longtime connection with Thomas. She couldn't quite figure it out. All she knew was that they weren't related, because she'd asked—and for once Thomas had answered, rather than telling her it wasn't her job to ask questions.

Back at the Warehouse College, Marcia rushed straight to class. It was a historical seminar about the twentieth century in literature, for which they were reading a lot of dull realistic novels. The loner protagonists, men and women both, slogged through urban hellscapes halfheartedly pursuing alcohol or sex. They were insatiable, peevish malcontents whose moral stance was wholly transactional. Nothing much could be said about them other than that, but her professor was bent on saying it anyway. Mr. Whiskey came with her and sat in the desk next to hers, twitching his nose and whiskers in the musty classroom. Despite his invisibility, he gave off a kind of guardian vibe that kept people from sitting on him. Usually someone took the desk next to Marcia, but today everyone stayed away. A couple of people stared at the empty desk, looking hostile and upset.

Back at her dorm room, Mr. Whiskey walked around sniffing in all the interesting places. He touched the radiator with his paw. He jumped on her desk and sniffed the books, pausing to examine the tape-patched spine of *Men Built It out of Wood*. "There's something here," he said.

"It was my father's," said Marcia.

"I like it. Hang on to it," said Mr. Whiskey.

"I will. I *did*," said Marcia, picturing it on her bookshelf in Round Stone in 2018, where it had sat for years.

The cat scrambled up on a plant stand and looked out the window for a bit. Finally he settled himself into the depression in her beanbag chair. "I've never seen one of these. The man I loved did not have one," he said of the chair.

"Real people don't have them. Only students and kids," said Marcia. She could see him quite well. The cat struck her as more material now that they were alone.

"I haven't been to college before," he said, "so I might be way off base, but there's something sketchy about this place."

"What?"

"Let me count the ways: lame lecture, pit of a classroom, uncomfortable seats, weird-looking students. Some of those people were forty. Or older. You were the only one listening."

"They're nontraditional," explained Marcia.

"Three or four of them slept through the class. The professor may have been high. Didn't you notice this before?"

"Not really, no," said Marcia. In truth, when she'd gone to college, she had been so happy to be parted from Nina and the Noisetteses that she hadn't looked at any of it too closely—the full-ride scholarship announced by a handwritten line on a blank on a postcard, the weak curriculum and transitory population of underprepared students. She was afraid if she asked too many questions, there would be a poof of sparkle dust and it would all vanish.

The more adult Marcia nodded and said, "You're right. I was too young back then to be very discriminating. Or wary."

"Another thing," said Mr. Whiskey, "at the donut shop. Thomas saw me. He pretended not to, but he knew I was there. I think the bald lady did, too."

"What do you mean?" said Marcia anxiously.

"They see me just like you do. They can probably hear me. I don't know if that's good or bad. They *seem* all right. But I couldn't read them."

"What about Silvestro?"

Mr. Whiskey gave a wide pink yawn and said, "I was invisible to him, at least. But let me tell you, girl, you shacked up—are about to shack up—with a genuine bozo. An Italian with no guile in him. He's totally what he seems to be. Thomas was trying to size him up, too. All that silly jabber about the dismembered clown? He really meant it. He didn't just get struck by a thunderbolt when he saw you; he got blown up by a *cannon*."

Suddenly it hit the more adult Marcia: "Oh, my God. I can't go through that courtship again. It was awful. He came into Homerun Donuts every day and ordered crullers and talked like that. He was like a slobbery puppy that wouldn't give up trying to get in my lap. It just wore me down, so I finally said yes, I'd go out with him, and then—" A sick feeling overwhelmed her. "Then I yielded my virginity to him—and I liked it! He was good in bed. *Really* good."

She was shaking, and she put her head in her hands. "The best climaxes of my life!" she moaned. "Why do you think I tolerated him for all those months? But if I have to go through that again, I'll probably have a heart attack from the sex at my age. Besides, I need to get back to now. Something is happening with Howie. I don't know what, but he wouldn't send me a message with a pickup truck unless it was bad."

"If you want freedom—a new life—and safety for your son— you have to put now on hold," the cat reminded her. "But the good news is that then *is* now, and *now* is then. Which automatically puts the real now on hold. You don't have to do a thing except be you. Your heart *is* twenty-two and will hold out. I didn't know you were such a slave to sex, though. But I hear you. I don't want to personally witness that show. I never did know what to do when the humans started rolling around. Sit there and watch? Bite their feet? Hide under the bed?"

He thought for a second. "We didn't jump quite far enough ahead, obviously. How much longer till Silvestro's accident?

Marcia made a calculation in her head and told him.

"Let's do this," said Mr. Whiskey.

And they did. At the last second, as she was thinning out and starting through the straw, she heard him ask, "What happened exactly? What kind of accident?"

"He stepped on a . . ." said Marcia.

And then there was only the roar of time.

My fear of the desert began before my parents divorced and my
mother left. Her disappearance one night while I was sleeping
didn't frighten me. I was raised by nannies and tutors: my
relationship with her was, if anything, even more distant than
my relationship with my father. Actually, I did see her leaving
that morning. I woke early to the warbling of wrens and looked
out my window to see the car being loaded with more bags than
anyone would travel with, and then there she was in the drive
with her dogs: a black cocker whose name I've forgotten and a
long-haired red dachshund, Pimpernel. She looked ecstatic to
be leaving, a snap to her walk. The driver touched her arm, a
gentle warning about lateness. Then she got in the car, a dog on
each side in the leather back seat.

I didn't miss her much. She loved those dogs but was
otherwise shallow and grating to be around. She chewed loudly
and stared at me with narrowed eyes when we had Sunday
brunch together. She called me Gordon, my middle name,
which was also my father's name, so it was confusing. She asked
what I was thinking about and then ridiculed my answers—so
I learned to make things up. "The desert," I said one day, out
of desperation. She laughed louder than ever and then stopped
and said, "You know the stories, don't you? Did any of your
nannies tell you? The tribe of sorcerers that live there? The
Desert People, they're called. Immortal avengers. They're as old
as time and have special powers, and you don't want to mess
with them." She was looking at us both as she said this. She
wasn't pretty enough to be a trophy or smart enough to be an
asset. If she had depth, it was invisible. My father's acquisition
of her was inexplicable, unless it was all about sex, but he didn't
hold on to her long. She thrilled at the thought of making
people feel bad. She was a vampire in that way, sucking the
happiness out of others like blood. Genetically, the resemblance

is there: I was not the only member of my family to discern the pleasure in extreme unpleasantness.

—MEMOIRS OF SOCRATIES LOVE

Powers Commonly Ascribed to the Desert People

Invisibility

Flight

Shapeshifting

Ability to freeze adversaries

Second sight

Superhuman stretch

Running at the speed of light

X-ray vision

Prognostication

Mind control

Poison spittle

Turning adversaries into toads or vermin

Mind reading

Time-travel

—THE INFORMATION HATCH

Chapter 15

"A Pop-Tart," she finished when the roaring of their passage died down. They were back at Homerun Donuts, but they were outside the shop now.

"What's that? Some kind of explosive?" said Mr. Whiskey.

"It's a breakfast pastry that you warm up in your toaster."

"No one dies from stepping on a pastry. Unless . . . was there a trip wire in it?'

"It was just a brown sugar–cinnamon Pop-Tart. Frosted. That was what started it."

The cat changed the subject. "Are we coming or going?" he asked, eying the Homerun storefront.

Marcia looked down at her shirt. Other than the ball cap, the Homerun uniform was a plain white T-shirt and a pin-on badge. Below her badge were small spots of grease, or possibly icing. She pulled the end of her sleeve up to her nose and sniffed. "We're not coming; we're on our way home," she said. "This shirt's dirty. And smells like donuts. I'm not much of a laundress, but I always went to work in a clean T-shirt. Thomas was strict about cleanliness. Mostly because of the city health inspector. But also his acne."

They started walking. The architecturally conglomerate cityscape spread before them and in all directions. Marcia thought about what it would be like soon, not to be bound to Holliday College or Round Stone or Nina and Kirk and their kin. She could *almost* believe in it—that it was going to happen, that she would be free to build her own life. It was a high-winds day, and the sleeves of her shirt rippled against her arms, which felt strong and alive, like small, active lizards were living under her skin, breathing in and out like accordions and running around.

"I feel so young. I never noticed how much aging takes out of you," she told Mr. Whiskey.

"Try cremation," he said. "It's a lot worse. Unless you get lucky and reconstitute."

The way he locomoted through the city was new and must have been related to his less material condition. She was not carrying him, exactly, but neither was he exactly walking or flying. He was part of her, but not. The best way she could describe it was that it was like having an invisible nonexistent sidecar attached to you, with a marginally visible (to you) reconstituted cat riding in it. Once again, she considered, for just a second, the possibility that she had gone off the rails mentally.

"You're totally sane," Mr. Whiskey reassured her.

"How are you moving?" she asked him.

"I'm not sure. It's just something that happens now. Where are we going?"

"Silvestro's," said Marcia. "My feet are insisting on going there, so he and I must be living together now. Which means I'm also pregnant. So is Howie in me? Or on What Island? Or both?"

"Don't overthink this," said the cat.

They had to take the L to get to Silvestro's apartment. They got off at the nearest station and walked to his building. A clock in the window of an office lobby told them it was three fifteen. "He's still at work," said Marcia. "He works for Burroughs Software Solutions. Named after Edgar Rice Burroughs, the pulp-fiction writer. Creator of Tarzan and a lot of pulp sci-fi. Moon maids, spacemen, previously frozen cavemen/professional wrestlers. Racist, I'm sorry to say—I'm not sure how I know that. Burroughs was born in Chicago, and the company founder is a fan of his work. I don't know exactly what Silvestro does. Every time he talks about Burroughs Software, he lapses into Italian, so I just tune it out."

"You're speaking in present tense, I notice."

"Then *is* now," agreed Marcia. "I can feel it."

Inside the apartment, Marcia got herself a glass of water and put some in a bowl for Mr. Whiskey. She gave him a salad plate of pastina with cream poured over it. He ate it hungrily. "You still have a good appetite," she remarked.

He didn't say anything but trotted around the apartment, noticing the things she'd moved there from her dorm room: the beanbag chair, the hot pot, her few pairs of shoes, her schoolbooks. He found *Men Built It out of Wood* and sniffed it again. "I really like this book," he said. "It elicits considerable purring."

"The college didn't want me moving out of the dorm. They made a lot of noise about it. At first they said they were going to revoke my scholarship for immorality. But then they backed off."

"Good for you, asserting yourself."

"I didn't do anything. They just changed their mind."

Mr. Whiskey jumped on the couch and stretched out on his side. His length was impressive. The couch was cream-colored faux leather, and against it, Mr. Whiskey's gray fur took on a rich blue tint. "Tell me about this wrongful-death settlement," he said. "How did that happen?"

Marcia cast about in memory. It had been such a long time. But it also hadn't happened yet, which was strange—and if they were successful in saving Silvestro, it never would happen. She found that, as with their last hop, she still retained the knowledge of the older future Marcia but also the younger, current Marcia. Howie and Cor-Spamkeer hovered on the edge of her consciousness, but they were less insistent than in her 2018 life: a ghostly outline of danger rather than the real thing.

"So after Silvestro died, I went to see a lawyer. I'd told my adviser at the Warehouse College that I might have to miss some classes because my boyfriend had died and I had to move back into the dorm. There didn't seem to be any Marcos coming to take care of the legal affairs; none of them showed up to help. Then I figured out that I was pregnant. *Am* pregnant." She patted her still flat belly and thought about Howie. It would be nice to see him again when he arrived in nine months, even though he would be much smaller than the last time she'd seen him and unable to talk. At least he'd be safer.

"The baby was a big complication. My adviser didn't know about it. She recommended an attorney named Fortress to help me figure out how to handle Silvestro's last things and get him buried. I thought the name 'Fortress' sounded reassuring. I went to see him, and he took charge of everything—the funeral arrangements, terminating the lease, liquidating Silvestro's possessions. He didn't know about the baby until I threw up at the funeral. When he discovered that I was carrying Silvestro's baby, he told me that I—my baby—had a good chance of winning a wrongful-death suit against Burroughs for the Pop-Tart on the floor when they were unveiling the bust."

"What?" said Mr. Whiskey.

Marcia continued, "He helped me sue Burroughs on behalf of Howie, and the company settled out of court. Fortress negotiated the trust arrangements. I agreed to go to Round Stone—I had no idea Nina would move there. Fortress kept trying to talk me into investing individually, too, but I had enough on my mind, and I didn't have anything to invest except my Homerun Donuts paychecks. I guess I do now—I mean, I will in the twenty-first century. Even though there was the trust for Howie, I still saved for myself. I've got some money. I have it in 2018, I mean."

"We could hop to Round Stone in 2018 and bring it back."

"But wealth isn't going to save me from being tied to Round Stone and Nina. Only keeping Silvestro alive will do that. We have to stay on track."

Mr. Whiskey closed his eyes and went to sleep for a few seconds. Abruptly he woke up. "Why did the settlement require you to go to Round Stone?" he said.

"It didn't *require* me to go anywhere. But Howie got three times the money if we chose Round Stone. I wanted to be sure he was well provided for."

"Hmm. Very strange," said the cat. And then, sounding somewhat panicked, as if he'd just thought of this: "What day is it? *When* is Silvestro going to die? We need to make sure it doesn't happen."

Marcia went to Silvestro's desk, where he kept a small flip calendar. "Tomorrow," she said. "It's tomorrow!"

AT JUST AFTER SIX, they heard Silvestro in the hall; he was singing something by the Kinks. He had a good voice that carried, even when he wasn't being intentionally loud. The second day of his appearing at the donut shop came back to her. She'd heard him quite clearly outside, speaking in a euphonious foghorn voice to a passerby, and recognized the voice before the bell on the door jangled and he rushed in, full of passionate love talk. He wanted a cruller for here and an old-fashioned to go. In the back, Thomas heard, too, and he came up and kept a watch on things. In later weeks, after she and Silvestro had started dating, Thomas probed her surprisingly personally about her new boyfriend, and he often came up from the kitchen or office and engaged Silvestro in chitchat about Italy and the software company. It was more than idle conversation—he was trying to gather information. Silvestro didn't appear to notice or be bothered by this, though. He was perennially voluble and not terribly private.

Marcia was flattered that Thomas cared enough to want to look out for her.

Now, hearing Silvestro in the hall, the young Marcia felt a mix of anticipation and dread, but the older Marcia was worried. "How do I keep from doing something that will change things?" she asked Mr. Whiskey.

"Isn't that what we're here for?"

"I mean, things we don't want to change."

"There's not much you can do; just follow his lead," said Mr. Whiskey. "He doesn't know his days are numbered. Here today, dead tomorrow. Or not dead, if this works."

"OK," said Marcia. And when Silvestro swept in and flew toward her, she let him embrace her and kiss her wetly. Then he picked her up and carried her around the apartment, which was something she'd forgotten about: he'd liked to tote her around, crooning at her and telling her about his day in Italian.

Mr. Whiskey watched with no expression. But after a minute of this, he said, "See if you can get some of this office stuff in English. It might help us tomorrow."

"Silvestro, honey?" said Marcia tentatively. She wriggled around to indicate that she was ready to be put down.

"*Mia cara, voglio portarti tra le mie braccia per il resto della mi vita come un fascio di preziosa lavanderia.*"

"Could you try to speak English more, so I can understand you?"

"I want to carry you in my arms for the rest of my life. Like a clump of the most valuable laundry," said Silvestro.

"What were you saying about the office? About Burroughs?"

"Tomorrow is *un giorno speciale.* They are dedicating a representation of Edgar Burroughs—it is a *busto* of the head. He arrives at nine. *Poco dopo,* there will be a speech. They have asked me to make a PowerPoint of this *dedicazione* because Mr. Alvaro has a voice *molto dolce,* and maybe people do not hear this speech and need to read the letters on the screen. So I have made this production, and it is mine to run the slides because it is an important speech."

"Get him to put you down," said the cat.

"Put me down, please," said Marcia.

Silvestro obliged. For having a desk job, he was quite strong, but he could lug her about for only so long.

"Ask if you can come to the dedication."

"I'm afraid to alter things too much," she whispered to the cat.

"Fine," said Mr. Whiskey. "But it would give us an excuse to show up tomorrow and get rid of the Pop-Tart. How *did* he die, exactly?"

"Later," whispered Marcia. Because Silvestro had produced a bag of carry-out food and a bottle of wine, and it was time for dinner. She set the table while he laid out the food. It was fish and chips, coleslaw, and biscuits. And a piece of cheesecake from the deli down the street for dessert.

Mr. Whiskey hovered about while they ate, and Marcia quietly slipped bits of fish off her plate and dropped them—the minute she let go of them, they became more translucent, as the cat was. She assumed that in the case of anyone who couldn't see him at all, they would just disappear. Silvestro was staring across at her and didn't notice, or he would have been very upset to see her dropping pieces of fish that vanished into thin air before they hit the floor.

After the cheesecake, they cleaned up, and while she wiped the counter, he came over and put his arms around her and pressed his crotch against her backside. His erection was unmistakable. And welcome, she had to admit.

The cat made himself scarce while Marcia and Silvestro decamped to the bed. There Silvestro gently undressed her and kissed her all over her chest and then pulled off his own clothes more briskly. As Marcia watched him, things came back to the older version of herself: the shock of all that dark body hair against his creamy light skin; the long, surprisingly silky-feeling penis that at this moment was rearing defiantly from the dark tumbleweed at his groin. He jumped onto the bed and proceeded to please and take care of her, as he'd promised that first day in the donut shop. It was all exactly as she recalled: the disconcerting feeling of plunging headlong into a hedonistic pleasure fest and simultaneously watching from a remote observer's station, berating herself for her weakness: how could she be ensnared by mere sex? Today, added to it all, was the knowledge that a teeny-tiny Howie was in her somewhere, in the general vicinity where Silvestro was poking. She hoped it wouldn't traumatize him.

Afterward, Silvestro got up and wandered to the kitchen for a glass of tea. He started reciting, apparently from memory, the speech he was to project in his PowerPoint the next day. His voice carried through the apartment: "Today we recognize our debt to Edgar Burroughs, our namesake. True son of Chicago, true entrepreneur. He saw a niche no one had yet noticed: a niche with no ape men, so he filled it with the most famous ape man of all. And the moon maids. And *uomini* of the caves. I mean, the cavemen. At Burroughs Sotware solutions, we are following in his footsteps."

"It's 'software,'" whispered Mr. Whiskey, who had reappeared and jumped up on the bed with Marcia. "Not 'sotware.'"

He nipped her arm rudely, and she sat up, pulling the sheet around her to cover her nudity.

"Listen. How *did* Silvestro die?" he said.

"He stepped on a Pop-Tart that someone had brought in for breakfast and dropped on the floor near the AV booth while they were dedicating the bust. This was after the speech, so he started to go to the men's room on the next floor for a paper towel to wipe off his shoe. But there was a line for the elevators because everyone had come down to the gallery level for the dedication, and now they were all going back to their offices. He took the stairs, and he tripped and fell down one flight, hit his head on the railing, and cracked his skull. He was hospitalized for a week, and then he died. He was conscious for a while when I saw him in the hospital. That's the reason I know all this."

Mr. Whiskey listened and then said thoughtfully, "Let me sleep on this. There's something funny. Silvestro's pretty fit and athletic. If he can keep his balance carrying you around the apartment, I have trouble with him falling on the stairs. And who brings a frosted toaster thing to a dedication ceremony? You know what I think? Someone deliberately arranged an 'accident' because they wanted to get rid of Silvestro."

"Why?"

"I don't know. But we have to be on our toes tomorrow to make sure they don't get to him. And then we're going to get you right back to your new future, your *liberated* future, the second we've saved him."

"And we'll check up on Howie? Why can't we just go now?"

Mr. Whiskey stared at her.

"Oh, right. For a minute I thought we'd already saved him. The time change is messing me up."

She remembered then that she had a history quiz to study for, and she put on a T-shirt and clean underpants and got to work, even though Mr. Whiskey had implied that the classes and faculty at the Warehouse College were not very high quality, and she could probably turn in anything and still get an A.

And so went the evening, with Marcia studying various American acts and multinational treaties and Silvestro playing *Fallout* on his PC until everyone, including the cat, fell asleep.

I was determined to have more than my fifteen minutes of fame. I wanted something enduring. Fifteen *centuries* of fame. Something without precedent, to make people remember. My father's success had withered in the end because he'd made the mistake of selling what people wanted: readily available airline flights, comfort, low prices, with the option of luxury fares to flaunt wealth for those who wanted that. But no market share is eternal: the competition is always salivating at the prospect of getting some of yours. When competition got fierce, and then regulations got tight and economic ups and downs stressed the travel industry, his airlines (not "his" in toto; he held portions of several) started to take shortcuts. Cut, cut. Snip, snip, snip. Then people were no longer getting what they wanted. And to make matters worse, there were crashes and incidents. Planes grounded. Lawsuits. Falling share prices, bankruptcies. Finis.

Soon, he was old. Friends had deserted him. He lost the use of his legs. He began to have doubts and talk about chimeric notions he'd always discounted: generosity, compassion. Of course, it was too late, but he'd recognized something: that laying all your bets on the desires of others—for transportation or anything else—missed the boat.

Did I say that he was old when I was born? My mother was wife number three. After she packed up and left with her darling hounds, it was just the two of us. And the household help. I was nine then. I was fifteen when he lost his grip and, together with the airlines, crashed.

One day a few years after that (I was around seventeen), having it out with him over a small family matter in his townhouse, I gave his shoulder a shove. Not meaning to—but it was enough to topple the old flyweight out of his chair. He planted facedown, and I watched blood pool around his head like a crown. A carmine circle shaped like a saint's halo in an antique painting. I shouted for his aide, who came running and picked him up, swabbed him clean. He was lucid and unfazed. Not even a concussion. But it sent me a message: Don't build your fame on a pile of money, and don't build on human wishes, which are transitory and fickle; you will surely fall. Build instead on things eternal: the body's frailty and a lake of blood. Build on what everyone most fears. Build on what no one wants. On what anyone would do anything to avoid. Then, you will prevail.

—MEMOIRS OF SOCRATIES (SICKRABIES) LOVE

Chapter 16

In the morning, Marcia woke just as Silvestro was leaving. He was dressed in a dark jacket and smashing tie. If you didn't know what a goof he was, you would be struck by his Leonardo DiCaprio looks and European flair, especially the bright tie and bicycle-toe wingtips.

No sooner was he out the door than Marcia pulled on clothes, and she and Mr. Whiskey ran to catch the train—rather, she ran and Mr. Whiskey traveled via his urban locomotion in the hypothetical sidecar. Fortunately, Marcia was young and looked great when she rolled out of bed and ran out the door without doing anything more than running her fingers through her hair and slapping her face to freshen it. She was adorable: tight shirt, butt-hugging pants, big breasts, and dark, mussed bedhead. When confronted by the middle-aged security guard at the tall, glass-walled Burroughs Building, she simply said she was going to be late for the dedication and had forgotten her company ID, and he looked at her breasts and pretty young face, smiled, and let her pass.

Mr. Whiskey didn't get stopped because he was invisible.

They found the gallery level just as the ceremony was starting. There was an AV booth at one end, and Silvestro was already in it; he didn't see them come in.

Marcia scanned the room. "Where's the Pop-Tart?" she asked the cat urgently. "I don't see it!"

He trotted around the perimeter and then dashed into the thick of the assembled employees. Marcia had had no inkling he could move so fast. Around and between and even through people's legs he shot, like a gray fur projectile. There were more well-turned-out professional women than Marcia expected, which made her momentarily jealous. There were sixty or seventy employees in all. She'd thought Burroughs was an intimate operation of mostly grungy young male geeks; she must have missed a lot about Silvestro's company by not asking him to translate from the Italian.

The cat came bouncing back, panting, and said, "Over there. The lady with the blond updo in the gray pencil skirt and stilettos. She's got a plate with a perforated square thing. It looks like a dehydrated sandwich."

"That's it!"

At first Marcia couldn't find her in the crowd. But then she saw her, making her way toward the AV booth. Mr. Whiskey had described her to a T. Marcia wondered how he knew about pencil skirts and updos. She herself was barely conversant in these things: Nina had often laughed at her clogs and called them "Midwestern staff-nurse chic."

Arrived at a spot near the booth, the woman stood facing the podium and the still veiled bust. She looked around casually and then dangled her hand low at her side. In it was a paper plate with the Pop-Tart. If she set it down, it would be right in Silvestro's path when he exited the booth.

Mr. Alvaro was just finishing: "So to sum it up, at Burroughs Software Solutions, we are following in his footsteps, filling the unnoticed niches, meeting the public demands and going them one better. I thank you all for being part of our visionary team. And now, with no further ado, here's Edgar!"

Off came the covering, and there was the *busto*. It was of a young Burroughs, with a forehead that sloped back gently, heavy-lidded eyes, a straight, strong nose, and a rounded chin. There was not one extraordinary thing about him other than the fact that he looked so unremarkable. Marcia wanted to laugh because it looked like Mr. Alvaro had just unveiled a bust of an insurance salesman or a school superintendent. A couple of people did laugh underneath the short burst of polite applause. The blond woman clapped, too. Then she artfully leaned over amid the applause, set her Pop-Tart on the designated spot, and soon hurried away.

The last slide stayed on the screen for a minute and then went blank, and the projector turned off.

Marcia was trying to get over to the other side of the room and grab the Pop-Tart before Silvestro stepped on it, but there were so many people, and it was harder than she'd expected. Silvestro emerged from the booth, and suddenly the cat was rocketing away again. As she watched, a man appeared out of nowhere and muscled up against Silvestro, sending him stumbling toward the pastry, but at that moment, Mr. Whiskey intervened. Somehow, despite his lack of substance, he nudged Silvestro in the other direction. Oblivious to having been rescued, Silvestro recovered his balance and moved toward the elevator, cheerfully greeting colleagues and stopping a moment to pay his respects to the newly dedicated bust. Then he joined the cluster of people waiting to get on the next UP elevator. Marcia and the cat stood a short distance away, out of view, waiting to make sure he got on.

And then the man they'd seen earlier, who'd tried to shove him onto the Pop-Tart, reappeared. He tapped Silvestro on the shoulder, smiled, and whispered to him, nodding at the door to the stairway. Silvestro assessed things—the number of people waiting and the poky progress of the two elevators up to the eighth floor and back down.

After a minute, he headed for the stairs.

"There's someone in the stairwell waiting to push him," said the cat. "Let's go!"

One thing about Mr. Whiskey—he never hesitates, thought Marcia, and for the briefest of seconds she found herself comparing him very favorably to Orson, who had been fearful of not just fireworks on the Fourth of July but also brooms and the garden hose, even though no one had hit him or sprayed him with water in all the years she had him.

"Aren't you afraid?" she whispered to the cat.

"Fear is an absence. Reconstitution has made me too impenetrable to be afraid. Still, I don't much care for the snapping of a trash bag when you shake it open to line a wastebasket," he admitted.

Marcia opened the door and peered into the stairwell. Silvestro was halfway up the next flight. It was him for sure: there were the pointy Italian shoes.

Mr. Whiskey scooted through the door. Marcia followed.

"Look!" the cat said in a loud whisper. Another pair of shoes was descending toward Silvestro. Marcia thought she recognized them, and her thoughts went in a million directions.

"*Buongiorno*, Signor Donut!" called Silvestro cheerfully to the approaching shoes—his would-be assassin's.

"Silvestro! Watch out!" shouted Marcia.

He turned and looked down at her. "My love!" he exclaimed. He spun around and took the stairs back down two at a time to greet her. Meanwhile the man on the stairs above him had turned and was bounding back up. When he reached the next floor, he ran out, and the heavy emergency door slammed behind him.

Silvestro wrapped Marcia in an embrace. "My beautiful woman. You fill my heart like a bucket to see you with your messy hair. But what are you doing here?"

"I'm so proud of you. I just wanted to see you," she lied.

"And what was your boss doing at the *dedicazione*?"

"So that was—"

"It was Signor Thomas. Why is he here?"

Marcia's thoughts were in chaos. Thomas Cook? Killed Silvestro? Why? It wasn't possible. She started to object, to question Silvestro, but before she could, she felt the cat's claws in her shoulders and saw the tail start to windmill.

"We have to go now! Before anything happens to Silvestro!" cried the cat.

The transition went faster this time. She was in the straw and thin as a wire. And Silvestro was in the straw with her. They were entwined, melded stickily, like two strands of a Twizzler. "I'm getting better at this," trilled Mr. Whiskey. "Three of you! You, him, and Howie!"

But something was wrong. The progress was fast, but within it, something long and slow and awful was unfolding. She could feel it, looming and crashing at her and engulfing her. Her heart was bursting; her chest was compressing; her mind was evacuated and rubberized, and for a brief flash she thought she would die—and then she wanted to die. Her whole body was trying to rip apart but also to pack itself into something the size of a saddle-soap tin. Maybe it was the pregnancy. After all, somewhere in the accelerated voyage, she would have given birth.

But she felt no joy, as one should at having a baby, only the faint residue of something she'd once seen that had made her *briefly* happy—a rare moment of happiness in her life after her parents died: a cow lying in a pasture on a sunny day when she had been in the car with the Noisetteses, driving to one of their many boring family excursions that had made her feel so left out. Marcia had looked out the window and seen a brown-and-white cow, and the cow had looked back at her. The cow had opened its mouth, like it was laughing. It was mooing, and though Marcia could not hear it across the distance, she felt like the cow was conveying a message to her, telling her she'd see her parents again someday.

The cow reverie faded. The straw was expelling them. Then she was out. She felt herself plumping back up. She could hear Silvestro's foghorn voice as backdrop. But she couldn't see. Her vision was shrouded, and another voice was speaking to her. Speaking to her alone. Right in her ear. It was her father, Dale. She almost wept to hear his voice. She *was* weeping. There were tears running all over, but her eyes wouldn't open.

You've made a mistake, my dearest little Turtle Turd. You'll see. But don't worry. Nothing is done that can't be undone, nothing broken that can't be fixed. You and the cat will find a way. But in the meantime, watch out. . . .

"WATCH OUT. SEE IF you can stop her thrashing around." It was Nina speaking. "I'm afraid she's going to throw herself off the couch. Does anyone have a handkerchief? Her face is sopping."

"Sì. Here is one." It was Silvestro's loud, musical voice.

Marcia opened her eyes. Nina and Silvestro were leaning over her. Forty-something Nina, of the frosted blond bob, was mopping her tears with the handkerchief. And fiftyish Silvestro was peering at her worriedly. How gray and haggardly rugged he looked—more Pacino than DiCaprio now. A tan, anxious Kirk hovered behind them. "Should I call an ambulance?" he said.

"No, no, she sometimes faints like this," said Silvestro. "It is always happening these last few months. I think it is because she is thinking about Howie. But it is worse in the nights, when she is tired."

"Where am I?" said Marcia. And then felt stupid for talking like an amnesia victim in a TV drama. She was starting to feel more herself, though her father's words still lingered in her mind: *"You and the cat will find a way."*

"You're at home, Marsh," said Nina.

"But this is *your* house," said Marcia. She sat up and looked around. It definitely was Nina's house, though the furniture was all wrong. It had the spaces. And the seating—though it was different seating. It had the real Persian rugs. As further evidence, on one of the end tables was the ornamental silver tray that Nina used to carry her energy knobs around.

"Are we in Round Stone?"

"Boy, is she out of it," said Kirk.

"Shhh!" said Nina. "For God's sake, Kirk. She just fainted. Of course she's disoriented."

Over in a corner was the cat. He was watching the scene, now and then lightly grooming his chest and shoulders. Marcia waited for the others to notice him, but one by one they all looked in the direction she was staring, and no one said anything. So he must be invisible in all times but the actual, true, original one where they'd started.

"What are you looking at, *mi amore*?" said Silvestro.

"Nothing. I'm just really tired," said Marcia and lay back down.

"I'll get her some soup. I made some last night, and I brought you leftovers," said Kirk.

She remembered suddenly that Kirk was a horrible cook. "*Please,* don't bring me soup." She sat back up. "I think I'm OK, actually."

"Marsh, do you feel up to finishing our game?" said Nina. "Or should we go home?"

"Game?" She thought for a second, trying to remember, and while she was straining to recall, the cat whispered, "Botticelli. I think you should continue. I'm not sure what's what yet, but the only way to figure that out is to stick with the script. Which, apparently, is a game of Botticelli."

"I think I'm OK," said Marcia to Nina. Though she didn't feel OK at all.

"I don't know how to play," she said to Mr. Whiskey.

"They don't, either," said the cat. "Just go along with it."

She waited to see if they'd noticed her talking to herself and then remembered that in all other times but the original one, her conversations with Mr. Whiskey were on a different plane and couldn't be heard. The Noisettes-Pettysaleses and Silvestro were all still waiting for her to say yes or no.

"Let's play," said Marcia.

Nina smiled. "Wonderful. I'll get us some more wine first. If you don't mind me rooting around in your kitchen?"

No one minded.

Nina went to the kitchen and came back with a newly un-corked bottle of malbec, which she poured for the others, and a glass of ginger ale for Marcia. "No wine for you, Marsh. Not after that scary spell," she said.

"I'm really fine," said Marcia, sipping and getting bubbles up her nose.

"Should we start over?" said Kirk. "I don't remember where we were on that last one."

"Good idea," said Nina. "Do you want to go again? With a new person?"

Kirk was sitting on a brocaded loveseat, shoes off, sock feet draped over Nina's lap now that she'd sat down again. Marcia was on the sofa, and Silvestro sat in a leather recliner at an angle. Marcia had started to understand that this was her furniture. She had a clear memory of picking it out with Silvestro and of look-ing at this house with him and the Realtor. She remembered wad-dling through it, pregnant, and talking about the floor plan and the aging sewer line. She knew that Silvestro was a tech executive with a company just outside Bixby, that he'd done an online MBA and quickly moved up, and that she'd gone on for an MA her-self and ran the museum at Holliday College at a generous salary. But she also remembered her other life, working in High Cultural Endeavors for a lowly hourly wage. Her memory of that life was much better.

She pulled out her phone and looked at it. It was the same day in 2018 from which she and Mr. Whiskey had embarked when they'd time-traveled back to the donut shop. There were no calls or messages from Howie, but there was a series of increasingly demanding messages from Nina about the Botticelli game this evening. So they'd come back to exactly the same day they'd left from. The difference was that now Silvestro was alive. And they were married.

Not the only difference, though—there was the house. She wondered if Nina and Kirk lived in her house from the other life. "Nina, how are things on Funnel Street?" she asked cagily.

Nina blushed and said, "Just because you have that cushy museum job and Silvestro makes a wad of money doesn't mean you have to rub it in."

"There's nothing *wrong* with Funnel Street," said Marcia. "Lots of good salt-of-the-earth types live on Funnel."

"I take it 'salt of the earth' is not a compliment?" said Mr. Whiskey. He had strolled closer. Now he jumped up in Nina's lap and sniffed at Kirk's ankles. "Why does he smell like butter and lighter fluid?"

"It's the spray-tan chemicals, I think," said Marcia.

"What's that?"

"He goes into a booth, and they spray stuff on his skin, and it turns him orangey brown."

"Ah," said the cat. "I can see more colors now than when I was a basic cat, but I don't know all their appellations." He touched Kirk's ankle with his paw. "Orangeybrown, orangeybrown," he repeated. "I will remember. This smelly human leg-end is orangeybrown."

"D," said Kirk, oblivious to the fact that an invisible cat was insulting his ankles. "I'm thinking of someone. My name starts with D."

"Are you the work of art by a famous Italian named Michelangelo?" said Silvestro.

"It has to be a real person," said Nina. "Not a statue."

"Sometimes—do you ever wonder how we all ended up here in Round Stone?" asked Marcia. She was struggling with the difficulty of being able to retrieve only patches of this new life. By contrast, she recalled her original life quite well, and she remem-bered all her time trips with the cat to date. But whole swaths of *this* life were utterly blank. What had happened?

"In the past months, since she's been having these spells, she is forgetting everything," Silvestro explained to Nina and Kirk.

"Surely not *everything*," said Kirk.

"No, she has not forgotten *this* place, this city. She knows that in the evenings of the *primavera*, the sun will blaze above the western rooftops of the Round Stone and plunge into the River Sawgash like a slice of *patata cruda* into a vat of the very hot oil, where it will cook to a crisp, so it can rise in the eastern sky *la prossima matina* like a perfect golden round *disco* like a Pringle."

"So how did we end up here?" said Marcia.

"It is the hand of fate that has brought us such wonderful jobs," said Silvestro dramatically.

"And then Nina heard about your good luck and got a job here, too," said Kirk. "And then she and I met, and the rest is history."

"And such nice raises for us, *tutti gli anni*. Every year," said Silvestro.

"Oh," said Marcia. She considered: wonderful jobs? Large salaries and annual raises? At a small-town college? It it all sounded like a ridiculous fantasy. She had no memory of it. But it struck her that her mission with the cat had been a failure. Silvestro was alive; there was no wrongful-death settlement. Yet she was still chained to Round Stone, apparently, and to Nina. And once again, money seemed to be keeping her here.

"Is there a pet cemetery in Bixby?" she asked impulsively.

Silvestro looked away, and Nina and Kirk adopted distant, pitying expressions. Then Kirk grabbed his wineglass, swigged from it, and said, "OK, let's go, people. D. No statues. Real people."

"Are you an actor?"

"I'm not DeNiro," said Kirk.

"A musician?"

"Nope, not Drake."

"Are you dead?" said Silvestro.

"I'm not Princess Diana."

"Your turn, Marsh," said Nina.

"Hmm," said Marcia, "are you a blackguard?"

"It has to be someone real," Nina corrected her.

"Blackguards are real," said Kirk.

"What's a blackguard?" said Mr. Whiskey.

"A bad person," said Marcia.

"I'm not Dennis the Menace," said Kirk.

"He's not a blackguard, just a bad kid," said Marcia.

"He's fictional," said Nina.

"I'm not Dillinger," said Kirk.

"Who's that?" said the cat.

THE GAME CONTINUED interminably, with Nina apparently making the rules and Kirk getting drunker and seeming less and less certain of who he was. In between questions and drinks of wine, he sucked on a hard candy.

"I'm sorry, but I simply can't stand this," said Mr. Whiskey. "Wake me when it's over." He went to sleep.

Marcia looked at her phone. It was terribly late—after one thirty. They'd been playing since midnight. "Does Howie have a curfew?" she said.

Silvestro erupted. "Oh, my son! Howie! *Che cosa terribile!*" He sniffed hard and seemed to be trying not to cry.

Marcia felt awful about upsetting him so badly. Perhaps the dog would comfort him. In the past of her *other* present life, the one she could remember, the one where the Pop-Tart/stair thing hadn't been thwarted, the one where he'd died, Silvestro had always professed to like dogs, although he wasn't allowed to have one in his Chicago apartment. Marcia had sometimes entertained him with her father's favorite comic dog plots. "Do you want me to go get Orson?" she said.

"Aaagh! Orson! Why did we ever adopt this wicked animal?" Silvestro shouted. He began carrying on in his native language. None of them could understand him, and Marcia wanted to follow Mr. Whiskey's lead and simply go to sleep to escape it all, but then Silvestro stopped suddenly. "I *must* make her understand," he said apologetically to Nina and Kirk. "Maybe then she will remember. If her memory has not been destroyed by all these years of grief."

He turned and looked directly at Marcia. "*Mi amore*, you must remember so you can move on. It was the wicked dog, Orson. Inside him was a vicious steak."

"Streak," corrected Mr. Whiskey, but only Marcia heard him.

"He did not like that we loved each other and our baby Howie more than a dog, so one day, he ripped Howie's throat out, and he died. Howie's little onesie was bloody red, like the tomato."

Marcia looked around. At Kirk. Nina. Silvestro. Back at Nina. It was true, she saw. It explained why she could only remember bits of things. PTSD—or something. It also explained the "bad trip" getting here—she'd had Howie, and loved him, and then he'd died awfully.

Mr. Whiskey was awake now. She looked over at him. He'd gotten up and was pacing, stiff-legged and agitated. His paws made a patting sound on the tiled windowseat where he'd been lying. His tail whipped and switched furiously. "Oh, boy," he said. "Oh, boy. Oh, *most* unsettling. *This* is a heck of a curveball. I definitely didn't see this coming."

Where was I? Oh, yes, I definitely had not seen this coming: the apparition of Susan with her punctured diaphragm. But I have not been straight, Dear Reader, about how profoundly infatuated I'd become with Dale Farrar. A friend of the heart—someone who accepted me for who I was. It was a bromance before we knew the word. It was an utter joy to be in his company, from my perspective. And from his, I believe he was drawn to my need and fulfilled by it in a way that his many other casual friendships had not fulfilled him. Had I imagined that we might stay together forever—that in some way we might become partners? That Susan would vanish and it would be just the two of us? I think I had.

But then my door rattled and opened. A long-haired girl stumbled in, contraceptive device in hand. Her thin robe gapped open, but she didn't notice; she was looking at the diaphragm. I saw a tidy raspberry-tipped breast. Aroused yet revolted, I slid my gaze down, but then I was looking at a thicket of black hair.

And then those fateful words: "There's a hole in it."

I saw into the future: there would be a baby. Dale would belong not just to Susan but to it. A girlfriend could have been nudged out of the picture eventually, so I could have him all to myself.

A child was another story.

In hindsight, I believe my meeting and becoming friends with Dale was fate. It had almost changed the direction of my life and caused me to give up on the ambition I'd formed at seventeen—my ambition to acquire fame by the most dramatic means possible. An astonishing means. An unforgettable means. A mortal means. I would have given it up for Dale if he hadn't become a father. I know I would have.

But not if I had to share him with his offspring.

—MEMOIRS OF SOCRATIES LOVE

Chapter 17

Howie was dead.

Her son, dead. Howie, her son, was dead. He was dead? He'd died as a baby. The knowledge was crushing. Splintering. He had not learned to sing "Twinkle, Twinkle, Little Star," making a diamond with his dimpled toddler thumbs and index fingers. He had never eaten a Popsicle or gone to the zoo and laughed at the monkeys or seen *Toy Story*. Not had a potty chair or a car seat. Never had a school picture taken. Silvestro had not taught him to ride a bike or shoot a basket. He had not tied his shoes, sat on a pony, or "graduated" from kindergarten; he hadn't even had a birthday cake or an X-ray. She had not sunk her head in her hands in despair at his first cuss word or pink slip from school, or, later, his totaling of their most reliable car. She had not lifted him every day and carried him on her hip until one day, suddenly, he was so heavy that she couldn't pick him up anymore. Not taught him to do his taxes (or would Silvestro have done that?). Not filled to bursting with pride at the young man he'd become and simultaneously felt a shiver at how dispassionately time replaces each generation with the next and how scrawny her arms were now.

"Did he learn to say any words before he died?" asked Marcia faintly. It was all she could muster. Everyone was watching her reaction. Even the cat. His whiskers twitched.

"He could say 'bow-wow,'" Silvestro offered. "'Bow-wow' because of . . . that *wicked Orson!*" He started to cry softly. "He adored the Orson, but this *cane vizioso* murdered him!"

"Come on, guy. You're drunk. Let's get you to bed," said Kirk, leading him off. Neither of them was very steady.

Mr. Whiskey watched them go. "Want me to follow them and see what I can find out about your new-to-you life?"

"*No!* Stay here," said Marcia.

She glanced nervously at Nina, but Nina could not see the cat or hear this conversation. "Marsh, you've had a bit of a rough evening, haven't you?" she said and smoothed Marcia's hair with weird, mechanical strokes.

Marcia jerked away, but Nina took her elbow, got her up, and guided her to the bathroom. She stood with her and, as Marcia washed, chattered on and on. Which made things that much worse.

It was quite a bathroom: a jungle of gleaming, elaborately curved plumbing fixtures against glaring white porcelain imported tile. "This must be a bitch to clean," Marcia said, interrupting Nina's dialogue about the dog.

Nina stared at her. "You have Cindy come in once a week."
"Oh."
"Toothbrush time!" said Nina brightly. She put a pea-sized squeeze of Close-Up on Marcia's toothbrush. She turned it on and waited while Marcia buzzed it around her mouth, rinsed, spat. She felt like an automaton going through the motions.

They went to the bedroom, and she let Nina help her undress and get into a sleep T. "Do you remember those flowered catsuit bell-bottom pajamas you had? The purple-and-white ones?" Nina chuckled.

Marcia did. She had worn them once to a sleepover she and Nina had been invited to. Nina had trendy sleep shorts, but Marcia had the flowered bell-bottom catsuit, and the other girls laughed at her and said she looked like a hooker at a garden party.

"Where did your mom get those pajamas?" Marcia said.

Nina hedged and then admitted, "The Salvation Army, I'm pretty sure."

Marcia sat on the edge of the bed. The comforter had a stiff gold ruffle that scratched her bare legs. Nina sat next to her. The cat had vaulted onto a sculpted lowboy with opalescent drawer pulls. He reached down and batted at one of the pulls with a white-dipped paw, then drew up and sat regally, staring down Nina, who had no idea he was there.

Marcia gave him a watery smile. Then she happened to look up. Directly above him was a sixteen-by-twenty portrait of chubby infant Howie playing with a yellow ball.

She erupted in a fit of crying.

Nina patted her leg and said, "Marsh. Marsh. You'll get through this."

But Marcia couldn't stop now; she was overcome. The crying went on for a while, with Nina consoling robotically and Marcia sobbing and soaking the front of her sleep T, until suddenly something snapped in Nina. "Marsh!" she said rudely. "Enough, all right? Do you realize this happens *every* time we come over to play Botticelli?"

Marcia's tears abruptly ceased. "Really?"

"Ask her why she keeps inviting herself over, then," advised the cat.

"So why do you keep inviting yourself over to play Botticelli if the same thing happens every time?" said Marcia, her grief ebbing.

"Old habits die hard, I guess," said Nina. She stood up. "I ought to be going. You just need some sleep. I'll call you tomorrow to check on you. Kirk's already put Silvestro to bed."

"We don't sleep together?" In Chicago they'd snuggled every night, and she'd loved to rub her nose around in his chest hair and smell his man-and-cologne scent.

"You always ask that, too," Nina said impatiently. "No, you don't sleep in the same bed. Don't ask me why. I've never pried into your marital relations."

"Silvestro is an *excellent* lover," said Marcia defensively.

"I know. You tell me *that* every time, too. He's got a long, silly penis and he's a total wildcat with it."

"*Silky* penis," corrected Marcia.

"Who's got a silly penis?" chanted Mr. Whiskey.

Nina paused in the bedroom doorway on her way out. "I don't know why it always seems like I ought to stay here in this house and you ought to go to Funnel Street," she mused.

"Because this *is* your house in the real present time," muttered Mr. Whiskey. He made a graceful leap from chest to bed, just as Nina exited.

Marcia closed her eyes and tried to put all the pieces together—dead son, separate beds, her life an endless loop of museum work Monday through Friday and on weekends, drunken Botticelli games with Kirk and Nina that ended in orgies of grief. Add to that an electric toothbrush and ostentatious faucets and a cleaning lady named Cindy: it was the closest thing to hell she could imagine.

"Why can't I remember anything about this life?" she asked the cat. He'd curled up on her stomach, and his respirations matched hers, his furry flanks rising and falling with each of her breaths. Compared to Nina's awkward pats, so full of undisguised ambivalence, he was pure comfort.

He purred—raspily and then warming up to a full-body rumble. His claws pulled in and out, kneading her side through her shirt, but even though they pricked, she didn't mind.

"It's grief," said Mr. Whiskey. "You humans think lust can make you lose your mind. Lust or greed. Jealousy. But those are lightweights next to grief. Grief hijacks your whole self. It drops in unannounced and refuses to leave and overturns everything and makes you feel like you're alone on an island the size of a tortilla. There's no room for memories when you're stranded on a tortilla."

"That's why you can't remember the person you used to belong to?"

"I didn't *belong* to him. We just loved each other. It was a man who lived in a house. I remember that much. He had . . . a car. Wheels. He used to—" The cat laid his ears back in frustration. "It's all *blank*," he said angrily. "It's just gone. I want to remember, but I don't know where he is, or who he was, or when I died, or anything right before that or after, until I reconstituted in your living room."

"That's kind of how I feel," said Marcia. "But I can remember the other life. My real one."

"I can't even remember that. It has taken some getting used to," sighed Mr. Whiskey. "You're not like *him*."

"Ah, I'm sorry," said Marcia.

"It's OK," said the cat. "You can't help it."

SHE CAME WIDE AWAKE at four fifty-four. She opened the curtains and there it was, the moon, hanging like a fingernail paring caught on the hazy gray weave of the lightening sky. She preferred her moon larger, rounder, but nevertheless, it was magical to see it still out and about in the early morning.

An idea had erupted in her brain. This was what had awakened her. "Mr. Whiskey!" she whispered.

"Huh?" said the cat sleepily. He'd abandoned the bed for a private cranny between the lowboy and a wastebasket in the corner.

"Do you think Orson was planted?"

"Pine trees are planted. Not dogs. They whelp. In litters."

"I meant 'planted' like put there intentionally. Like someone left him for me to find so he'd kill Howie."

"He didn't kill Howie in your real life. Howie grew up and went to What Island. Orson only killed Howie in this weird alternate life," argued the cat. "Why would *anyone* want to kill Howie? And if they did, why wouldn't they just take him and tie bowling balls to him and throw him in the Sawgash River?"

"Don't say that!" shouted Marcia. She was on the verge of tears again, but she forced them back. "When Nina and I were in the bathroom, she was going on and on about Orson. Which wasn't very sensitive, and I know she's not sensitive—but still, she knew it would hurt, and she refused to shut up about him. She wanted to know if I had any idea how Orson had ended up in the street the day I picked him up."

"That was a long time ago."

"That's what I said. Also, in my real life, she's the one who told me about Eternal Paws pet crematory and showed me the flyer and convinced me to take him there."

"So she made you cremate him."

"*If* he was even cremated."

"Where did you take him again?"

"Eternal Paws. But it's a fake. A front. It's really a megachurch in Bixby. The Pious Body of Formally Doomed Souls."

Mr. Whiskey had still been curled in the corner, but now he got up and sauntered over to a spot near the bed and pandiculated. He gave a slow blink, arched his back, pandiculated again, and then savaged the carpet with his claws for two long minutes before regaining his composure.

"I have not heard of this trick: a church posing as a pet crematorium," he said.

Marcia agreed that it was unusual. "What do you think they'd gain from doing that?"

"Other then cremation fees and a lot of dead-dog ash, I really don't know." The cat swiveled his ears. "Do you hear that?"

"What?" she said, and then, "Oh." It was Silvestro, singing. He still had a marvelous voice at fifty, or whatever he was. The singing, in Italian, grew louder as he strolled through the house, apparently coming to find her. She had the fleeting sense of being pursued by a gondolier.

After a moment, Silvestro poked his head in the door. "Marcia! My darling," he said. "How are you this morning? Are you happy again like the American clam?"

"Here we go," said Mr. Whiskey.

"I'm a little better," Marcia admitted to Silvestro.

The cat said to her under his breath, "I just thought of something. Ask him what happened to Orson's body when he died."

"Silvestro, sweetheart?"

"What is it, my heart?"

"Remember after Orson . . . died?"

"I strangled that *cane vizioso* with my bare hands when he killed our Howie!" said Silvestro angrily.

"Whoa," said Mr. Whiskey.

"You certainly did," agreed Marcia, though she had no memory of this. "But what happened to his body?"

"Ah, you were so, so sad, and I was so, so mad. I would have chopped him in tiny pieces, but our dear friends, Kirk and Nina, carried him away for us to have him *cremato* in Bixby."

"Burned up in Bixby," translated the cat unnecessarily. "I'm getting really creeped out here. Ask him where the ashes are."

"Where are his ashes?"

"*Lost.*"

"Lost?"

"They send me the wrong ashes. The Orson is lost. They are the ashes of a *cat!*" said Silvestro disdainfully. "So I can never do what I wanted to do to the Orson, to throw his burned bones in the sewer. But still, I did it. I *pretended* these were the ashes of Orson, and I cursed them and flushed the cat down the toilet."

Mr. Whiskey looked very ill. "I think we need to get out of here, fast," he said. "We've got to go back to Chicago and kill him before *any* of this stuff happens."

"My beautiful wife. Let me comfort you." Silvestro stretched his arms toward Marcia. He was looking aroused.

"Don't let him get you with his silly penis!" cried Mr. Whiskey. One great leap, and he was on her shoulders, and it was happening again. "Flush *me* down the toilet, Marco?" said Mr. Whiskey. "Just wait and see what we're going to do to *you*."

The tail, the transition, the straw. "Grab that box!" shouted the cat at the last minute, and Marcia saw it on the nightstand, a sleek cloisonné case, and grabbed it.

Her body like a piece of fettucine, pulling and being sucked back by the force of time until she was expelled from a horrible, false future into a past she *could* remember.

It was the donut shop again, and they were on the street. There, inside, was Thomas, glistening dots on his face, talking to Mae. He was pointing to the old-fashioneds. He turned and looked at her through the window. She couldn't read his face.

Other Powers Less Frequently Ascribed to the Desert People

    Omnilingual

    Telepathy with animals

    Superhuman hearing

    Superhuman sight

    Immunity to every illness in the world

    Going without food or water for centuries

    Telekinesis

    Shrinking adversaries to the size of troll dolls

    Resurrecting the dead

—THE INFORMATION HATCH

Chapter 18

"WHAT ARE WE doing here?" said Marcia.

"We have to kill Silvestro so we can avoid that hideous alternative future and save Howie."

"We just got through saving Silvestro. Now we have to kill him? Why can't we just go back to the dedication of the *busto* and let him step on the Pop-Tart?" said Marcia, confused. *And get pushed down the steps by Thomas.* She still couldn't believe or make sense of that part—that Thomas was the one who'd originally killed him.

"I'm afraid it's not that easy," said Mr. Whiskey. "I'm sorry. It's just not possible. Believe me, I tried, and this is where we ended up. It's like one of those menu options you can see in your software program, but they're in halftone, so you can't click on them, even though you keep trying like an idiot. I kept trying, and this is where we are. We're just going to have to kill him ourselves."

"I don't want to kill Silvestro."

"Don't worry; you don't have to do it alone. I'll help you. But first we have an important task to complete."

"What task?" Marcia glanced again at the shop window. If they were here at the donut shop, there must be a reason. "Am I supposed to be working?" She looked down at her clothes, which were civilian garb, not her donut-shop uniform. She was in jeans and a green slub sweater, very lightweight, with three-quarter sleeves, that she remembered from all those years ago. In the green sweater, her form was outlined appealingly, and her hair was pure raven, and her eyes were deep pools of sapphire.

She had noticed before that her clothes and cell phone didn't time-travel. She always came out of the straw in period-appropriate clothes and accessories. If she left 2018 with a phone, she arrived in 1997 without it. The same principle worked in reverse.

"Look in your pack," instructed the cat.

Marcia reached into the backpack, which had appeared with the slub sweater on arrival. There was a package of Suzy Qs; she used to eat those all the time, even though Thomas's donuts were much better. There was a pencil pouch, a hairbrush, some mashed tampons, a folded-up sweatshirt. A map of Chicago.

"Keep looking."

She poked around further and found a paper bag. It felt lumpy, full of rocks and metal.

"Now go into the donut shop and ask if they know anyone who buys jewelry," said the cat.

Thomas had vanished to the kitchen, but Mae was running around wiping tables when they entered. She was so intense and wiry, it was frightening. Marcia had never been able to figure out her age. Someone else was behind the counter, a girl Marcia remembered dimly.

"That would be Renata," said Mae, turning from her wiping and coming over. She looked directly at the cat, and Marcia could tell she saw him. She remembered what Mr. Whiskey had said about being visible to Thomas and Mae.

"How did you know . . . ?"

Mae shrugged her square, bony shoulders and smiled mysteriously. Her eyes quite literally twinkled. "I have a certain gift. Gifts. I'm skilled in the old folkways. With a bit of clairvoyance thrown in."

"Ask her," prodded Mr. Whiskey.

"You need to sell some jewelry?" said Mae.

"No," said Marcia, who was wearing the only jewelry she'd owned in 1997, a tin pin shaped like a lizard.

"Yes," said the cat.

"Which is it, no or yes?"

"Look in that paper bag," the cat ordered Marcia.

Marcia was about to look when the door to the kitchen opened and Thomas came out. He said something in a low voice to Renata, and she took off her ball cap and left. He yelled to the guys in the back not to overknead the dough. His eyes met Marcia's.

He's looking out for me, she thought. Even though she didn't know why. Even though there was something strange about him that she couldn't grasp, and he'd murdered her lover and baby daddy. Even though (she could see it on his face) he was frustrated with this new turn of events.

"Open the bag," said Mr. Whiskey.

Marcia uncrumpled the soft brown paper and looked inside. She reached in and pulled out a ring. A diamond in a square art-deco setting. There were matching earrings. A sapphire pendant. Another diamond. A heavy gold necklace. A string of pearls that looked real. Another ring. And another, with a stunning opal.

"Try it on," said Mae.

It fit Marcia's finger. All the rings fit her.

"They're Silvestro's gifts to you," said the cat. "That guy was making great money, and he was crazy about you, and he kept giving you jewelry, hoping it would make up for Howie, which, of course, it couldn't. Fortunately your tastes run to the mildly bohemian, and you liked vintage. So they predate the '90s and they time-traveled just fine. Notice that the case they were in didn't make it, though. Hence the old twenty-five-K-in-jewels-in-a-brown-paper-bag trick."

"How did you know what was in the case?"

"Nina," said the cat. "I knew because of Nina. She couldn't take her eyes off it. I can't always, but sometimes I can read that chick's mind. She was jealous that you had a husband who gave you such expensive jewelry, to put it mildly."

"I still don't see what this is all about. Why did we bring the jewelry here? Why am I selling it?"

"Investments," said Mr. Whiskey. "I didn't forget what you said about the lawyer, Fortress, trying to get you to invest. I think it's worth following up on, since we had to come back here anyway to kill Silvestro."

Mae got a napkin from one of the tables and wrote an address on it and a name: *Schaeffer.* "It's a family-owned pawnshop," she said. "They'll give you cash without questions. Then you and Mr. Twitchy can go talk to the financial adviser."

"Whiskey," said the cat.

"Who would trust their money to an adviser named Whiskey?" said Mae.

"And then you'll come back here. On Wednesday," said Thomas. "In your usual clothes for your usual shift. We'll take care of getting Silvestro here and making sure the shop is empty. And when he walks in the door—you know where the gun is."

"You want me to shoot him?" Marcia was feeling very weak. "Couldn't I give him a poisoned donut?"

"It has to be the gun," said Thomas.

"It has to be," said Mae. "What did you think it was there for?"

"Robbers?" said Marcia timidly.

"Donut-shop robbers!" snorted Mae. "Like that's the scourge of Chicago."

"Sorry, but you threw a big wrench in things when you decided to save Silvestro."

"But the gun was there long before that," Marcia objected. "Twenty-three years ago, when you taught me to shoot it."

"This *is* twenty-three years ago," sighed Thomas impatiently.

"Well, twenty-one, actually," corrected Mae. "A couple of years have passed since you started working here."

"And you screwed things up, and you've got to shoot him," said Thomas.

"That's right," agreed Mr. Whiskey.

"It is," said Mae.

"You have to shoot him," they all three agreed.

They took the L to the pawnshop, which was not far from Silvestro's apartment. Mr. Whiskey floated along invisibly in the hypothetical sidecar. On his advice, she'd slung the pack with the jewelry in it on her left shoulder, and he locomoted and hovered on that side as a buffer. People instinctively avoided the space where he was. This made Marcia feel better about carrying around thousands of dollars in gold and fine jewels in a brown paper bag in her backpack.

It was a mild early-summer day: light humidity, but nevertheless fresh and verdant-feeling, even in the city. On the way from the train stop to Schaeffer's, they passed a park with sprinklers spraying. A car radio was playing that song about absent cowboys that she'd forgotten, but now she remembered how much she'd disliked it. There was a rival donut shop, much busier than Thomas's place. A few fast-food places with long lines inside, which told her it must be around lunchtime. Just as before, she felt young and lean and tight. But also worried in a way she had never been until after she'd had Howie and been responsible for another life. If shooting Silvestro was the *only* way to save Howie (and to save Orson from being a killer), she would have to do it, but it was an impossible choice, and she couldn't understand why none of them—Thomas, Mae, the cat—understood this. She didn't exactly love Silvestro, but she couldn't help but feel fondness toward someone so goofy, so blindly affectionate. And there were his sexual talents—she was going to have to give that up again. Again!

The neon sign in front of Shaeffer's was unlit; the shop was closed. The hours listed on the door were 1 P.M. to 9 P.M. This seemed to aggravate Mr. Whiskey tremendously. He gave a loud, sick-sounding meow, and then another and another. What a cat-erwauling! He had not done this before. Orson had barked and whined moderately and squealed shrilly at moments of peak terror, but none of his vocalizations had been this grating. Marcia covered her ears.

Inside the shop, there was the trundling of feet. Someone opened the door, and the cat shut up and shot in. Marcia followed.

"Welcome!" said the man with the feet—Schaeffer, she assumed. He closed and locked the door. "Thomas said you had jewelry?" He was thirty or so, with short black hair in a crown around his balding head and a brown plaid shirt with a Cross pen in the pocket. He had a slightly wilted appearance, as though he slept in his shop and had just gotten out of bed. He smelled like coffee and cardboard, but his expression was astute. Businesslike. He didn't look at the cat or say anything about the ruckus that had brought him to the door, so Marcia couldn't tell whether he knew there was a cat.

Mr. Whiskey was looking around. He had spotted a group of big-game trophies. The most impressive of these was an adult bear, stuffed, in an upright position, with claws displayed in attack. There were also a moose head and a couple of bucks' heads and a fleabitten-looking bobcat. "Incredible," said the cat. "This is truly incredible." He strolled over and circled the bear, his hackles up slightly. He sniffed its feet and then touched it with his paw and backed away. Then he jumped onto a display counter to examine the bobcat. "I'm beginning to feel better about this cremation thing," he said aloud to no one.

Schaefer seemed oblivious to the cat's perusal of the trophies. He was focused on the matter at hand. He gestured at Marcia's pack. "Let's see the jewelry."

She got out the paper bag and started to open it, but he gave a dismissive wave. "I don't need to actually *see* it, see it. I just need to *get* it. I can give you twenty-five thousand."

This carelessness about the bag's contents made her wonder. "Is that what they're appraised at?" she asked cleverly.

"It's what I'll give you."

"It's what he'll give you," echoed the cat. He was crouched down next to the bobcat, which dwarfed him. Marcia had thought of him as large, but he was not so big after all—or else the bobcat was a giant of its species. "Has anyone ever offered you twenty-five thousand for anything?" Mr. Whiskey pointed out. He jumped down and came over and sat by her ankle.

"No, but they might be worth more," said Marcia.

Schaeffer didn't react to any of this, so he was either a remarkable actor or he couldn't see or hear the cat. He wasn't one of them—whatever "they" were. Donut people. People like Mae and Thomas who could see invisible cats.

"I'm just wondering if they're worth more," said Marcia to Schaeffer.

"This is a pawnshop, not Christie's," he said. "I already talked to Thomas. And got the cash." He went over behind a glass case full of sporting knives and rummaged under it and came back with another bag—this one large, of brightly colored plastic, with pictures of farm animals and some writing in German on it: FERNSEHEN BEGINNT MIT KINDERSENDUNGEN.

"What does that say?" she asked curiously. She was enrolled in Exploratory German, but they hadn't learned much.

"'Television begins with children's programming.'"

"Oh."

He opened the bag to show her. It was full of money—twenty-dollar bills in stacks, each rubber-banded. The fact that they were small bills meant that the bag was very full. "Do you want to count it?"

"It's fine," said Marcia, who was feeling weak again. Somehow, receiving a bag stuffed with cash in exchange for gifts given to her by a man she was going to shoot on Wednesday was making her feel like she was accepting blood money.

"Sure?"

"Yes."

"Have it your way," he said and handed her the bag. "Don't spend it all in one place." He grinned and then said awkwardly, "Thomas said you were cute. But I wasn't expecting a black-haired knockout. Do you have a boyfriend?"

"As a matter of fact, yes. And I'm either pregnant with his baby or will be by Tuesday night," she said, having just realized that if she was going to shoot Silvestro and Howie was going to live, then she would have to be pregnant before she left for work on Wednesday.

Schaeffer's jaw dropped. "Oh. Oh. I'm sorry. I didn't know."

"No biggie," said Marcia.

But it was, she thought. It was big. Howie was here, or soon would be. Right here, with her. He'd been dead, but no more. That was the magic of Mr. Whiskey. She looked in the bag again. Then she grabbed it and swung it around. Twenty-five thousand dollars! She was going to invest it for Howie. Maybe it would allow her at some future date to walk away from the settlement so she wouldn't have to stay in Round Stone.

Schaeffer followed them to the door, looking sad, and locked it behind them after they exited. He thought maybe I was the one, Marcia realized.

"Little does he know you're an about-to-be murderess," said Mr. Whiskey, reading her mind. "A *pregnant* about-to-be murderess. How many pregnant women shoot their lovers in donut shops?"

"Not funny," said Marcia.

Mr. Whiskey rode along in the sidecar in silence for a while, but just before they got to Silvestro's apartment building, he announced, "Well, *I* thought it was funny."

On that morning after Susan stumbled into my room, Dale rattled my door at dawn and asked if I was packed—they were leaving in an hour.

I could not resist, even though I knew our friendship must come to an end. Our futures were laid bare. Fate had taken charge. He would go back to America and be a husband to Susan and father to her baby. It was the decent thing to do, and he had no ability to be anything but decent. Though he hadn't guessed yet that parenthood was his future—even Susan had no idea—I felt certain enough to stake my life on it.

And I would go home, having at least made a truce with my fear, with no more appreciation for my fellow human beings than I'd had to start—even less after the abuse heaped on me by some of the set crew. Nothing from my experience in the desert had changed my proposed course. I'd begun to take notes and map strategies.

We embarked for the wind sculptures, and it proved to be a disappointment: a few outcroppings of stone weathered by natural sandblasting into the rough semblances of a fish, a parrot, a three-legged wolf, a gosling, and a deformed pig with a dorsal fin. Dale, eternal optimist, had quite a good time and regaled us with stories of animated anthropomorphic dogs in deserts, but the rest of us were less than thrilled. It was just he and Susan and I and our desert guides, an odd couple, a May-December pair, but they knew the desert all right. There was a third tourist along with us—Beverly? Belinda? A good-looker, to whom I would have paid more attention if I had not been so despondent about saying goodbye (forever) to Dale.

Back in civilization, we celebrated over our last dinner, at a coastal inn on a terraced patio, where we ate an incredible meal of prawns and a delectable flatbread. Dale and Susan were going home the next day. The other tourist—Barbara?—had disappeared, but our guides stayed and dined with us. The man was thirty-some; the woman was older. Funny, if they told us their names, I haven't retained them. They were solicitous of Susan, almost as though they knew. They discouraged her from the wine, steering her toward some Italian soda. She was happy to go along with their recommendation and did not drink that night.

—MEMOIRS OF SOCRATIES LOVE

Chapter 19

WHEN THEY GOT to Silvestro's apartment, Marcia rummaged in her backpack for the key. She dumped the Suzy Qs on the hall floor while she was digging for it.

"What's this?" said the cat, sniffing the cellophane wrapper warily.

Marcia tried to explain about junk food, but Mr. Whiskey couldn't grasp the concept. "You really eat that?"

"Didn't the man you used to live with eat stuff that was bad for him sometimes?"

"He was good at finding free food. He didn't spend money like you do. He ate what he could get."

She stopped rummaging. Her heart jolted at the thought of Howie and whether he was getting enough to eat, since he wasn't allowed to have porridge roll. More importantly, how safe was he now on What Island, in the future world of her real, middle-aged life? The pickup-truck emojis had signaled trouble. What kind of trouble? She hoped against hope that his bodyguard was keeping him safe.

But—*awful* thought—what if she shot Silvestro, and it ended up killing Howie again instead of saving him? Or what if, in this new version of the past they'd entered, she never did get pregnant? She'd told Schaeffer she was having a baby, but how did she know for sure? What if shooting Silvestro would cause Howie to never exist? She pushed down a sob.

"Are you OK?" said the cat.

"Yeah, fine." She'd found the key and unlocked, and she lifted the cat, snatched up the Suzy Qs, and carried them inside.

The apartment looked just as they'd left it when they'd departed to save Silvestro. That was a consolation, anyway: it was nice to be in a place that was familiar and to have her whole memory back. She remembered all of her real life and all of this Chicago life from before—except for the mysterious new parts about selling her jewelry for twenty-five thousand dollars and shooting Silvestro, which were later add-ons.

She opened the Suzy Qs and offered Mr. Whiskey a bite. He sniffed and refused. Instead he went to the the fridge and meowed until she opened it.

Inside, she discovered the leftover fish and chips from her last Chicago meal with Silvestro. So this was the day after that meal. It was the day he'd originally had his accident. The day he'd stepped on the Pop-Tart and Thomas pushed him down the stairs and he ended up in the ICU, dying soon afterward and leaving her pregnant and mildly bereft. But it was also the day of the do-over—the day they'd saved him by preventing the Pop-Tart fiasco and rocketing him to safety. *That* day had sealed Howie's death warrant and made Orson a killer. They were here now to undo the redo. She could only hope that it would work.

She thought about all this as she got a plate and broke the fish in pieces. She put the plate on the floor in front of Mr. Whiskey. "Is this the same fish that you and he—?" he asked.

"It is. It's been in there twenty-one years. Do you think it's all right?"

"Negative twenty-one plus twenty-one and one day, so actually, just a day. It'll be fine. I'm getting really accurate," he said proudly. "I got us right back, exactly when we needed to be." He puffed his tail and arched his back, and his confidence reassured her.

She watched him eat hungrily. He purred and then lobbied for cream, so she gave him some. He looked up at her when he was done, licking his chops contentedly. The early-afternoon sun spotlighted him as he sat and washed his face with his paw. When he'd finished, he said, "I guess we'll find out what happened when he comes home this evening."

"If he comes home."

"He will. I think. I don't understand exactly, but it's kind of like double jeopardy. He can't die the same way twice. I'm not even sure the Pop-Tart would have been there this time. If it was, he likely wouldn't step on it. If he stepped on it, something would keep him from going up the stairs. Or from falling. Or, at least, from dying."

Marcia tried to point out that he hadn't died yet at all, so it wouldn't be repeating anything if he died now and double jeopardy wouldn't apply, but the cat was adamant. There could be no Pop-Tart tragedy, and there was a 95 percent probability that Silvestro would show up after work.

"Let's take a nap," he said. "That fish made me sleepy."

It didn't take much to convince her. Sleeping would let her forget the repellent task ahead—and she definitely wanted to forget it. In fact, she wanted to not do it, but it was becoming clearer and clearer that there was no choice if she wanted to save her son.

They lay on the leather couch, woman and cat, and in no time, they both fell into the kind of deep, unreserved sleep that only young people and small mammals can succumb to.

THE NEXT THING she knew, she was standing at the foot of a flight of steep stairs. And a dark form, cloaked in a foul, jaundiced miasma like the smoke of burning tires, was stomping down the steps, coming for her. "Who are you?" she cried out. And when it gave no answer, just loomed nearer and nearer, she drew on all her strength and shouted triumphantly, "You can't hurt me. I have *Mr. Whiskey!*"

And woke to the cat licking her face.

She looked around and discovered that she was on Silvestro's couch.

"That's what you get for eating crap and going to sleep in the middle of the day," scolded the cat. "Listen, it's after five thirty. Sly will be here any minute."

Marcia leaped off the couch, grabbed the bag of money, and ran around looking for a place to hide it. It was a typical bachelor apartment, and there wasn't a lot of furniture. Nothing with deep drawers.

"Can't you just leave it in your pack?"

"He gets into all my stuff."

"The suspicious type?"

"No, just a romantic bonehead. It makes him feel close to me."

"Give that to me," said the cat.

She put the bag on the floor, and he grabbed the plastic handle in his teeth and dragged it away into the utilities closet, the door to which was so slightly ajar that only a cat would have noticed. After a minute she went to look for him. He was sitting inside the closet, but the bag was nowhere to be seen.

"Where is it?"

"Try to find it."

She poked around behind the heating unit and some frayed straw brooms and a metal rod someone had stuck in there. She looked up, and down, and in every crevice, but the bag of money was nowhere. "Where is it? How did you do that?"

The cat made a self-congratulatory noise and said, "I haven't lost my basic-cat skills. I can still hide with the best of them. Same principle works for bags of money. You'll never find it until I want it to be found."

His ear flicked. "Silvestro. Hear him?"

In a minute, she heard him, and then he was unlocking the door.

She saw instantly that he was not himself. Usually he strode in with a lot of arm swinging and hearty breathing; it was something the older Marcia remembered about him fondly. He'd been so full of vigorous life. But now Silvestro entered quietly. He gave her a wan smile and said, "*Mia bellissima fidanzata.*" He began to weep softly.

Marcia stood woodenly. She had not seen him like this.

"Go comfort him, idiot," said the cat.

She went over and embraced him tentatively, and he collapsed into her arms, trembling and emitting a lot of cologne-scented tears. Eventually he stopped, sniffed, recovered his composure, and explained, "Today, this morning, I am showing the Power-Point for the *dedicazione*. And then I finish, and I want to go pay my respects to the *busto* because it is expected. But there is a pastry on the floor, an American Pop-Tart. I try to step over it, but it is not there! Like a ghost has kicked it. The *fantasmi* are playing with me. I go on the stairs because the elevator is too full, and then I see him. A man is coming to kill me. But then there is no man. The man and the Pop-Tart. They come and go like magic. I am so upset, I think I am going crazy, and I fall and almost crack my head. And then I think, if I die, possibly another man will take you and *fare l'amore* with my beautiful woman."

"No way," said Marcia, feeling thoroughly awful at this lie. "*Not* going to happen."

This satisfied Silvestro, and gradually he reverted to his normal demeanor. He made them a squash frittata and poured some wine, and they ate. He stared into her eyes and gushed over his relief that his life was good and she would never let anyone else make love to her. Then they went to bed, and Silvestro's excellent technique distracted her from the reality that on Wednesday she was going to murder him.

Mr. Whiskey waited with delicacy in the adjoining room until they were finished. Then he crept in and curled up by Silvestro's gym bag at the end of the bed. Just before she fell asleep, she heard him whisper, "Who's got a silly penis?"

WEDNESDAY MORNING FOUND her in Politics of Modern Europe at the Warehouse College. It was an exam day. She had a dim memory of this exam from the first go-round and wondered if she would do better or worse than before on the Poland essay. She wasn't sure whether she'd studied this time. In her original life she had, but having just popped back to 1997 for a short bit, would she have access to her earlier knowledge, or did the redo require her to restudy? She asked the cat what he thought.

"It doesn't matter," said Mr. Whiskey. "You could write a limerick about kielbasa and still get a good grade. They *always* give you A's. Like I said before, there's something sketchy about this place."

Marcia's T-shirt and cap were in her pack, and after she turned in her blue book, she went to the second-floor bathroom and changed her top, and then she walked, and the cat rode in the sidecar, to Homerun Donuts.

At first she was confused because it seemed to be business as usual at the donut shop. The Bismarcks and apple fritters were always the biggest sellers. It was no different today, and Thomas was his familiar distant self, though every so often she caught him watching her.

But around three in the afternoon, at a point when the shop was empty of customers, he sent the kitchen guys out to scout and locked the door and put a CLOSED BY ORDER OF THE CITY OF CHICAGO HEALTH DEPARTMENT sign on it. "That ought to keep people away," he said.

He gave her some busywork to do, cleaning mixer parts with a toothbrush and vinegar. Mae arrived in a flurry with a bag of fragrant Greek food, and Marcia remembered the day Thomas had come to her dorm room and she'd eaten her first gyro and received the command to come and work at the donut shop. They offered her some food now, but she and Silvestro had begun the day with coffee and almond biscotti and fresh honeydew, and it was all sitting, a sweet and fruity lump, in her nervous stomach.

The clock ticked away. Tick. Tick. And now it was four thirty. Mr. Whiskey was out like a light on an empty tray in the warmth of the donut case. Thomas called Marcia up front. Mae studied her and said, "We left a message for Silvestro. You're supposedly sick, and he's supposed to meet you here after work and take you home. The rush-hour noise will work in our favor. It will cover the gunshots. The kitchen crew will create a disturbance to keep anyone but your boyfriend from coming around. The cat will help guide him in. You'll have one or more clear, easy shots. Thomas says you're a natural."

"I can't do this," Marcia protested. She was shaking so hard, she thought she'd fall over.

"You have to. I don't think you understand what's at stake here," said Mae.

"Will it really save Howie?"

"It's the next step," said Mae equivocally. "You need to do it and not ask questions. You can't blow it." She looked directly at Marcia when she said this.

"Do I have to go back to Round Stone?"

"For a while. Not forever," Thomas said.

"With Nina?"

"Sorry," said Thomas.

"How do you know all this? How do you know about Howie if he's barely been conceived? He was never even born any of the times I've seen you," Marcia said, and then a light dawned. "Did you—can you—?"

"Time-travel?" said Mae.

"Do you?"

"How can I run a donut shop if I'm tripping around through the ages?" said Thomas.

"But you don't run a donut shop. Not always. That's not your main job, is it? It's some kind of cover for something else. Are you dead? Did you reconstitute?" Marcia pressed him. "Why did you kill Silvestro the first time? I get that it was him or Howie. But why would you care which one lived and which one died?"

"It wasn't necessarily either/or. Not until you and the cat re-worked the script," he said.

"But it was always Silvestro, from our point of view. He had to go. He would have distracted you. It might have interefered," explained Mae.

Marcia was about to ask what she meant by "interfere" when one of the kitchen guys banged on the door from outside and called, "He's coming! He's early."

"Quick," said Thomas, pushing Marcia behind the counter. Mae unlocked the door, and the cat streaked out.

Thomas handed Marcia some earplugs. "Put these in your ears. Don't want you going deaf," he said. He smiled and looked right into her eyes.

Mae grabbed a stack of napkins and set to filling dispensers, watching everything from the periphery. Thomas hovered in the kitchen door. "There's a loaded magazine in the gun. I checked everything. When you see him pass the window, get the gun and pull the slide. If you start to get cold feet, remember: Howie."

"Howie," echoed Mae.

Howie, said Marcia to herself. HOWIE.

"Go!" shouted Thomas from the doorway. He ducked into the kitchen. Silvestro was striding along, swinging his arms, back to his old self.

Marcia lifted the tray, found the depression and the slightly warm (from the case lights) weapon. It was heavy, but she held it securely and followed Thomas's directions. She dropped her arms below the counter so Silvestro couldn't see what she was holding.

The safety was off now, so she was careful not to point at her feet. At the same time, she marked his height in her mind in the vacant doorway so that when he passed through, she'd aim automatically at just the right level—at the heart.

The door rattled. Opened. The bell jingled. The cat slid in, dancing around Silvestro's feet, doing his invisible force-field thing to keep Silvestro from rushing in too fast. She couldn't look at her lover's face.

Silvestro paused in the doorway, trying to come forward but not quite able to because the cat was herding him back. A grin split his face. "My beautiful woman in the baseball hat!" he exclaimed. "Mr. Thomas said you were sick. But you got better so fast!"

"I did," Marcia concurred. Her shoulders tensed. *Squeeze*, she told herself. *Take your time. Don't pull. Aim. Squeeze. Pretend he's a fire, and you're putting him out.* Which was a little true.

"OK!" Thomas signaled the cat, and Mr. Whiskey leaped lightly aside. Silvestro stepped forward, arms opening. Marcia raised the Beretta, and before his expression could change, she aimed, squeezed, was swayed by the discharge.

Silvestro's face contorted. He reeled and fell, half on his back, half on his side. It was a perfect shot. If he wasn't dead, he soon would be. There was a circle of red in the center of his white dress shirt, and she looked away and said over and over to herself, *I saved Howie. I saved Howie. Saved Howie. Howie. Howie. Howie Howie Howie Howie* HOWIE.

Informant 12

"Now I've got it. There are two of them. A he and a she. I think. They're both—

"It's just . . . memory, you know. It's like trying to pick up a worm, it keeps convulsing and wriggling away. We work so hard at the scavenging. You should come with us sometime.

"The Desert People. People say they're tele-kinetic. I don't know. They engage in operations. That sounds like they're spies, but they're time-management specialists.

"I've talked a lot today. Sorry. Did I answer your question?"

Chapter 20

IN NO TIME, Thomas was bounding to the door, locking it, and lowering the security shutters. Marcia hadn't even realized the shop had these—she always arrived after opening and had never given any thought to the apparatus above the storefront windows. Thomas knelt by Silvestro's body. It looked so large and lanky, sprawled there on the floor with limbs akimbo and the ribbon of blood snaking across his shirt, and she couldn't help but feel the terrible weight of this loss: of his ready, silky penis; of such exuberant, affectionate, vibrant daffiness.

Thomas checked for a pulse and then tried again when he didn't find one, placing a finger at Silvestro's razor-nicked throat. He hovered a steady palm above the shapely DiCaprio lips to try to detect a breath.

"Dead," he confirmed to Mae. She nodded gravely. An eruption of tears welled up in Marcia, but she pushed it back down. She tried to comfort herself with the thought that now Howie would be safe, but nothing seemed certain anymore. Back in the future (the real present), he was still far away, under close watch on an island in a volatile region. The More-Tally was rising. What was happening to him now? *Was* anything happening to him if she was here, in the past? She glanced at Mae, who was staring straight down into her, as if she knew the answers to all Marcia's questions and incomprehensibly more.

Then Mae looked away, and Thomas scrambled to his feet and navigated behind the counter. He plucked the plugs out of Marcia's ears and took the gun from her and wiped it clean of her prints. He was handling it quite carelessly as he removed the magazine. In answer to her unspoken thoughts, Mae said, "Doesn't matter if his prints are on it. There's no record of us—we don't even exist here. But you're different. The last thing we need is for something to happen to you."

"Why? Why can't something happen to Marcia?" inquired Mr. Whiskey, but no one paid him any attention.

Thomas looked hard at Marcia. "Are you OK?"

"Does this mean Howie won't die?"

"Remember what your job is."

"Dispense donuts. Don't ask questions," said Marcia dully, and she felt sick. The pickup-truck emojis danced before her eyes.

"Tell me about What Island," she demanded.

"What island?" said Mae.

"How are you in on all this? Why do you see Mr. Whiskey? Did *you* send him?"

"Your job, Marcia," said Thomas gently. "No more questions. But no, the cat was a surprise. And Howie is in a safe place."

"Does that mean he'll live?" insisted Marcia.

"Tommy! We need to get rid of this corpse over here," prodded Mae.

"Right," he said and then turned back to Marcia for a second. "Job well done, kid. Unpleasant but necessary, and now it's finished. And remember: you didn't really kill Silvestro. You just returned him to his previous state. If anything, you gave him a few more years."

"Cat-flushing years," grumbled Mr. Whiskey.

Marcia suddenly felt very sweaty. She wanted to get away, to get out of the donut shop, to run away—anywhere. But if she tried to bolt, Thomas and Mae would likely stop her.

It was a trap. The whole thing: her job here, which had happened because Thomas had commanded her. And shooting Silvestro—the same thing. If she'd really had a choice, if they hadn't pushed her into it, would she have done it? Her lover's supine form with the red stain on his front was burned into her mind.

She did the only thing she could do to get away at least for a minute: she said she had to pee.

The Homerun bathroom was a storage closet with a sink, toilet, and brick-and-board shelves with stacks of donut boxes and white baker bags (which was probably a health department violation, storing them in the bathroom). She splashed her face and dried it with toilet paper because there was no paper towel.

What did it all add up to? Why was she here? She'd tried to save Silvestro in the first place because she'd wanted freedom from the wrongful-death settlement—freedom to live her own life and raise her son where and how she chose, not chained to a narcissistic frenemy and meaningless, menial work. Yet it had all gone wrong. Why? It was the older Marcia asking these things. Especially, she was asking herself, who were Thomas and Mae, really? Where had they come from and why? And, for that matter, *when*? They didn't seem evil, yet they'd interfered in her life almost from the day she'd left the Noisetteses', insisting that she work at the donut shop, killing her lover, and eventually forcing her to kill him again. Yet they'd also known—must have known—of her ill-fated plan to save him from stepping on the Pop-Tart, and they'd looked the other way. Whose side were they on? Why had they attached themselves to her? What did they care if she was rich or poor, free or in prison for murder, and why had they gone to some lengths to help her sell her jewelry and make sure she wasn't implicated in Silvestro's killing?

Worst of all, if she didn't know who they were or whether she could trust them, how could she be sure they were being truthful about Howie?

Then her breasts started to tingle, and any doubts she'd had about whether she was pregnant in this alternate 1997 were put to rest. Boob tingles were something she'd endured through the entire pregnancy. And these boob tingles felt distinctly like the kind fetal Howie had caused.

He was alive! For now, at least—and she would do everything she could to keep him that way. She patted her stomach and tried to remember how many weeks along she'd been when Silvestro died the first time. Not many.

When she came back from the bathroom, Mae and Thomas and Mr. Whiskey were gathered in a secretive knot. The body was gone; the floor gleamed. A mop was nearby. They looked a little guilty.

"Where's Silvestro?" asked Marcia.

"Oh, don't worry about that." Mae adjusted her cap and stepped behind the counter. "It's all taken care of. I'll handle things from here. You go on home. Get some rest," she advised.

"What home? Where do I go now?"

"Whiskey knows. We filled him in. You just go with him," said Mae. "But before you get out of here, do you want to take that gun? You may need it where you're going."

"Where am I going?" said Marcia.

"It's not really a question of where; it's when."

"Are we going back to 2018?" she said hopefully.

"Not yet. Go on," Mae urged her. Thomas nodded in agreement: *Take it.* So Marcia lifted the old-fashioneds tray and reluctantly picked up the gun—the instrument of Silvestro's death—which Thomas had replaced there and slipped it into her pack. "But—" she started to say, thinking that it wasn't a good idea to be toting a murder weapon around with her.

"It's taken care of," said Mae.

She took a deep breath, lifted the pack onto her shoulder, and hurried out to the sidewalk with the cat.

Outside, she stood in a daze. A minuscule blood spatter on the hem of her work shirt caught her eye and stopped her dead. She started to tear up again.

"Quit that. We have things to do" said the cat,

"Where to now?"

"Back to the apartment. You'll have to relive the funeral and some of the aftermath. Thomas says it's important to get as close to the original events as possible before we leave."

"How can there be a funeral? The body is gone," said Marcia.

"It's at the mortuary."

"But I *shot* him. Isn't there an investigation?"

"It's taken care of," said Mr. Whiskey firmly. "Thomas has connections everywhere, and the police have already just about put it to rest. All you have to do now is go with the flow."

Which is what she thought they'd been doing ever since the cat had shown up in her living room.

THE "FLOW" TURNED out to be getting her things out of Silvestro's apartment and back to the dorm as quickly as possible. They started walking briskly in the direction of the L station. Marcia was still in shock and barely noticed that a violent wind had blown up and that the sky, looking like a pot about to boil, was spitting down angry wet drops. Storefront banners were whipping and flapping, and paper was blowing around; a cardboard French-fry basket hit Mr. Whiskey, locomoting next to her in the sidecar, and made him hiss.

"I didn't know you could do that," she said, coming out of her fog for a second.

"What, hiss? Another basic-cat skill. I apparently haven't lost those," he said, "just transcended most of them."

Then she remembered that it was the lawyer, Fortress, who'd made the arrangements for moving her things. She explained this to Mr. Whiskey. Thomas must have overlooked that detail. "Maybe I should just go to the Warehouse College and tell them what's happened and let Fortress send someone to take care of it all. Like I did the first time. Since Thomas says we need to get back on the original track."

"Fine," said the cat, sounding annoyed.

"Besides, I don't think we could do much at the apartment. You can't move furniture, can you?" said Marcia, thinking aloud.

"Only in theory," said the cat. Then he added, "But what about the money? The twenty-five thousand? You didn't have that the first time. Maybe we should get it first."

"Oh. Right," said Marcia.

Neither of them thought it a good idea to let Fortress's hired movers handle the bag of cash, so they hurried on to the apartment. Inside, Mr. Whiskey ran to the closet and dragged it out. "OK. Let's go," he said.

"Wait," said Marcia. She stood staring at the table where she and Silvestro had eaten last night and this morning. He had dressed it with elegant simplicity: a paisley tablecloth and a white vase with a plastic stem of something roselike. She remembered how he'd cried, imagining himself dead and picturing her with another man. And how she'd persuaded him that it would never happen. How he'd brightened and recovered himself then and put out a bowl of kalamata olives, her favorite. While she'd munched and tried to avoid thinking about her commission to shoot him, he'd stood in the narrow apartment kitchen in his dress shirt, oblivious, applying his smooth European hands to slicing zucchini, whisking eggs. Blotches of dried sweat had stained the underarms of his shirt. She'd noticed them and wondered because he was not a sweaty guy. And then she'd realized that he had been frightened by the vanishing Pop-Tart and the near miss in the stairwell. A premonitory frisson of his mortality had shaken him, and he'd turned to her for comfort. And then she'd killed him in cold blood. Raised the gun, pointed, squeezed. In the end, she had done what Thomas asked her to without hesitation.

She went into the bedroom and gazed at the rumpled sheets of Silvestro's unmade bed. The cat came along. "You did what you had to. For Howie," he said.

Marcia spun around angrily. "Thomas wouldn't even say for sure if it saved Howie. No one has to kill someone," she shouted. "I don't understand why they made me shoot him. And I don't get why Thomas killed him in the first place."

"Ah," said Mr. Whiskey. "It's the old mystery of how a small evil prevents a great one—or opens the way for good. I'm sorry. That's all I know."

"I don't even know why I've been trusting you."

"Don't cry again," he warned. "It's messing me up. I'm programmed to respond to your tears—another of those old basic-cat skills. It brings out the primitive in me, and then I don't think straight. Anyway, you need to focus on the greater good."

"What's that?" she snapped. "Saving endangered species? Solving the poverty puzzle?"

"Following your instincts," he said simply. "Going through the open door. *Your* greater good is doing what's been set for you. That's why I'm here. I think." He turned and trotted out of the bedroom and back to the plastic bag on the floor and sat down by it and waited until she came and got it, and they left.

Marcia's recollections of Silvestro's original final arrangements were clouded at first. Was it grief again, dimming her memory? Had she grieved for him in 1997? She did not remember. She recalled feeling sick all the time from the hormones and being afraid: twenty-two, not even having graduated, soon to have a child. How was she going to support the baby? She'd dreaded the Noisettes family's reaction when they found out she was pregnant by a dead Chicago foreigner (they hadn't said much).

If she'd grieved in '97, which she might or might not have, it was real and acute this time. She was more practiced in loss now: from little losses like fleeting chances to bigger losses like a comfortable car dying or a favorite work-study student leaving High Cultural Endeavors for grad school. There were the big ones: not just her parents but also Orson's death, Howie's departure for What Island. The largest loss of all, though? The life she'd given up in exchange for Howie's security: a life of freedom to be herself, to live wherever she wanted, work with whomever she wanted doing work that was as meaningful or meaningless as she decided it would be. A life anywhere, *anywhere* other than Round Stone, far away from Nina. The life she'd been trying to recover. Unfortunately, that effort had so far led only to disaster and death.

Gradually the grief gave way to a shiny, painful present clarity that the original events had lacked. This feeling stayed around and hovered over her move back to the dorm. It was all so easy once the Warehouse College connected her with Fortress. He immediately took over everything. But Marcia wondered: How did the people at the college know him? Who was he working for? Was he in league somehow with Thomas and Mae? These were questions she hadn't asked the first time.

This same painful clarity colored her initial appointment with him. She saw that he was younger than she recalled, sort of a poser, with a persistent facial stubble and a confidence that was probably overinflated. Why had she believed, back then, that he had her welfare at heart? But on second reflection, he showed more interest in her financial well-being than anyone had to date. "Once we get all this other stuff cleared away, I want to talk to you about investing," he kept repeating. "You can never start too early."

The painful clarity hovered over the funeral, which was mostly as she recalled it. Same Catholic chapel. Same pudgy, clever priest, same trite homily. The older Marcia had never gone back to visit Silvestro's grave—an omission that, she now realized, had been thoughtless: not to have taken Howie there at least once.

At the funeral, she sat in the family pew with Fortress, who was determined to stick to her like a soggy leaf to a shoe. She wore the same black peasant skirt and cable-stitch sweater as before. There was no other family today. There had been none in '97. The cat sat up next to her in the pew, erect, attentive, horrified. "This is crazy," he kept saying. "This is just *crazy*. What is all this? Up, down, kneel, down, up, kneel. Can't humans stay in one position? Is Silvestro really in that box? Who are those men carrying him around? What are they doing? Why are we all singing? What's *that*?" he said as the priest swung the censer.

"Shh. A censer," said Marcia.

"It's smelling up the whole place. This is insane. Did they do this to *me*?"

"We only do it to people," explained Marcia. Mr. Whiskey looked relieved, but disappointed, too.

Graveside, at the cemetery, she vomited just outside the lawn tent.

"And what might this be?" said Fortress, looking down at the mess on the ground.

"Suzy Q and a green vegetable," said Mr. Whiskey, but Fortress couldn't hear.

"Wait! Are you pregnant?" Fortress whispered.

"Yes."

"It's Silvestro's?"

"Of course."

He all but rubbed his hands together in glee. "*Fantastic* development," he said and thrust a hankie at her to wipe her mouth, and another business card. She already had two. "Make an appointment and come and see me again tomorrow. We need to talk about this. And about investing." Marcia nodded and tried not to throw up again.

One small difference between the original funeral and the redo was the cat. In his previous incarnation he hadn't observed human funeral customs, and he was scandalized by them and quite vocal about it. Another difference was that this time, her grief was much greater. It turned out that the older Marcia truly missed Silvestro and mourned for him in a way that the young

Marcia hadn't at the time, and still didn't. Most of all, though, she grieved for herself: on account of Silvestro's death, she'd forfeited the life she might have had but never would. If she'd known at the time how much she was going to give up because of it, she would have been devastated.

As it happened, Marcia didn't have to make an appointment with Fortress because he barged into her dorm room the next day, just as he had in '97, disheveled and almost manic. He'd been negotiating on her behalf with Burroughs Software Solutions. Since Silvestro's accidental death was the company's fault, Marcia's unborn child had a legitimate wrongful-death suit. She would have to sign away Howie's right to sue the company over the accident in exchange for a substantial sum, to be placed in trust and administered by an anonymous third party. There was a clause requiring her to live and raise Howie in some town other than Chicago, that place yet to be determined by the yet-to-be-assigned trustee. She'd be allowed to finish her degree at the Warehouse College first, of course.

"What if I refuse?" she said to the cat. "If I say I don't want the settlement, I'll be free."

"And poor. Raising a son with no money. If you take the settlement, you know what will happen. If you don't, you have no guarantee that Howie will turn out like he did in Round Stone. You'll be working two jobs, scrambling to pay rent. Here in the city? Who knows what kinds of influences he'll be exposed to? Poor, deprived, angry, with an overworked, stressed-out mom—he might end up a delinquent. Remember why you agreed to the settlement last time?"

She did. "But that's only one scenario, the one you described. It might all be *better*."

"Want to risk it? Besides, the more you deviate from the script, the more likely you are to mess things up—like when you saved Silvestro and Howie ended up dead."

On this, she had to concede that the cat was right.

The last time she saw the lawyer was a week after the funeral. This, too, was as she recalled the original events. They met in his office to sign the settlement agreement. The Burroughs representative explained that she would be raising Howie in Round Stone. It hadn't sounded bad the first time: a small college community near the Sawgash River with a stable population. She'd had no inkling, of course, that Nina would follow her.

"Don't forget about the twenty-five K," whispered the cat after the documents were signed. This time, unlike the first, she had money.

But Marcia didn't need to remind Fortress. He'd already made an appointment for her to meet with his own personal financial guy. They took the train to the adviser's office on East Fifty-Second, and Marcia opened an account and listened to him talk about risk tolerance and asset classes. He helped her pick a mix of blue-chip stocks and some promising but riskier investments. She only vaguely understood what they were doing. She showed ID and filled out paperwork. When she came to the address part, she hesitated.

"We're out of here and back to 2018 as soon as you're done," said the cat. So she filled in her future address on Funnel Street. "You're sure we're going back to *that* house, not Nina's?" she asked him.

"I am not going back to Nina's house ever, if I can help it," said the cat. He twitched the skin on his back, and his fur rippled like a field of short gray grass.

It may sound as though I had no respect for my father, Gordon—in my last mention of him, I was gloating over the memory of him facedown with blood puddling around his head. And I do believe, of the two of us, I was the smarter, better man.

Still, I'm grateful. He prepared the way, as it were. He had a nose for money much more sensitive than mine. Without his money at my disposal, I would be no one. Nothing. And he taught me certain vital principles. For instance, Efficiency vs. Productivity: Productivity is by far the more desirable of the two, he said. A little looseness in the machinery? A little waste—not that big a problem, so long as it serves the interests of productivity. "A shrewd entrepreneur is always thinking in terms of more," he advised me. And though I rejected much of what he told me, I hung on to that.

So I've learned to quantify my achievements. Always thinking about more. An incredible word, by the way: a word that, since the Middle Ages, has filled four of eight slots in that old parts-of-speech schematic. A word that appears in idiomatic phrases without number. A word that can even be a proper noun. Sir Thomas More, for instance, who filled quite a few of slots himself: author and statesman, saint and martyr, to name a handful. Of whom it might be said, "Thomas was beheaded, and then he was no More."

—MEMOIRS OF SOCRATIES LOVE

Chapter 21

MARCIA ARRIVED BACK in 2018 with her cell phone, in Bermudas and her favorite sandal clogs that left her toes open to the warm Round Stone rains. Something hard was poking her side and bruising her hip.

They were in the front yard of her house on Funnel Street, and it was warm—late spring or the end of summer. Actually, it wasn't rain but a high-tech sprinkler wetting her toes and watering her straggly, sundry perennials. She had no memory of such a sprinkler and hoped she hadn't come back to a *different* new nightmare life, where instead of a cleaning woman and fancy faucets she had a gardener and fancy sprinklers.

What now? She'd been so sure saving Silvestro would free her from Nina and Round Stone. And then she'd been sure that killing him again would return things to how they'd been and save Howie. But now she wasn't sure of anything. Was this her original life? Most importantly, was Howie still alive?

She looked to the cat. He was alert, watching a figure coming up the driveway. "I know that person." he said, twitching his ears.

It was the letter carrier, with Marcia's mail. She looked familiar to Marcia, too. "Hi, there," she said and stared awkwardly at Marcia's hip, then shoved a pile of letters at her. She looked down at the spot where Mr. Whiskey was sitting on the sun-warmed sidewalk and frowned.

"Does she see you?" Marcia whispered.

"Of course I do," said the letter carrier, and Marcia understood then that she really was back to her true, present life.

According to her phone, it was Saturday, so she didn't have to be anywhere. Inside, she leafed through the mail while the cat strolled around, sniffing. There was a promotional postcard from Holliday College touting the launch of Tuition Redefinition. There was something from a company called PPP. It was stamped TIME SENSITIVE, which meant it was probably junk. There was a flyer from Floods, advertising a giant sale on ring bologna. Floods was always trying to compete with Stowes, but they just didn't have the cachet. She threw the mail in the floor basket and walked around, checking things out.

"What are you doing?" said the cat.

"My eyes are your nose," said Marcia. "I'm seeing if anything has changed."

In the bathroom, the tub was still long, and it had the same mandala shower curtain with whorls of teal and goldenrod. In the bedroom, her bed was as she'd left it the morning they'd first traveled to 1997 Chicago. On the back porch, the door was still cock-eyed from having been broken into. The birdbath in the backyard was still cracked and dotted with pasty turds. In the basement, the freezer's absence was still so apparent it was like a headline had been left off the front page. There was the unblemished rectangle of lighter cement where it had sat.

"What's this?" said the cat, placing a tentative white paw across the line where the dark, dirty floor turned clean.

Marcia explained. Then she started talking about Orson in his frozen red blanket and how she'd kept him in the freezer until she'd delivered him to what she had thought was Eternal Paws for cremation.

"You *froze* him and then *burned* him?" The cat grew agitated and walked around making a low, growly sound. "When did they steal the freezer?" he asked finally.

"Right after I took him to be cremated."

"Do you think someone took the freezer because they thought Orson was still in it?" said the cat. "Who knew he was in there?"

"Nina—but she's the one who pushed me to get him cremated. Plus she's too petite to steal a freezer."

"Then maybe the question to ask is who knew he *wasn't* in the freezer."

"Only the people at the megachurch."

"Hmm," said the cat. "Let me cogitate on this."

They went back upstairs. "You're very good on stairs," noted Marcia. "Did you live in a two-story house?"

"I don't know," said the cat wistfully. "I don't think so, but it's nebulous."

She was only half listening because her mind had turned again to Howie. She took her phone out of her shorts pocket. To her astonishment and relief, there was a message from him!

Mom, it read, *sorry if I scared you with that last message and the* 🛻*s. Nothing to worry about, it's all good. Things are bad on the mainland. The More-Tally keeps going up. But it's safe here.*

I'm staying healthy, eating tons of mekanize and boiled eggs. I've got quite a collection of interview material. There's interesting lore about some people who live in the desert. The biggest problem I've had is that some of these informants have terrible memories— either that, or the porridge roll does something to them.

Mom, I know I've probably told you this—but I thought I was here about the language, and turns out, it's the lore. Their forgetfulness aside, these people are fascinating. The interviews are like nothing I've done in the past. Research is all about being open to whatever there is, wherever you are. They don't teach you that in college.

I hope you're having fun with your new cat. What's his name, by the way? Give him a pat for me. I can't wait to meet him.

Your son,

Howie.

Marcia read the message twice. It had been sent just an hour ago. He was alive! He was busy learning exotic desert lore. And safe, far from Cor-Spamkeer, gathering previously unrecorded folk ways from interesting people—safe for the moment, anyway.

Also, he'd said he wanted to meet the cat, meaning he was thinking about coming home. Now all she had to do was figure out how to *get* him home.

She sat down for a few minutes, savoring the relief. The time-travel had tired her, and she was on the brink of drifting off when Mr. Whiskey jumped up next to her and bit her sharply on the ear. "Get with it!" he admonished her. "We didn't come back to now to nap. You have things to do. You have to bring Howie home. And I have to *get* home."

At that moment, *Nina Nuts* blared on her screen. The cat saw it, too. "Answer! See if you can find out why she sent you to Eternal Paws. The key to my past is in the origin of my ashes. If we can figure out where they came from, I might be able to find my human."

Reluctantly, Marcia answered. But at first she couldn't get her question in because Nina was being Nina.

"Marsh!" she said. "How *are* you? I stopped by to see you at High Cultural Endeavors the other day, but you were up to your ears in typing one of those endless reports they're always piling on you. What would Holliday College do without you?"

"Hire a replacement at a lower wage," said Marcia.

"Ha! Ha! Marsh, you're such a wag," laughed Nina giddily. Then she stopped laughing abruptly and said, "How's little Cinders Friday? Your kitty cat. Do you still have him?

It struck Marcia that even though it had been a long time—twenty-one years, in fact—since she'd spoken with Nina, she was already running out of patience. "I thought you didn't like cats. Why are you asking?"

"I have a coupon for a free pet grooming. It just came in the mail. Have you thought about having him groomed? I could drop over and give it to you."

"Oh, my God," moaned Mr. Whiskey.

Marcia ignored them both. "Nina, do you know anything about a sprinkler on my lawn?"

"*Eternal Paws*," said the cat in a stage whisper.

"Who are you talking to?"

"No one. The cat doesn't want to be groomed," announced Marcia. "It's not a good idea."

"How do you know? He might love it. And I don't have any use for this coupon—"

"Cinders Friday has Zarte-Haut syndrome," said Marcia quickly, calling on her sprinkling of German. "His skin is unusually delicate."

"Marsh, I've never heard of that," said Nina suspiciously.

"Neither had I, but then he just started flaking away before my very eyes," said Marcia. "Now he has to take prescription caplets and wear a protective body sock to keep him all in one piece. Grooming would destroy him."

The cat was glowering. Before Nina could ask anything else, Marcia blurted in a rush, "Nina, why did you want me to take Orson to Eternal Paws?"

"I didn't particularly care where you took him," said Nina. "I just wanted you to get him out of your house so—"

"What?"

"So you could have closure. And then that flyer appeared in my door. Normally I throw that stuff away. I don't know what compelled me to give it to you. It was almost like something was making me do it. And about the sprinkler? Kirk drove by and noticed your flowers were drying up, so he took our best sprinkler over. It's Hammacher Schlemmer."

Marcia bit the inside of her cheek and said, "Oh, thanks, Nina. It's good to have generous friends."

She hung up and announced to the cat, "We're going to Stowes. I need to restock the fridge." She stood, and the pain in her hip was so sharp that she gasped.

"Do you want to take that gun out of your waistband first?"

She looked down. Indeed, it was the Beretta that had been bruising her hip all this time. No wonder the letter carrier had looked at her strangely. She pulled it out of her shorts waist and weighed it in her hands. "Why didn't I notice this before?" she said.

"You've been preoccupied. But maybe with the wrong things. When I was a young cat, I could sit for hours outside a mole burrow, waiting for one of the little rascals to come out. I became a virtuoso moler. But I missed many birds and rabbits that way."

He lifted one paw, licked it, and put it down. "You may need the gun later," he said. "But put it in a safe place for now."

ON THE WAY to Stowes, the cat sat next to her in the passenger seat, making wide sweeps of his rough tongue over the gray fur that had started to look ruffly and unkempt, they'd spent so much time traveling through the straw lately. At the last minute, she'd grabbed the sprinkler from the lawn, shaking it to drain it first and then slinging it into the trunk.

"What are you doing?"

"*This* is going straight to the Goodwill," announced Marcia.

She remembered that on the day she'd rescued Orson, the back seat of her car had been full of bags she was taking to Goodwill. She wished Mr. Whiskey could take her back, just for a second, so she could witness it all unfolding. But time-travel was not about finding one small, errant puzzle piece. That was what memory was for.

She pushed on the gas, and they sped to the Goodwill, where she handed the still dripping sprinkler to a startled employee with the words "Friends don't force friends to water their flowers." Then they sped to Stowes and got fish and fruit and bagels and milk and ground lamb for the cat and a Stowes sandwich for Marcia. Old Mrs. Stowe was not there, but her daughter-in-law was, the one who dressed revealingly on the weekends and worked in Payroll at the college.

"How's business?" Marcia asked.

This provoked a rant from Young Mrs. Stowe. "You wouldn't believe how *low* Floods is going to steal our customers," she told Marcia. "It used to be they would just shoot at our fireworks stand with cheap bottle rockets all summer. But now it's gotten bitter." She looked around the store quickly and leaned toward Marcia confidentially. "There's something you should know. I was looking at some files in the auxiliary shadow backup system the other day. I noticed something strange about your son's fellowship. Have you been wanting to locate him?"

Marcia nodded eagerly.

"Here's the thing . . ." She lowered her voice to an inaudible whisper.

"Wait. What?" said Marcia.

But just then, the bell on the door jingled and Young Mrs. Stowe turned to greet the new customer. Marcia waited around, but people trickled in steadily, requiring Young Mrs. Stowe's attention, and finally Marcia had to go, before the lamb and milk went bad.

They drove home, and Mr. Whiskey ate a plate of browned lamb lightly seasoned while Marcia toyed with her sandwich and tried in her mind to hear what she hadn't been able to hear in person. What had Young Mrs. Stowe said? What did she know? Also, what was the auxiliary shadow backup system?

After the cat was finished and had fallen asleep, she went and rummaged through Howie's files, but she still couldn't find the original fellowship offer. She tried to FaceTime him. No luck. She tried messaging, but it stayed undelivered.

I see upon rereading my earlier account that I haven't always been clear, dear Reader. Neither have I presented things entirely chronologically. My mother would have pronounced this memoir a failure for those faults. But that was because she misunderstood. She believed I was just a lackluster clone of my father: a budding businessman. And a businessman must be clear; he must do things in the necessary order. However, I was no businessman. I was a visionary. And a seeker after immortality. Or do I mean "immorality"? Perhaps the two quests are related.

But striving for glory is always a risk, isn't it? I would have been better off if I'd been more like my father. I could have lived quite comfortably, taking only modest chances. My father's airline interests had failed, but the family wells ran deep. Wealth was the dominant gene. The Loves had money. We were money. I might have learned the art of finance and spent my time making more of what we already had.

But there was that urge that kept bubbling up. The desire to make something. Something eternal. Something sublimely, terribly, unforgettable. Outlandish and out of bounds. Only Dale caught a glimmer of it. But his goodness kept him from grasping it fully.

And then, he turned away to his family.

There is a point in life when one's course is sealed. It comes earlier than you might think. Dale's inveterate niceness was inscribed before he could talk. My penchant for malignancy was set many years before I watched my mother drive away with her dearly beloved dogs—leaving her very not beloved son behind.

I write this to pose a question: Do you wonder if my affection for Dale could have reformed me? No. Yes. Maybe. The only chink in my armor was our friendship. But he had to be all for me. I am, it seems, not incapable of change, but only when it's change on my terms. At heart, I am a black and possessive soul.

—MEMOIRS OF SOCRATIES LOVE

Among the experts recruited by Jaytie Limes in the transformation of Kanz-_ika was a select group of architects from Europe, Asia, and the Americas. Initially they were tasked with several government projects in the capital, but it was quickly apparent that Limes's real purpose was to engage high-level experts in the design of his sprawling prison/execution complex, Cor-Spamkeer. Only a few trusted members of this group saw the plans for the whole complex. The others were divided into task teams to design and oversee construction of the prison's various functional units: multiple intake halls; a two-story administrative office building; "dormitory" housing for up to 25,000; detention cell blocks; killing antechambers; three killing complexes; canteen and stores; infirmary; morgue and crematoria; and the rumored "transfer room," where select bodies were taken for unknown purposes. The original plan was adapted and expanded to keep up with Limes's goal of an accelerating More-Tally. A majority of the dead were cremated on-site, but as corpses piled up and furnaces in the crematoria malfunctioned repeatedly, bodies were intermittently shipped to nearby uninhabited What Island and buried in mass graves.

Despite the superior design, Cor-Spamkeer's facilities proved insufficient to meet Limes's quotas, so construction began on satellite killing facilities. All were called Cor-Spamkeer and distinguished by colors: Cor-Spamkeer-Red ultimately spawned five additional smaller "corpse-maker" complexes: Jade, Violet, Aquamarine, Tangerine, and Crystal White.

—THE INFORMATION HATCH

Informant 12

"I don't know why none of us thought of it. If we
had made more of a ruckus, I would not be here
talking to you. *They*, the ones I'm telling you
about, were smarter. We were all headed to the
same place, but they were saved. Rescued. Removed
and sent away because they sounded like . . . I
don't know. They were so *loud*. A lot of my memory
of that time is gone, but I'll never forget their
screaming.

"Maybe that's the lesson. As simple as that. How
does that go? Squeaky wheel. They got the grease.
Because they sounded like a horde from hell. It
was the Desert People who saved them.

"You need to know this about the Desert People. They reuse, recycle. They can put *anything* to
use. Look at us here. Scavenging. We were rotten
through and through, but they found a use for us.
Now we spend all our time looking for what we can
never find. How's that for irony?

"I'm so lucid today. My memory's on fire. It must
be the extra porridge roll."

Chapter 22

ON THEIR WAY to Bixby, it started raining. This made Marcia feel at least partially vindicated about dumping an almost new hundred-dollar sprinkler at Goodwill. She was unusually edgy. It was the hemmed-in feeling of being back in Round Stone after the exhilaration of being twenty-two again and running around Chicago with a supernatural cat.

And always, there were her fears for Howie.

When the clouds rolled over the sun and the rain began, the cat went to sleep on the passenger seat, head between his paws. Marcia grew increasingly despondent; each sweep of the wipers sounded like a dirgelike iamb from a poem by Poe. Then suddenly Mr. Whiskey woke and announced, "It's OK. Your being stuck in Round Stone, the danger to Howie, my separation from the man I love—they'll all end soon. Nothing is forever. The natural impulse of life is toward liberation. Preservation. Harmony. Reunion."

"The natural impulse of life is toward death," said Marcia darkly.

"Quit that," said Mr. Whiskey. "It's a lovely afternoon. We're on our way to Bixby. We hope to discover what happened to Orson and maybe, just maybe, where I came from. And anyway, even if life does lead to death, death can also lead to life. Reconstitution. New powers. Potentiality from beyond the grave. I'm the living proof. Though technically, I'm dead."

Thus chastened, Marcia drove over the Sawgash River bridge. She glanced at the banks below and noticed some people fishing.

The cat read her thoughts. "Wait! Is *that* where fish come from? From those people who hold sticks out over the river?"

Marcia knew a lot about fishing because, in addition to being an amateur historian and an expert on cartoon dogs, Dale Farrar had liked to fish and used to take her along, when he wasn't stoned or watching TV. She described the premise to the cat.

"So you put booby-trapped food, or something that looks like food, on the end of a string, and the fish gets hauled in by its mouth? Isn't that animal abuse?" spluttered the cat after she'd filled him in.

Marcia explained that the fish Mr. Whiskey ate was not caught this way; it was mostly fished or farmed commercially. Nets, traps, big boats, hatcheries, canneries. "All these years, and I never knew," he mused. "It really is eat or be eaten out there, isn't it?"

Driving into Bixby, she saw that it looked the same yet created a very different impression. The church grounds, which before she'd understood to be a cemetery, now looked like an agrarian tract of rolling green dotted with small yurt-like tents that she had somehow mistaken for dog headstones the first time. Possibly the congregation lived in the tents. The church building looked the same, but where before it had seemed bleak and utilitarian—a facility to char dead pets—she was seeing it as a church now. Holy ground. When she'd expected a pet crematory, that was what she had found. Now that she knew it was a church, she picked up on a saintly vibe.

"You do realize the people here deceived you?" said the cat. "Made you think they were a crematory? Overcharged you for getting rid of a dog blanket? They can't be *that* saintly. Is it possible that my ashes were delivered to you because there were no Orson ashes? You still don't know for a fact that they actually cremated him."

"One way to find out," said Marcia and parked and they got out of the car.

Just as they were about to enter, her phone blurped. Howie! He was FaceTiming her! She moved away from the door and pressed the green video-camera icon, and his face emerged on her screen like a troubling vision: unshaven, unglued-looking. What Island "nets" swarmed around him. His eyes were glazed, and bits of something dried—mekanize?—were crusted around his mouth.

A lag, and then, in a voice suffused with deep dread, he moaned, "Mom. MOM!"

"Howie! What's wrong?"

"Mom, remember what I told you about the people here all being from somewhere else? They're *dead*, Mom. That's why none of them are native What Islanders. They were dead when they came here. And everything I told you about their language? It's not really shifted; it's what dead-speak sounds like to the living. I got away from Shyl for a while, so I was able to talk to them more. They have terrible memories because technically they are brain-dead, along with being dead in every other way except appearance. But I got more garbled bits and pieces from them, and this is what I figured out. Shyl and Crumb and I are the only living humans on the island. That's why the islanders don't care about houses or money. They don't need to because they're dead. Remember I told you the porridge roll was some kind of natural speed? Well, that's not right, obviously, because dead people don't need speed. It's . . . I don't know what, exactly, maybe some kind of reanimating elixir? It keeps them active and bodied so they can go around scavenging."

Marcia's thoughts went a million ways. Either he was delusional, which would be terrible, or, equally bad, he was trapped in the midst of some genuinely bizarre zombie horror show. "Howie, you need to come home *now*!"

"I can't, Mom. That's the other thing. I don't think Crumb or Shyl intend to hurt me, but I'm a prisoner here. I mean, there's no one to help me get off the island because there's no one else who's alive. The islanders just go around eating their porridge roll and carrying their sacks. I didn't want to tell you about the scavenging, but I know about that, too. It's *life*, Mom. That's what they're looking for. They're hunting for artifacts of living. It's like reverse archaeology, but it's sad. They died and were buried—probably here on the island. And something reanimated them, and now they go around looking for clues to what it was like to be alive—but their memories are so foggy that they don't find much, and when they do find something, they can't make sense of it."

No sooner had he finished his sentence than the call ended, and she was left looking at his stricken face (so handsome, so like Silvestro), covered with gnats and facial hair. She tried to call back. Again. And again. But he didn't answer, and all breath deserted her. What had her son gotten dragged into? Would he be killed, too, and zombified, to wander around with a sack speaking pig Latin?

The cat jumped up and sidled against her in an attempt at comfort. When she finally stopped shaking and remembered where she was (Bixby) and why she was here (to find out about Orson's ashes), he said simply, "If you want to help Howie, my guess is there's nothing you can do but go forward. Anyway, we've done enough back, Marcia. Let's go."

Just inside, in the narthex, a maroon wall with a mirror confronted them. Without thinking, she picked up the cat and showed him himself—something she used to do occasionally with Orson.

The cat stared and muttered something. Then he said, "Put me down," and she did, and he stalked along the wall and into the foyer, refusing to look back at her.

Out of nowhere, a woman appeared. Her expression was distracted and vaguely otherworldly. Marcia recognized her as the "grief counselor" she'd talked with before. Lisa. But instead of the poorly sewn jacket, now she was in jeans and an off-white tunic that made Marcia think of priests' vestments. It had long sleeves with diagonal points that fell over her hands and a high neck and fitted shoulders. Embroidered in a most beautiful cursive, in shimmering blue thread over a neat square breast pocket, was one word: *Lifted*. When the woman smiled at them, she looked like a benevolent alien.

"Pick me up again," said the cat.

Lisa didn't react at the cat's speaking, so Marcia assumed she was not one of "them." Something about her had made Marcia imagine that she might be a donut person. Apparently she was not, so anything Marcia and the cat said would be inaudible, though because they were in the original time, Mr. Whiskey was still visible.

"Pick me up," the cat repeated.

"I thought you were mad at me."

"Anger is a secondary emotion. Primarily, I am shamed. In the mirror, I discovered my appalling avoirdupois. You've been feeding me too much."

Marcia bent and lifted him. It was true that he'd gained a few pounds.

Lisa had been watching them curiously. "You are aware that your cat is *animalis beatus*?"

"He recently transitioned from fish to lamb," said Marcia. "Is that what you mean?"

"Ah, yes. *Manducans feles, agnus*," said Lisa, nodding.

"What's 'Lifted'?" Mr. Whiskey asked on the other plane.

"What's 'Lifted'?" Marcia asked Lisa, staring at the blue embroidery on her tunic. The blue glimmered in an entirely unthreadlike way. The script was beauteous.

"We are the Pious Body," explained Lisa. "The Pious Body of Formally Doomed Souls. But we have, praise our saviors, been Lifted."

"What's that?"

Lisa's expression grew misty, and her voice dropped half an octave. "We come from remote regions on the other side of the globe, where we were cast into darkness and danger. There was weeping and gnashing of teeth. We were indeed doomed. We sweated blood as we watched, all around us, souls just like us get picked off and led away to die. We remember almost nothing of that time except that it was full of terror. But our cohort here all shared this: we were louder than a hog slaughter."

"That sounds awful," said Marcia.

"Tell me about it. It *was* awful. While others were biting their lips and going to their deaths with stoic dignity, we made noise. A TON of noise. The more scared we were, the more noise we made. An onslaught of decibels. An assault of horrendous shrieking. In fact, afterward, some of us suffered permanent hearing loss. We were banshees crying a warning about our own impending deaths. We shouted, screeched, and howled. We yowled, shrilled, screaked, and keened unendingly. We were not about to go quietly if we could raise holy hell.

"We made so much noise that our saviors heard from miles away, and once they got wind of it, they were right on it and came and got us. So we were saved: given a reprieve through a magical transportation."

"You mean transmutation?"

"No. Trans*por*tation," insisted Lisa. She seemed to think Marcia wasn't getting it. "All hope had been entirely lost. We'd stood on the edge of the abyss, staring into our inevitable future of not-being, and quaked at the prospect and screamed, like the cowardly babies we were, until our throats were raw.

"But then it happened—we were *lifted*." She gave a balmy smile. "That's the transportation part. We flew above the abyss and across the ocean. Darkness turned to a new dawn. We were seized from our dark dungeon and *lifted* to the green hills around Bixby by our salvational spirits. They made us a holy bargain: they'd set us up with a church in Bixby, and in exchange, after they instructed us in the art of the chiphole, we would serve as their backup prayer team. They already knew we could make a racket—it was just a question of training us to make it for *their* purposes. Ever since, we have been a community given to assisting our rescuers and upholding their good goals through prayer.

"Unfortunately," she added, "they set us up with the church but didn't give us an operating budget. They expect us to be fiscally self-sufficient. It's left us hard up for cash."

"This is a regular church, right? It's not a cult?" asked Marcia dubiously.

"It's the Pious Body," said Lisa and left it at that. "True piety outshines all excess. All fanaticism and aberrant creeds. We align ourselves now with the beneficent desires of our rescuers until the day we finally go home, wherever that is. In the meantime, we act as agents and accept all donations and paying commissions."

"What kind of agents?" said Marcia testily. "Dog-burning, ash-stealing agents? I never got Orson's ashes back. I got ashes, but they were the wrong ones."

"I remember you came here with your dead dog. But you have found a blessed new companion," Lisa replied evasively.

"Truth," said Mr. Whiskey.

"I want to know what happened to my dog! I want his ashes!" demanded Marcia.

"Come with me." Lisa pulled them into the same back room where before she had taken Orson's body, supposedly to put him in a vault. But there was no vault here. There was nothing mortuary-like at all. It was a windowless room about ten by ten, with more of the Con-Tact-looking "wallpaper," a desk, a laptop, an office chair, a tall fake plant, and a pair of framed prints of raccoons frisking around in woodsy brush. The prints had pink garage-sale price stickers in the corners.

Lisa spoke in a loud whisper. "Shh. I'm not supposed to be telling you this. Our market research suggested that this would be a good area for a pet crematory. Round Stone and its environs are in a "dead spot"—oh, sorry, I didn't intend that pun—a dead spot for disposal of animal remains. And there's the retired racehorse sanctuary right here in Bixby. So we were trying to break into the business, but we hit a bump with the startup funds. We needed an incinerator that would take a whole horse, and we didn't have the cash, and our credit, I'm sorry to say, isn't the best because basically, we're illegals. We took a vote and decided to start small, with just dogs and cats in our firepit, until we had the capital to go whole horse, as it were. You were our first client, the first person to respond to our flyers."

"So you burned Orson in your firepit?" said Marcia. She was feeling more than a bit ill.

"Oh, yes! He burned beautifully!" said Lisa. "It was a very nice fire. We all gathered around and intoned, and though the hair didn't smell great, it was quite spiritual.

"But unfortunately, before the ashes were cool enough to remove, a storm front moved in and drenched them and turned them to mush. We tried drying them out on screens, but they just turned into crispy ash-globs. We were afraid you would be angry and want your money back, so we dispersed the globs over our lovely green space, where they dissolved and the spirit of Orson was freed to run and play. Surely you felt him as you drove in?"

"No," said Marcia angrily. "I'm pretty sure I didn't."

"And we found you some substitute ashes that weren't all globbed up. We didn't think you'd know the difference. How *did* you know, by the way?"

Marcia looked to Mr. Whiskey, and Lisa picked up on her glance. "Oh," she said slowly. "I think I see." She reached over and laid her hand on Mr. Whiskey's back. "I have heard something about this. It does not often happen, but it can . . ." she trailed off.

"That's all I can tell you." She was still whispering. "I know what you're going to ask. Where did the ashes come from that were delivered to you?"

"Yes, where?" said the cat.

"Where?" said Marcia.

"We liberated them," said Lisa. "We prayed until we had a vision of a delivery car transporting ashes to veterinary practices; we went a few counties over, where no one would recognize us. And then our sister followed the driver until he stopped, and while he was making a delivery, she liberated a resin box of cremains. You see how nicely it turned out? If she hadn't freed your cat, he'd be sitting in a box in someone's utility room."

"You *stole* me?" said the cat.

"You stole him?" said Marcia.

"'Stole' is so judgmental. But, you see, we didn't have a choice, did we?"

Marcia did not agree. While she was still trying to process Lisa's extraordinary revelation, Mr. Whiskey suddenly asked, "Where is everyone? If this is a megachurch, where's the rest of the Pious Body? All we've seen so far is one person. And where's the person who stole me? Also, where was I going?"

Marcia relayed these questions to Lisa.

"I am not allowed to tell you the identity of our sister who acquired your cat; that is confidential information. And even she did not know the destination of the ashes. But I can tell you where the rest of the Pious Body is. They are supplicating and petitioning," she said. "They have gone to their chipholes to pray."

"Chipholes?"

"Their private spiritual spaces. You saw them when you drove in."

"You mean those white tents."

"Well. But they're *holy* tents. Chipholes," repeated Lisa.

"Does she at least know a direction? Maybe a county?" Mr. Whiskey said, but Marcia ignored this. "What kind of prayers?" she asked curiously as she stood to leave, wondering for a moment if they took requests.

"Just to be transparent, we're typically paid for our prayers. If you'd like, I can give you a rate sheet. No prayer is too small, but we do have some larger accounts. For instance: for Kanz-_ika. That one's our bread and butter. Much evil is afoot in Kanz-_ika. We are praying all day long for Kanz-_ika.

"We have a sliding scale if you can't afford our usual rates," added Lisa a little too eagerly.

"Or we can work out a payment plan!" she called after Marcia as she and the cat headed out the door.

On the way out of Bixby, Marcia rolled down the windows. Indeed, they could hear the members of the Pious Body in their tents on the grassy expanse, intoning something urgent and impelling, though the words were lost in the overhum. She noticed Mr. Whiskey's ears swiveling.

"Is your reconstituted hearing as good as a normal cat's? What are they saying?"

"It's better than a normal cat's. Shhh. They were humming some kind of liturgical moondance music, but now they're speaking." His ears pricked and he listened intently, and then she saw his feline expression, if there was such a thing, change suddenly.

"'Exit Right Now or You'll Die!' That's what they're saying."

"Oh," said Marcia and reflexively stepped on the gas.

"Can you push that floor thing harder?" said the cat.

"The accelerator? Sure," she said and sped up to eighty, and they cruised out of town with the cat at high attention.

After a few miles, he relaxed. "I don't know what that was all about, but I think it's OK. Maybe it's just one of their chiphole chants," he said and then, "What do you think a chiphole is?"

But Marcia was on another track. She was noticing that the pure, cloudless blue of the late-summer sky was exactly the same shade as the dress she had worn at Nina's wedding. Their forced sisterhood had required her to be Nina's maid of honor and stand up with her as she said her vows to Kirk. Marcia had handed Nina the ring and followed her around managing her seven-foot train. Nina's measurements were so proportional that her gown had needed no alterations. But Marcia's sky-blue dress had to be specially sewn to accommodate her big boobs, which Kirk kept referring to inappropriately as "the Boobsey Twins." Now Marcia looked at the sky, remembered Nina's intrusion on her adult life here, and the wedding, and the dress, and the "Boobsey Twins," and wondered how much the Pious Body would charge to pray for her release from Round Stone.

They reached the Sawgash River bridge. The fishers were still out on the banks, but something had just happened. She slowed to watch. They were riveted to their phones and shouting. A few were pointing, and she saw, rising in the sky, in the same direction where they were pointing, an expanding black plume, the only stain on the otherwise pristine blue.

When she got home, she learned from a flurry of texts and the local news what it was: Stowes had blown up and was burning to the ground. And Young Mrs. Stowe, the only one in the store at the time, was missing.

Informant 12

"A pen. That's what it was called. I remember how
it was used. I used it for my work, but I don't
know what that means. What is work? Is it like
scavenging?

"What? No, I don't know 'money.'

"You have no idea what it's like. I would give
anything to get it all back. I cried when the pen
suddenly emerged where we were digging. I didn't
tell you that before because it didn't seem important, and I was a little sensitive. I cried for
a long time. I held it in my hand. Something told
me it was a way of making things permanent. But
nothing is permanent. We are proof of that.

"Did I tell you that the Desert People woke us?
We were asleep, but they needed us. For you, so
you wouldn't be lonely. So you'd have something to
keep you occupied for as long as you have to stay
here. You can stay as long as you like.

"To scavenge, you know, doesn't *require* porridge
roll, but that helps us. It gives us the desire
to get up every day. Not that we sleep like you
do, now that we're awake. We've watched you sleep.
It's beautiful. You're so peaceful when you sleep,
and then you wake up every morning without magic.
Without porridge roll.

"I don't know what's in it. They say food is
life, but I don't think life is in it. It's not
like when I had a pen. If we work hard at scavenging, the Desert People will reward us by letting
us stay awake.

"I used the pen every day for my work. It felt so good just to hold it, even though I couldn't remember what I did with it.

"Maybe you could scavenge with us sometime so you wouldn't be lonely. Maybe you'd find a pen, too.

"You'd never die if you stayed. Not the way we did."

Chapter 23

At home, Mr. Whiskey dashed into the house and disappeared the minute she opened the door. The city of Round Stone had a Twitter, and someone was on it live-tweeting the fire and the rescue efforts. Still no sign of Young Mrs. Stowe, who had discovered something in the auxiliary shadow backup system, who might have figured out how to get Howie home. But now she was missing. Marcia felt like a million things were caving in at once, not a few of them ashy: Stowes was burning to ashes. Orson's ashes were lost, dissolved in the soil around Bixby. A dead ash-cat was her only confidant, and the only person who might have been able to help rescue her son had probably been killed in the explosion at Stowes.

She stomped around the house, yelling for Mr. Whiskey. She found him in the bathtub.

"We learned *nothing* about where I came from. An entire afternoon in Bixby, wasted," he moaned accusingly. "All I know is that I was stolen from a delivery vehicle. I feel worse than I did not knowing anything."

"You want me to feel sorry for you because you can't remember your origins? Do 999,999 out of a million cats remember their origins? No, I don't think so. Sorry I can't join your pity party. I've got my own problems," snapped Marcia. "And why are you in the tub?"

"I came in here to get some peace and try to think. At least I've figured out the chipholes. It's a mispronunciation of 'chapels.'"

"Chipholes. Chapels. This is all insane," said Marcia impatiently. "Can't you help me?"

"I don't know how," said the cat sadly. "I may have run up against the limits of my new powers. It was only a matter of time."

THE NEXT DAY was Sunday. Marcia had expected to hear from Nina, but there was nothing from that quarter. She'd spent a restless night agonizing over Howie. Young Mrs. Stowe was still missing, now presumed dead: it was awful to think of her being blown up, but worse still to think that Marcia's best chance at rescuing Howie had gone to the grave.

Early in the morning, while the town was quiet, Marcia drove over to Stowes. The cat was depressed and didn't want to come. "Maybe you need to eat something," said Marcia. She offered him scrambled eggs, but he refused, saying, "I'm nothing but a fat lump of dead cat, forgotten by all who loved him and not properly laid to rest. I shall not eat again." This made Marcia feel even guiltier than she did already about having been sharp with him the night before.

There was only one vehicle at the Stowes lot, Old Mrs. Stowe's pickup with the sticker on the cab window that said FOLLOW ME TO THE BEST SANDWICHES IN TOWN. The still smoking, soaked remains of the store were barricaded for safety. Old Mrs. Stowe was standing beside the barrier, a package of something under her arm. She was a sizable woman who had towered once but who in her sixties had begun caving in through the shoulders and torso. Against the backdrop of the store's wreckage, she looked more like a tragic king—Lear or Oedipus taking in the devastation they'd set in motion—than an elderly maker of locally famous sandwiches.

Marcia went and stood beside her. "Old Mrs. Stowe, are you all right? I'm so sorry for your loss."

She held out the package Marcia had noticed under her arm. It was the Sunday *Post*. "They brought the paper," she said dazedly. "The store is gone, but they still brought the Sunday paper for us to sell." She handed one to Marcia. "Here. You were always a good customer," she said.

"Thank you. I'm so terribly sorry," repeated Marcia awkwardly.

"Look. The deli case is the only thing that didn't burn up. It's aircraft-carrier steel."

"Do they know what happened?"

"A homemade bomb," said Mrs. Stowe, and then added thoughtfully, "I never heard of a store-bought bomb, come to think of it. We sold everything else, but we never sold bombs. The whole place went up in seconds. My daughter-in-law was the only one here."

Old Mrs. Stowe touched Marcia's arm and said, "You work at the college still?"

Marcia nodded.

"Well, Young Mrs. Stowe has a lot to say about that place. She's a whiz at getting into the auxiliary shadow backup system, and she finds out a lot of dirt. People making salaries they shouldn't no way be making for teaching classes about Instagram, and a different high-dollar administrator for every word in the dictionary. And now they're in a tight spot and raising tuition, and I bet you won't see any of that money, and neither will she."

"Probably not," Marcia agreed, thinking that Young Mrs. Stowe was especially unlikely to see any of it, since she was dead.

Mrs. Stowe began to weep wheezily. Then she stopped just as suddenly and wiped her face with her hand. "We still got Young Mrs. Stowe with us," she said. "That's the miracle in all this."

"You found her body? It was . . . intact?"

"We still got *her*. Alive as you. She had a feeling and stepped outside, or we'd be picking up pieces of her right now," said Old Mrs. Stowe. "It was a miracle. She saw a vision in her brain of a bunch of hippies in tents. Then they all came out and yelled at her to get out or she'd die, and it scared her, so she ran out of the store right before the bomb exploded. Then she drove out to the Casey's at Bixby and bought a bunch of lottery tickets because she figured it was probably the luckiest day of her life. That's why no one could find her until this morning. She bought the lottery tickets and went to that casino next county over and gambled all night while we were out here looking for her finger bones in the ashes. She won eight hundred dollars." Old Mrs. Stowe sounded neither compassionate nor judgmental about her daughter-in-law's behavior; she was still in shock about the store.

Marcia didn't want to trouble her further by telling her what she and the cat had heard the Pious Body chanting right before the explosion, so she said a circumspect goodbye and went to her car. Back home, she grabbed the newspaper and her phone and went inside. To her dismay, she'd missed a call from Howie's alternate phone number. She called him back, holding her breath that it would go through. She unfolded the *Post* while she waited for him to answer and skimmed the sobering headlines while the phone rang. Once. Twice. Four times. Then voicemail. She hung up, heart careering around, and stared at the paper:

MORE-TALLY CLIMBING RAPIDLY

GRUESOME DISCOVERY:
UNINHABITED ISLAND HOME TO FRESH MASS GRAVES

COR-SPAMKEER "DEATH PRISON" VICTIMS
BURIED IN ISLAND PITS

Shakily, Marcia read. The island was cut off to all traffic except Jaytie Limes's military transports. According to the article, it was uninhabitable and had not, in modern history, ever been inhabited—so Howie was right that he and Shyl and Crumb were the only living people on the island. For years, the bodies of prisoners who died in Cor-Spamkeer had been trucked to the coast and shipped over the water for disposal, but now the morbid trickle had swelled to thousands.

This was what had happened to Howie's interview subjects. They weren't just any dead people. They were Limes's victims who had been executed and shipped off for disposal. New aerial photographs of What Island's rough terrain revealed vast areas that had already been covered over with fresh, rocky dirt and others that were being dug or had been dug: large rectangular pits like fatally shallow basements, waiting for the dead.

Wave after wave of sheer icy electricity washed over her. For long moments, she thought her heart would stop. She tried again to call Howie—and again it went to voice mail. She pulled up her NooNews app. They had aerial drone footage of the mass burials on What Island. There were mounds of dirt where previous graves had been filled in, and then the view shifted to a rectangular pit, larger than any swimming pool. Soldiers in khaki were lifting inert bodies and tossing them in. And other men, down in the pit, were arranging them in rows for maximum space efficiency.

Something caught her eye, and she replayed the video and then played it again. Was it? She couldn't be sure. There was a rocky hillock at the edge of the mass grave. And beside it, a flash of washed denim and cardinal red. Howie's red jacket? His favorite red jacket? None of the soldiers would be wearing red, and there was no one else on the island. No one living.

She watched again. The pit. The soldiers. The bodies. And then the flash of red, a form she could hardly make out. About Howie's height, with a small old person holding his arm and either following or guiding. Crumb? Disappearing behind the hill before Marcia could be sure of anything.

She replayed yet again. Did the person move like Howie? It was so long since she'd seen him (though it wasn't actually that long; it just felt like it from all the time-travel). *Was* that his jacket? Had he taken it with him? He'd been packing; he'd dropped his bag with a thump, but it wasn't his bag dropping; it was Orson keeling over dead. She hadn't paid any thought to what jacket Howie was taking after that. If Orson hadn't died just then, she might be certain now.

She called him again. It rang and rang and went nowhere.

She went back to the NooNews app and looked for the link to the video, but now she couldn't find it. If it was Howie, he'd been within a few yards of the soldiers. He'd seen the mass graves. Had he known this for long? Was that what he'd been trying to tell her in that mysterious message with the pickup-truck emojis? She wished she hadn't been so preoccupied with the cat and trying to save and kill Silvestro. Maybe she would have insisted earlier that he come home. If she had, he might be safe now.

She went to find the cat. He was asleep in the bed, even though it was eleven in the morning. She sat down next to him, and he started purring. She loved his purr. It rumbled and rolled; then he gave a breathy sigh, and then more rumble. Roll. Rumble. Sigh.

He kept purring, and she put her arms around him and breathed in his warm, clean cat scent. "I'm glad I have you," she whispered.

She was getting up to go try calling Howie one more time when she heard the cat say, "The red jacket is not in the closet. He took it. Reconstitution has allowed me to see color, remember. And also to see through you. I'm not yours, Marcia. You don't *have* me. I belong with someone else, and I need to figure out where he is. I'm not going to stay here forever. I'll have to go soon. Time is almost up."

Chapter 24

It was not as hard to get ready for work the next day as Marcia expected. She'd thought that being gone for twenty-one years might mess with her motivation, but she jumped right out of bed and grabbed her pull-on black office pants. She chose a pink blouse—pink looked great with her dark hair. She was trying to focus on the superficial—the alternative was to obsess about Howie and the mass graves on What Island. She'd tried every way she could think of to contact Young Mrs. Stowe, but the other woman was avoiding the local press and refusing to answer calls or return emails.

"Wow. You look very dressed," said Mr. Whiskey when he strolled into the kitchen at the smell of eggs with cheddar. He must have forgiven her for her sharpness the other evening. He also seemed to have forgotten about not eating.

"The man I loved was not a good dresser. But I didn't mind," he said.

"Did he work in an office?"

"I believe he telecommuted. Or maybe he was unemployed. He drove around in a pickup truck. I remembered that the other day."

"A truck like Old Mrs. Stowe's?"

"I have not seen her truck, so I don't know if they're alike," said Mr. Whiskey and began gobbling the eggs and skim milk she set out for him on the chopping block. No word about his being overweight.

"There's something wrong with this cream," he said after a minute.

"It's nonfat milk, to help you slim," said Marcia.

He lapped the rest of it and then looked up and said, "We can go back to the old stuff—just don't give me as much of it."

As Marcia was gathering up her things to go, he said, "Knowledge is like a second tail, you know: having it gives you more to balance with, or to brandish if you need to intimidate someone. How much do you know about Jaytie Limes? He seems to have sprung out of nowhere with a penchant for killing people, but full-blown sociopaths don't just drop from the trees like ripe nuts. So I'm wondering, who was he before he was what he is now?"

Marcia stared at him. "I never thought about that," she admitted.

The cat puffed in a know-it-all way. "Contrary to popular lore, curiosity did not kill my relations. It made us wise and helped us retain our edge. If I were you, I'd stop kicking myself over letting Howie go. You couldn't have stopped him. And for goodness' sake, quit poring over the media coverage of the executions. What good does that do? Instead, get some curiosity and start learning something about Limes and Kanz-_ika. The more you know, the more tools you have in your tool kit. The more tools you have, the more rodents you can get. Ancient cat wisdom," he said and licked his fur nonchalantly.

Marcia thought about this as she drove to work. He might be right.

Fortunately, given her agitated state, little was expected of her that Monday. Everyone knew where Howie was and what was happening there, and they tiptoed around her. Even the work-study students left her alone. She checked the next-semester enrollment stats and pulled old files for shredding. Then she just sat.

She remembered what the cat had said. Might as well research Jaytie Limes and Kanz-_ika. She started with *The Information Hatch*.

"Jaytie (often J. T.) Limes is a Eurasian revolutionary. . . ." This was basic. She knew all this. She skimmed ahead.

In the mid-'80s, Limes, under another name, led a bloody coup in
Kanz-_ika. He then renamed himself "Limes" for unknown reasons.
His true identity is a deeply guarded secret and has been eradicated
from all international records. Through a practiced strategy of legal
suppression and destruction of documents, he has eliminated
all information relating to his family, birth, childhood, and young
adulthood. He might as well have been dropped by a stork or
spontaneously generated from under a cabbage.

—THE INFORMATION HATCH

She Googled around but could find nothing that added any
insight to this. The cat was right: full-blown sociopaths didn't
just fall out of trees, but whatever Limes's origin story was, he'd
scrubbed it from the Internet.

Just before lunch, her phone rang for the first time all day. She
expected Nina, but it was Kirk.

"Marcia! How are you?"

"OK," she said cautiously. In fact, she was frustrated. She'd
been trying to track down Young Mrs. Stowe, but the Payroll Office phone tree kept sending her in a loop, and no one there would
reply to her emails.

"Nina's got a shit show at the office, and it's our day for lunch at
the Holliday Club. Want to go for a late one with me?"

Marcia had known Kirk for almost twenty years, and they had
never had lunch. Also, she knew that Nina had stopped going to
the Holliday Club; she said everything they served there tasted
like either Rotel or Jimmy Dean. She felt certain that Nina and
Kirk didn't have a standing date there or anywhere. Nevertheless,
whether because of Mr. Whiskey's urging to be curious or just
because she was bored and upset at the same time, she said yes.

"One thirty. See you there," said Kirk.

She decided to look up the Warehouse College on *The Information Hatch* while she was waiting. There, she had better luck:

"The Warehouse College was an unaccredited diploma mill operating in urban Chicago from the late 1980s through 2004."

That confirmed what Mr. Whiskey had observed: that the place was sketchy, the faculty incompetent, and her grades inflated. Though it didn't explain why she'd been offered a full-ride scholarship via a handwritten postcard. She puzzled over this for a few minutes, but her thoughts soon boomeranged back to Howie.

At one fifteen she walked over to the Holliday Club. Kirk was already there, at a table in the back corner. He rose and embraced her lightly. "Marcia. This is a terrible time for you."

She nodded and waited to see where this would go.

The waiter arrived, and Kirk ordered shepherd's pie and pickled onions. Marcia ordered the massaged portobello with cheese lace.

Kirk said, "I can't imagine everything that must be going through your mind right now."

"I was wondering if the cheese lace would taste like Rotel," she said.

"Ah," he said, smiling weirdly. Then he leaned forward, glanced at her blouse, and said, "I like a woman in pink."

"Oh, ho. Which one?" said Marcia cleverly.

Kirk chuckled. "Such an effervescent spirit you are, even with tragedy crashing down upon you."

His phone went off just at that instant, and he spent the next ten minutes painstakingly typing a message. By then the food had arrived, and he tucked into his potatoes and lamb while Marcia, who was not at all hungry, tried to figure out a way to sneak the cheese lace home for the cat. Finally she just wrapped it up in a napkin and stuffed it in her purse while Kirk watched.

"Aren't you going to eat your mushroom?" he said.

"No," she said sadly. "It reminds me too much of Orson."

He nodded and stared at the mushroom. "I see what you mean. Orson was very special," he agreed in a strained voice.

They spent several silent moments gazing at her mushroom and reflecting on the specialness of her dead dog. Then Kirk started trying to cheer her up by telling her about an albino Scottie he'd had as a boy, Alastair White. "I have a picture of him back at the office. Would you like to walk back with me and see it? It's right on your way."

Keeping the cat's advice to be curious in mind, Marcia agreed. Their lunch had come quickly. Kirk had bolted his food, the conversation had been sparse and halting, and she still had twenty minutes to kill. He chattered to her about Tuition Redefinition while they walked. "Isn't it really just another tuition hike? Why all the hype?" she asked.

Kirk clucked and said, "There's a lot more to it than that. Every time you raise the cost of something, you implicitly redefine both the product and the consumer/supplier contract. Not to put too fine a point on it, but you disrupt the *entire value chain* and then create *new* links. It's nothing to be taken lightly."

Marcia admitted that she'd not understood this.

"How could you? You've been suffering," said Kirk. "You've lost a member of your family. I still can't believe he's gone."

"Howie?"

"No, Orson," said Kirk.

His office was in a quiet corridor at the end of the third floor of the Finance Building. "Come in," he said. "Have a seat." Other than his desk chair, there was only one place to sit, a wide, leather-upholstered guest chair, so she sat in it.

"Here's Alastair White," said Kirk, plucking a pewter-framed picture from a shelf. He brought it over and held it out to Marcia. It showed a befuddled-looking white fuzzball of a dog on the end of a low stone wall. Its tail stuck out at an angle like a white phallus or a bleached carrot, neither quite up nor quite down. Its pink-lined ears were cocked. Its nose was a shiny black bulb, and its head was a long trapezoid like a goat's. It had wet, dark eyes and a large lump protruding from its snowy beard.

"That's not an albino. His eyes are brown. And what's wrong with his chin?"

"A tumor," said Kirk. "It was inoperable without removing his whole lower jaw. It disfigured him for life."

"Did it get larger over time?" asked Marcia. She felt a little like Mr. Whiskey, saying this.

Kirk stared at her with an unreadable expression. "A *lot* larger," he said. "So large that Alastair White had to be put down."

The expression in Kirk's eyes was a blend of grief and something else, but before she could figure out what the other thing was, he put down the picture and, to her amazement, embarked on a hysterical confession: "Marcia, I know how hard losing Orson has been for you. Nina doesn't understand. She's never had a pet in her life. But I had Alastair White. He was everything to me—our bond was unbreakable, except by death. Then the tumor took him, and I grieved for years. I was a shell of a man. I married Nina and began a career, but I was a hollow, loveless soul, going through the motions. Only in my late twenties was I finally ready to heal and move on.

"One day, I brought a dog home from the shelter. I thought Nina would embrace him, but she threw a fit."

"Nina's never liked animals. She's even worse about cats," Marcia observed.

"Marcia, do you know what they do to unadoptable dogs?" said Kirk. "They whack them. *Whack* them! I just couldn't bear to return him, knowing he might be whacked . . . and then I heard Nina talking on the phone with you, and I knew how I could keep Mitey from going back to the pound."

"Mighty?"

"Mitey. He had mites when I got him."

Kirk continued, "You're a pushover, Marcia. Nina is always saying that, and she's right. You're too tenderhearted. I knew if you saw Mitey, you'd stop for him. I followed you when you left work one day and dropped him right behind your car."

"He *was* planted," said Marcia dazedly. "It was you."

"It was I. Did you ever wonder why he loved steak so much? I used to drop by on my lunch hour when you were at the college and feed him Ponderosa from a to-go box through the fence on days when you left him outside. Nina didn't let on—but I think she knew. She's always been jealous of you for being nicer than she is and liking animals and having a kid."

He went on. "I feel his loss, too, you know. You lost Orson once, but I lost him *twice*. Though the first time, he wasn't Orson; he was Mitey," he reflected.

Marcia was still processing this surprising confession when Kirk jumped in her lap. He straddled her and kissed her and simultaneously grabbed the Boobsey Twins. Marcia's memory of Silvestro's sexual skill was still fresh from the time-travel. By comparison, Kirk was pathetic. Half of her mind was thinking it was no wonder Nina was like she was, having to put up with this sort of gropefest in the bedroom. The other half was trying to figure out how to get him off her.

"Kirk!" she shouted. "Get off me."

"No!" he declared.

She decided to tip him off her. Her height helped. Feet planted, hands behind her. Push forward. Rock the chair. Harder. And then it was tipping over on top of them. Kirk was on the floor. Marcia scrambled to her feet. She grabbed her purse, which had acquired a cheesy smell, and made it to the door before Kirk was even upright.

"Marcia!" he called after her. "Could I just see his ashes sometime? Please?"

She was disgusted and wanted to run but didn't want to draw attention to herself, so she power-walked until she got to the stairs and then trotted down to the second floor, where there were more people and offices with open doors and she felt safer. By the time she reached the first floor, she was thinking again. What just happened? she said to herself. She'd intended to call the police, but already she wasn't so sure.

She weighed the importance of reporting Kirk's assault against the faint likelihood that he would try it on someone else who'd recently lost a dog.

"I think I'll wait a while," she said out loud to no one. She was outside now and walking briskly back to High Cultural Endeavors.

That was when her phone vibrated. It was Howie! FaceTiming!

She pressed the button to answer. Her son's face appeared. He was not at the sketchy temple. She saw rocks and dirt. Were those bodies in the background? No, they were moving. Four or five shadowy figures. Humanoid, moving like ritual dancers in a very stylized performance that included a lot of touching the soil. What Island undead at their scavenging. What else could they be?

"Howie! Where are you?"

"Mom, listen. I need to talk to you."

"I'm glad you called. I've got some good news. Young Mrs. Stowe knows something about your fellowship situation. She's promised to help get you home," lied Marcia.

"Shyl and Crumb want me to stay here. That's partly why I called, Mom."

"I thought they were holding you prisoner. And now you want to stay? And do what? Interview more zombies about made-up ancient legends? This isn't Stockholm syndrome, is it? Are you starting to identify with them?"

"Mom, *no*. I *want* to stay. Even if Crumb hadn't asked, I would have wanted to. And the dead here—they're not like you say, they're not zombies. They're real. *Human*. Listen to me. I didn't understand at first why they'd send me someplace where people spoke the same language (sort of) and there was nothing new for me to research. But then I realized: there is something new; it's *all* new. No one has done this before: lived with the dead and studied them; learned how they talk, how they think, what they do, how they understand their condition. No one has looked into their tacit knowledge and their explicit knowledge. There are no ethnographies or grammars. No archives of their lore. It's a linguistic and anthropological bonanza. More untapped material than you can imagine—the kind of treasure trove careers are built on. Mom, how is it even possible to understand life without knowing what the dead know? And I'm the *only* person who's ever gotten access to it. I'm staying here, Mom. That's final. Don't even try to convince me otherwise."

And before she could try, he ended the call.

Chapter 25

SHE ARRIVED BACK at her house with her thoughts still in chaos, to find Mr. Whiskey in a terrible state. He ran over to her in a very basic-cat way and wound around her ankles, shedding gray hair all over her black pants. Then he led her to the side window. She peered out and saw her yard, somewhat dried-up and crispy. Maybe she should have kept Kirk's sprinkler.

"What am I supposed to be looking at?"

"Death. Vacancy. Terror," sputtered Mr. Whiskey. "A boy just walked right into your yard and shot at a squirrel four times, and the last time, he hit it in the head and the squirrel fell over and jerked around. The boy waited until it stopped and then picked it up and went away, twirling it by the tail. He was *smiling!*"

The neighbor boy with his pellet gun.

"How can you allow this?" moaned the cat. "I've had a terrible feeling lately that something was going to happen. And now this!" He jumped up on the windowsill, hissed, and jumped down, his hackles up. "That could have been a cat. It could have been *me!*"

Marcia didn't point out that he was already dead. "I doubt he'd shoot you," she said. "And anyway, you don't go outside unless you're with me."

Mr. Whiskey wasn't reassured. "I still think something bad is going to happen," he said and retired to the living room, where he curled up by the bookshelf, head down and ears back, looking ultra-annoyed, until he soon dozed off.

She had been through so much and had so much to think about that she had to sit on the couch for a while. She didn't close her eyes, just stared at the wall, which needed new paint, and thought about Howie insisting that he was going to stay on What Island to study the dead. Her heart was broken, but what could she do? He was an adult man now. She no longer had a say. From there she thought about Kirk's bizarre behavior and his revelation about loving Orson, wanting Orson, feeding him steak on the sly, grieving over him. For a split second, she recalled one of Dale's favorite cartoon episodes: Doggie Daddy trying to get an unwelcome Snagglepuss out of the house to shoot him. She wondered if Kirk liked cartoons. Neither he nor Nina had a sense of humor. She missed her father: the way he'd laughed at every antic sequence, even if he'd seen it two dozen times. His conviction that funny things mattered. She could hear him saying, "There's more common ground between TV animation and world events than meets the uninitiated eye . . . but the world will forget the Holocaust before they'll forget their favorite *Scooby-Doo* episode." He'd meant it so seriously. It was silliness, but he'd believed it, and he'd loved her like crazy.

Her mind wandered along the gallery of cartoon dogs they'd watched together: Huckleberry Hound, with his gentle drawl and refrain of "Clementine." Muttley, hunching and sniggering. Precious Pup. Pongo and Perdita and all their spotted puppies. Deputy Dog. Dynomutt. Hector. Snoopy. Manfred. Astro. Pluto. Scooby and Scrappy Doo. Yippee, Yappee, and Yahooey.

They galloped and clowned and wheezed and connived and performed a variety of canine antics as they paraded through her mind. So many lovable canine characters. So many crazy plots. She knew them all, because he'd told her about them over and over. And over. And over.

His beautiful voice, with its cheery cadence. Everyone loved Dale. Everyone. Even the spoiled, wealthy, warped Sickrabies Love, whom he'd met in Africa while working as a driver on the location set for the space epic. They all adored Dale. Because he loved everyone indiscriminately.

All those dogs. No wonder when she'd seen Orson bounding along behind her, she'd picked him up. It wasn't just that she was a "pushover," as Kirk claimed. It was a no-brainer: she'd been programmed to love comical and poignant and endearing and scheming dogs. Orson was all these things. But he was dead, and his body was dissolved in the soil around Bixby. And now she had a cat who was also comical and poignant and scheming. And a consolation for Orson. But soon he was going to leave her. She didn't think she could take one more loss.

After a while, she was hungry. She remembered the cheese lace in her purse. She got up and picked the shreds of napkin off it and found Mr. Whiskey and split it with him. It was good aged cheddar and didn't taste like Rotel. She wished she'd asked them to box up the mushroom, but she probably would have left it in Kirk's office in the scuffle.

By now it was dark. She turned on the porch light to look in the mailbox. It had been a typical mail day. Nothing of consequence: another "time-sensitive" piece from the official-sounding PPP. She threw it in the floor basket.

Apropos of nothing, the cat observed, "Every so often, I miss my frenemy, Blackie Bad-Cat, even though he was a terrible blackguard. Perhaps we were codependent, and I didn't realize it. The way you and Nina are codependent."

Marcia was only half listening. Finally she took in the fact that the cat had spoken. "What did you say?"

"Blackie Bad-Cat was a blackguard."

"No, the other."

"I just wondered if we were codependent, like you and Nina. She needs you because you're someone she can feel superior to. Have you ever asked her why she followed you to Round Stone? The world was her oyster, but she chose here. Believe it or not, she prefers you to her family of origin. I mean, wouldn't *you* prefer you to Mrs. Noisettes? Nina really does think of you as a sister. And you need her—"

"I don't," said Marcia irritably.

"You do. To give you something to chafe against."

"You're not qualified to psychoanalyze me," snapped Marcia.

The cat jumped off the couch and stretched. "Maybe not. It's been a tough day for both of us. Me witnessing a rodent shooting. You defeating Kirk's attempt to mount you. We should probably get some rest," he said. Then he strolled off to a new favorite spot he'd found in Howie's room. Marcia got into her sweats and went to her bedroom. They curled up in their separate spheres and drifted off, each lingering in the state between waking and sleep just long enough to wonder if they were going crazy or if they really *were* hearing the Pious Body of Formally Doomed Souls in their chipholes, chanting.

IF ONE DAY could have an antithesis, the next day in High Cultural Endeavors was the antithesis of the day before. Everyone dumped buckets of work on her desk, and the always needy faculty outdid themselves. Marcia had a sign on the wall behind her desk that said, IS IT PLUGGED IN? IS IT TURNED ON? DID YOU REBOOT/READ THE DIRECTIONS/CALL MAINTENANCE/PUT PAPER IN IT/GOOGLE IT? As far as she could tell, no one ever read this notice or bothered to implement these suggestions, and she spent the morning running around solving software and hardware issues.

Right after lunch, Nina called. "Long time no yak-and-clack," she said. "Kirk's going out of town this weekend for a financial powwow, so you *have* to come over and drink some pinot with me."

Marcia really did not want to see her after Kirk's assault the day before. "Nina, it's a hard time right now."

"With Howie? Oh, Marsh. I know! But you can't control everything. You've given him wings, and now you have to let him fly."

She couldn't help herself. "Nina, the More-Tally is up to almost a million. They're dumping the bodies in mass graves."

"Oh, Marsh. Always so dramatic! It's the third world, right? That sort of thing is always going on there. Anyway. Friday. You *have* to come. No excuses. You can't tell me you've got to change the cat box or something."

"Cinders Friday doesn't . . ." Marcia started to say but caught herself. "Cinders Friday doesn't have a box. He has that skin condition, remember? The litter can tear up his paw pads. So he likes to go outside."

"Really! Outside? But what happens during the day while you're at work?"

"He holds it," said Marcia.

"He holds it?"

"Holds it like a champ. No diapers for Cinders Friday."

"Diapers—ha!" laughed Nina. "Well, if he can hold it all day while you're at work, he can hold it long enough for you to come over and drink some wine Friday night."

Marcia sighed resignedly and agreed to come.

THE DAY WENT ON. And on. Late in the afternoon, she finally got a few minutes to call Holliday's Payroll Office. Once again, she got thrown into the phone loop. Finally she got through, but the temp who answered didn't know anyone's name, and they'd all left early for happy hour anyway.

Still later, she was driving. She was almost home, and in just a minute she would have the comfort of Mr. Whiskey—his sardonic wisdom and reverberating purr.

Strangely, thinking of the cat made her feel more panicky rather than less. She sped down Funnel Street and careened into the driveway. She sat for a second staring at her house.

Something was wrong! She jumped out of the car and ran to the house. The front door was unlocked. She had locked it this morning; she always, always locked it. "Mr. Whiskey!" she yelled. "Mr. Whiskey!"

No answer. No saucy gray cat strolling out from some mysterious hiding place. She called again and again and ran around looking for him. He was not in the bathtub. Not under the bed or in the yard—though surely he wouldn't have gone out there after seeing the squirrel shot. Not in the closet. Not here. Not here.

But wait—what was that, right in the middle of the living room floor? Right where the cat had reconstituted that first night, where the resin vessel had busted and spilled his ashes?

He did *not* make waste.

But it was.

A turd.

A discreet pellet: caramel colored and shapely. Compact and dry and tidy. It had come out of Mr. Whiskey. One single, elegant, odorless, spherical deposit. Of course. Mr. Whiskey would not poop with fetor or sloppiness in his reconstituted state. He'd done it to send her a message.

But what did it mean?

Informant 12

"I understand what you're asking. I think. You're not one of us; you sleep and eat mekanize. I used to eat . . . I can't remember. Lucky you. You weren't dragged out of a pit and fed porridge roll and given a bag to go scavenging. But we heard you've decided to stay.

"I never gave advice before. But it's not right to let you just, without—I ate some extra today, to focus. Here is the advice. It is from all of us: think long and hard, because if you stay . . . I'm talking about choice. You will lose it.

"That might sound too negative. We like you. We'd like you to stay. Of course. But here on this island? We are not like you. You don't want to be us. You don't want to know too much about us. And really, there's not much to know. Just so you get it: we have no choice. You can't always believe that the Desert People have your welfare in mind. Their scope is larger. We're like pawns to them. And so are you.

"Still, I remember when you first came, you talked about burning dead pets. That was a shocking idea. No one would do that here."

Chapter 26

THAT NIGHT SHE barely slept. She kept listening for the soft sound of Mr. Whiskey's paws in the hall, the thud of him jumping from some high-up hiding place. The light swish of the comforter when he leaped up on the bed. Once she thought her phone blurped, and she lunged for it on the nightstand. But no one had called—it was fatigue and her overactive imagination.

She called Round Stone Animal Control on the way to work to report a missing cat. But she hung up when someone answered, realizing that if asked to describe him, she would either start wailing or let slip some absurd-sounding detail: "He's been trying to lose weight lately." "He sometimes gets around in an invisible sidecar." "He says knowledge is like a second tail." "He likes to cogitate in a dry bathtub." "He was stolen from a crematory delivery vehicle by a member of an impecunious megachurch." "He rose from the ashes and can time-travel."

Still, she hoped.

That someone would find him and bring him back. That she'd walk in the door tonight to find him waiting for a salmon omelet. Or that he'd be found in some remote location and she'd get that magic call, like winning the lottery. Like you heard about dogs who'd been gone for ten years suddenly popping up thousands of miles away, wearing the same bandanna around their neck they'd left home with. Dirtier, of course.

She was inputting the work-study students' hours for their bi-weekly checks and trying not to dwell on the cat or on Howie's decision to stay on What Island when she thought once more of Young Mrs. Stowe.

She picked up the phone to call but changed her mind, not wanting to risk the phone loop again, and instead took an extra-late lunch and meandered over to Payroll.

The Payroll Office was in the basement of the Finance Building. To avoid running into Kirk, she entered at the lower level. This was not just a little like Chutes and Ladders: you followed a zigzagging concrete ramp and then went through a creaking, ancient automatic door. Then into a low-roofed tunnel with walls padded in some kind of hobnailed rubber, and finally out into the brightly lit Payroll lobby with its long counter behind which worked the four college employees who knew how much *everyone* made here. Marcia had the feeling that upon seeing her, they recognized her not as Marcia N. Farrar but as $43.2K, single, one federal withholding allowance, life insurance at 2× base salary, with supplemental.

Only three of them were there today, two women and a man Howie's age. Young Mrs. Stowe was not among them.

"I'm looking for Young Mrs. Stowe," she said.

Three blank stares.

"Diana," said Marcia.

"Why?" said the woman who appeared most in charge.

Marcia didn't really want to tell them, and she was becoming an expert liar. "She has my parking hang tag. I need it back."

"You're not supposed to lend those, you know. You could lose your parking privileges if you get caught," said the in-charge woman.

They all laughed for some reason, and then the in-charge woman said, "Anyway, good luck getting it. She quit, so you'll have to go to her house." Marcia couldn't tell if this was said with relish or dismay.

"Why 'good luck'?"

"She's never home. She's always prancing around town in those bodycon slut clothes." They all laughed again.

"You should know better than to slut-shame a coworker. Especially one who was almost blown up last week," Marcia reproved them quite seriously. Then she asked, "Do you know why she quit?"

"She said she got PTSD from the bomb going off at the store," said the in-charge woman. "That's her story. Believe it if you want. Or not."

Marcia decided to change her approach. "If I wanted to find out some fellowship details from the auxiliary shadow backup system, how would I go about that?"

They all froze.

"Who told you about that? Diana? That's sensitive information. No one is allowed to access it," said the in-charge woman. "You get *fired* for that." The others nodded in firm agreement: the auxiliary shadow backup system was not accessible to mortals and support staff. If Marcia was reading their expressions correctly, it was better not to speak of it.

"You could try the store anyway," the in-charge woman called to her on her way out. "She's probably out there twerking in the rubble."

Marcia went back through the hobnailed tunnel and out into the full light of the almost-autumn day, no more enlightened than when she'd gone in. Campus planters were ablaze with asters and mums. She was trying not to think about Howie or the cat. Every minute since she'd first learned about the walking dead on What Island had been bloated with terror, and every second since the cat had disappeared had pierced her with loneliness. The landscaping crew were driving around on small tractors, pulling carts of mulch. She wanted to scream at them, "What do you think you're doing?" But this was not fair of her—the tractors and carts were their job. It wasn't because it was their idea of a good time that they were bent on shoveling two tons of red bark all over everything.

Back at the office, she settled into her afternoon routine. But soon the work-study students came and stood by her desk awkwardly. "Ms. Farrar? What's wrong?" they said. "You're acting so weird. Is Howie dead?"

She bit her cheek hard, tried not to shout at them, and explained calmly about the cat.

"Do you have a picture? We could post it on the High Cultural Endeavors Instagram," they offered helpfully.

Marcia shook her head. She didn't even have many pictures of Orson, come to think of it, though she had quite a few of Howie. But no number of photographs would bring any of them back.

After work, packing up to go home, she realized she had no one to take care of today. No cat. No dog. No son. Of all the depressing things she'd felt, this was somehow the saddest. No one needed her.

What the heck, she thought and drove out to Stowes to see if by chance Diana was there, though she didn't expect to find anything but a mound of ashes.

The drive to Stowes took her through her favorite part of Round Stone: houses older than the ones on Funnel Street but nicer—'50s ranches with flat green yards and birdbaths. Immaculately pruned trees. House numbers on the curb that always looked freshly painted. Down a gentle slope, over a concrete bridge that spanned a creek. And up and around a curve with a sign that said to share the road with the Amish. Then: Stowes. It was only singed, soggy remains now.

As luck would have it, both Mrs. Stowes were there, Old and Young, with the F-150. Marcia got out of her car, crossed the caution tape, and picked her way through the debris to where they were trying to wrangle the deli case—the one Old Mrs. Stowe said was made from an aircraft carrier—onto a very long, low cart or dolly. "I can help," said Marcia. Together she pushed and lifted with them until they got it onto the dolly and rolled it out to the truck, then muscled it into the bed and slid the dolly in next to it. The case stuck out the back about a foot, but Old Mrs. Stowe bungeed it horizontally, vertically, and diagonally. "That ought to hold it," she said with satisfaction.

"No, it won't," argued Young Mrs. Stowe. "It will fall out and cause a wreck."

Old Mrs. Stowe didn't respond, and Marcia decided that this was her opening. "Young Mrs. Stowe—" she said.

"If you're here to ask something about Howie's fellowship, I don't know anything," said Young Mrs. Stowe, glaring pointedly. "I'm done with that place, and I already forgot everything I ever knew about it."

"That's not possible," said Marcia.

"It is when you supposedly have PTSD from almost being blown up and you decide to sue your in-laws over it, even though they gave you a part-time job and the down payment for your house and babysit your kids whenever you want to go out to the bars," said Old Mrs. Stowe. "It's definitely possible. At least, that's what Mr. Injury Lawyer told her."

Young Mrs. Stowe glared at her, too. "Would you quit waving our dirty laundry around in front of her, please? Let's go," she said.

"Wait a second. Is this really aircraft-carrier steel?" Marcia asked, rapping on the smoke-tinged metal of the deli case.

Old Mrs. Stowe said, "Who knows? Old Mr. Stowe liked to think so. He was Navy in Vietnam. He missed being in a war after he was discharged. He sold soda crackers and tarpaulins all day. Then he'd go home and watch combat flicks or play those war games on the Internet."

Marcia said wistfully, "That sounds like my dad. In his spare time, he liked to watch cartoons."

"War cartoons?" said Old Mrs. Stowe.

"Dog cartoons."

"War and dogs go together," said Old Mrs. Stowe, nodding.

"No, they don't," said Young Mrs. Stowe.

"'Dogs of war,' Marlon Brando said it. It's Shakespeare," said Old Mrs. Stowe.

"You don't know jack about Shakespeare. If you can't put it in a sandwich, you don't know it from armpit hair," said her daughter-in-law.

"I know how to be decent, at least. My whole life just blew up, but I'm not suing anyone, am I?"

Marcia realized they were having some issues, but she decided not to probe.

"Let's go," insisted Young Mrs. Stowe with a sneer.

Old Mrs. Stowe ignored her and turned to Marcia. "Sorry if my daughter-in-law was rude to you. And thank you for helping us, Howie's mom. Is he OK?"

"It would help if I could figure out how to get him home. But I need some information. If Young Mrs. Stowe knows something—"

Young Mrs. Stowe shook her head. "I forgot it all," she repeated. "My whole memory is wiped."

Old Mrs. Stowe sighed and looked defeated. "She knows, but she's clammed up because of the lawyer."

"I'm sorry for everything you're going through," said Marcia. She said goodbye and got in her car and drove off.

AT HOME SHE felt smoky from helping with the fire-singed deli case, so she ran a bath and slipped into the steamy water. Everything that mattered in her life now boiled down to opposing possibilities. Howie would either come home eventually, or she would never see him again. Mr. Whiskey would come back to her soon, or she would never see him again. She tried to let go and not think about any of this, but from the leaky, imperfect vault of her memory, strange bits kept slipping out and floating into consciousness: gyros and the *busto* of Edgar Rice Burroughs. Animated canines gallivanting across the screen of the Farrars' portable wood-grain Zenith. Wiry Mae in a ball cap. Marcia herself handing over a pile of jewels to a mildewy pawnbroker in exchange for a bag full of money. The streets of Chicago, with Mr. Whiskey in the hypothetical sidecar. Muttley and ankle surgery. Her dad's patient instruction in the fine points of cartoon storylines and his conviction that everyone liked to laugh and would remember *Scooby-Doo* before the Holocaust. His untimely fall. A flowered catsuit from the Salvation Army. The courier bringing the ashes that would turn into Mr. Whiskey. Her hand reaching to take them. More wonderful than any bundle of cash.

When she was tired of soaking, she stood, drained the tub, dried herself. Friday night was wine with Nina. She did not want to go. How strange that Old Mr. Stowe liked war films—he did sound like her dad. Why was she thinking so much about Dale lately?

She brushed out her hair, put on lotion and her robe, retrieved *Men Built It out of Wood*, and took it to the bedroom, where she got into her sweats and climbed under the covers and opened it to the first chapter. She leaned across to the nightstand and got her reading glasses.

Dale had often read from it to her, but she hadn't taken the time to read it herself, thinking she already knew what was in it. She'd never asked him why he'd loved it so much, but reading now, she understood.

How funny and delightful and strange it was—all the things people had built, or tried to build, out of wood. Typewriters. Stethoscopes. A balsa-wood wedding dress. Motorcycles. Books. Streets. Marbles (playable). Basketballs (not). Kitschy things (outhouse keychains). Fake ones (Dillinger's gun). Noble things (a Norse burial ship). Good woods, luxury woods, extinct woods, soft or hard woods, junk woods. Wood clackers. Wood gambrels, wood rollercoasters. Wood flatware.

And, of course, buildings of all sizes and purposes, from yard sheds to cottages to lean-tos for livestock to the Old Government Buildings of Wellington, the Pagoda of Fogong Temple, the medieval churches of Vologda. Some still standing straight, testifying to the glory of wood. More gone now because . . . they were *wood*. People built them and used them, and they sometimes lasted, but mostly they rotted or burned or fed termites and carpenter ants.

It was an enormous relief to think about all that wood for a while. The stories were weird and humorous. She totally got why Dale had loved this book with its quaint, funny, poorly written anecdotes about human effort and absurdity—and, occasionally, success. It put everything in perspective. Wood *was*. Wood *worked*. Or didn't. People needed it, but it was good for only so much.

She read until she fell asleep, and for a short time, at least, didn't think about either Howie or the cat.

Chapter 27

Driving to Nina's, Marcia felt deeply the absence of Mr. Whiskey. She was trying not to think about everyone she'd lost or been separated from. Dale Farrar. Susan. Howie. Silvestro. Orson. And now, despite their short time together, Mr. Whiskey. So much of her was them. She was nothing without them. But yet she *was* without them. She existed apart. She kept on being Marcia.

"Let's sit out on the patio," said Nina when Marcia arrived. She was wearing a three-quarter-sleeve linen sweater under a flowing ivory wrap threaded with accents of burnt orange. A gold spike necklace. Flattering taupe capris. Strappy, expensive espadrilles. Marcia felt the way she usually did around Nina: large of foot, and démodéé. She had been too upset and reluctant about coming tonight to plan something to bring, so in the end, she'd shredded some old Brussels sprouts on a mandoline, stirred in a glop of Miracle Whip, sprinkled peanuts over the top, and crammed it in a Tupperware tub.

Nina took the Tupperware and pried off the lid. "Marsh! How thoughtful of you," she exclaimed. "I have some cheese and crackers and nuts and petits fours. This will add a note of healthful fiber."

They went outside on Nina's patio. It was not that great a patio—Kirk had made it himself, and he should have hired a contractor. Nina set the shredded sprouts amid the other food. There was the silver tray she used for her energy knobs. Now it had crackers on it. There was a glass dish of hard candies in cellophane.

"Do you like my wrap? It's Vance Corvelle," Nina said.

Marcia made an affirmative noise, and Nina whisked off the ivory wrap and draped it over a chair. The wine was already opened. "Grigio or noir?" she asked and then poured the red for

Marcia without waiting for an answer. She kicked off her espadrilles playfully and poured herself a glass of the same. Then she sat, and Marcia sat, too, though keeping her shoes on.

"To absent husbands and almost-sisters," said Nina cheerily. She raised her glass and clinked it against Marcia's and eyed Marcia curiously.

Marcia took a swallow and then another. The gemlike colors of the candy caught her eye. The wine was dry and very smooth and made her head swim pleasantly—a welcome feeling in light of the stress she was under. The candy was bothering her.

"Here we are," said Nina.

Marcia agreed. She chomped some nuts and cake: the wine had sharpened her appetite. Then some cheese on a Carr's. Then another little cake stuffed with jam. "Nina, why did your parents want to be my guardians?" she asked casually.

Nina's tone softened. "Oh, I know you've always worried about whether anyone wanted you. I can see why. But they *did* want you, Marsh. We all did. I wanted a sister, and they wanted another baby, but the stork apparently didn't have our address. They had just decided to get a parakeet when they heard about you. It was kismet: they had all the paraphernalia for a school-aged girl already, so they wouldn't have to spend money on a cage or those bird toys with bells. Besides, I was such a little altruist—they knew I'd open my heart to you. And I did. You were so much more fun than a pet! I could talk to you and tease you—and you talked and teased back! Plus, you know Mother—do you think she could have tolerated cleaning out doo-doo bird litter? With that smell? Marsh, you were long since potty-trained and just the ticket—the answer to all our needs. Do you see how wanted you were?"

Marcia was silent. She watched Nina open the Brussels sprouts and poke at them with a serving spoon, then put a few crackers on her plate and slice some cheese. She looked off into the yard and seemed to be thinking. Nina was not a person who did this often or who wore her emotions on her sleeve, but she looked . . . Marcia wasn't sure how she looked. Victorious was a strange word, but it was what popped into her head. Victorious and smug.

"Nina, did you follow me to Round Stone because you need me to feel superior to?"

Nina slowly turned. "What?"

Marcia backtracked. "Sorry," she said. "I didn't really mean that."

"I hope not."

They sat in silence for a few minutes. Finally Marcia spoke up. "You know about Kirk, right? You know he invited me to lunch the other day?"

A slight twitch of her mouth.

"He told me a silly story about a Scottie dog with a tumor and then invited me back to his office and went into a long spiel about how he wanted to get a dog and found Orson at the shelter and named him Mitey, but you made him take Orson back, so instead he dumped him in the street where I would find him, and I did, and I adopted him, and how he used to come over and feed him bits of Ponderosa through the fence."

Nina looked away coldly. "That's absurd," she said. "That dog went back to the pound. Kirk knew how I feel about pets."

"He didn't go back, and you know it. That's why you were always so funny about Orson, isn't it? Because you knew. Whether you wanted to or not, you knew that Kirk didn't take him back—that he arranged for me to find him. You knew that I adopted him. And you knew that Kirk still loved him, even though he was *my* dog."

Nina looked out toward the edge of the yard with no expression.

"Also, Kirk made a pass at me the other day."

Nina's head snapped around. She stared at Marcia with narrowed eyes for several long seconds. Then she laughed. "Oh,

Marsh! Don't lie to me. Kirk would never do any of those things! Dump a dog in the street? Name it Mighty?"

"Mitey."

"Feed it Ponderosa? Make a pass at you? You must be just *desperate* to feel like you're worth something, so you're making all this up.

"It's sad how you're always bumping up against your limitations," she continued, "but you know, we all have to accept the truth, even when it's not flattering."

Marcia stiffened and put down the cake she was about to bite into. It was not that good anyway. It was dry yet mildly oily, and the jam had a chemical aftertaste. It had probably come from Floods, and it couldn't hold a candle, cakewise, to the bakery items Stowes had sold. "Nina, what 'limitations' do you mean?"

Nina equivocated. "You dress like a retired schoolteacher. You have a nice figure—a little tall and top-heavy, but not impossible."

"Nina!" Marcia warned.

"And you're not very good with money."

"I'm fine with money," said Marcia firmly. "I have zero debt. I own my house. I have a plump emergency cushion and retirement with the college—" (She paused, thinking that this last might be at risk if they were raising tuition because of shaky finances). "I have an investment account with **PPP**." It had come to her suddenly that she knew what **PPP** was, that the pieces of mail she kept receiving from there were statements. They must be the fruit of her investing the twenty-five thousand dollars with Fortress's friend in Chicago in 1997, after she'd saved Silvestro and then killed him.

Ignoring Nina for a moment, she took out her phone and used her calculator app. At a fairly realistic long-term return, she might have an extra $125,000 she hadn't been counting on. It was the nicest thing that had happened to her in a while. "I'm fine with money," she repeated. "So. No weakness there. What limitations, Nina?"

Nina chose her words carefully. "Well, you haven't exactly made a huge success of your life, have you? Same low-paid job for twenty years. The house in that little working-class subdivision. Never married—you had that one fling with an illegal alien a long time ago and haven't landed a man since."

"He wasn't illegal," said Marcia. "He had a visa. He worked for Burroughs Software Solutions. He looked like Leonardo DiCaprio."

"Whatever. But then you had a textbook working-class out-of-wedlock pregnancy. Sis, I love you like family—but blood is what it's all about. And yours is basic. Your dad was a janitor, and your mom wore double knits and bracelets from Avon and drew birds and flowers for Drippy Greeting Cards."

Marcia felt heat rising in her. "Nina! You didn't even know my parents. Don't talk about people you never knew. And I'm not your 'sis.'"

"Marsh, don't be so sensitive." Nina laughed nervously and shifted the candy bowl. Marcia's eyes followed.

The candy. The gemlike candy in the bowl. Jolly Ranchers. She remembered that she'd seen them here before. And that night in the alternate time when she'd been married to Silvestro and they were all playing Botticelli—in this house, which had been her house—Kirk was eating Jolly Ranchers. Like the one outside in the plant saucer near her back porch, shortly before her freezer was stolen.

"Nina, why was Kirk hanging around my house?" said Marcia.

"I don't know what you mean, Marsh."

"He's the one who broke in, isn't he? He's the one who jimmied my back door."

"Kirk can barely hammer a nail. Why would he try to jimmy a door? Especially yours?"

"You tell *me*. Did he steal my freezer?"

Nina shook her head. "I know you're worried about Howie, but Marcia, this is uncalled-for. My husband is a rapist who abandons dogs and steals freezers? All I can think is that you've had some kind of psychotic break," she said coldly.

"These cakes are awful," countered Marcia, picking up one of the jam-filled nuggets. "One more good thing Round Stone will never have again—cakes from Stowes." For emphasis, Marcia crushed the cake in her fist, but then she had crumbs and jam all over her hand. She looked around and spied Nina's Vance Corvelle wrap. Casually she pulled it off the chair where Nina had draped it and cleaned her hand with it, rubbing the violet jam into the fine ivory fabric.

She was not going to let things go. "Nina, I don't care what you think. Kirk did make a pass at me. He had his mouth all over my face, and he was squeezing the Boobsey Twins. I'm not the one who's desperate. He is. And I know he was hanging around outside my door right when someone broke in. There was proof. He peed in my plant saucer, and then he dropped one of his Jolly Ranchers in it. He's the only person I know who eats Jolly Ranchers. Next thing I know, my freezer disappears. You knew Orson was in the freezer. You're the only one who knew that besides Howie. Was he trying to steal Orson's body?"

Nina was scowling, her face twisted and hard like a furious puppet's. "Just shut up! My husband would not squeeze your big ugly boobs or steal a frozen dog corpse. You've totally cracked." She stood and stumbled, forgetting that she was barefoot, and yelped as she stubbed a toe. "Excuse me. I'm going to go call Kirk and tell him what's going on. You stay away from me. If you so much as touch me or any of our things, besides my Corvelle wrap, which you've already ruined, he'll know who did it and call the police."

"Just call the police right now," said Marcia. "If you think I'm dangerous, call them."

"This is not a neighborhood where that sort of thing goes on," said Nina. "The police do not come here. I'm sure you see them patrolling and making calls on Funnel Street all the time. They do *not* come here," she repeated.

"Fine. Don't call them. Do you want me to leave?" said Marcia.

"Yes, I think that would be best. Go home and let your kitty out to do his business."

"He got out and ran away," said Marcia.

Nina laughed. "Even your pets don't go the distance with you. Ever wonder about that, Marcia? Well, I'm done pussyfooting around—you're a terrible friend. You don't like anyone. You've always hated me, even when the whole Noisettes family took you in and took care of you. You thought you were somehow better than us, but it was just the opposite, and now you're finally reaping the reward of your stupid arrogance. I hope your cat *never* comes back. I hope he gets squashed by a monster truck. You are so deranged I can't even talk to you!" She thrust Marcia's Tupperware and sprouts at her and more or less threw her out of the house.

Marcia sauntered out to her car and drove around the block to the side street nearest Nina's garage, where she sat waiting about twenty minutes just to be sure the police weren't coming. Nina and Kirk had a basement, but how much easier it would be to hide a freezer in your garage than to move it down steep basement steps. If you owned a truck or had borrowed one from Holliday College landscaping, you could drive it right in.

She slipped through the neighboring backyard. Nina's garage had a side door. Marcia knew the house quite well, having been to many events here over the years and having occasionally helped Nina with Finance Department barbecues and her annual Holliday College Black Tie New Year's Eve Soirée. She didn't have a key, so if it was locked, she was out of luck.

But it wasn't locked. Marcia opened it quietly and went in. She wasn't worried about Nina hearing her—the garage was at the opposite end of the house from the living room, where Nina was most likely to be.

Marcia had only been in the garage a few times, but it was as she remembered it: spiffy strap brackets and shelves for tools and auto supplies, a handy wall rack for rakes and shovels. The garden hose on its spool. A blue trash bin with *Noisettes-Pettysales* stenciled in white spray paint on the side. An out-of-commission bird feeder. The self-propelled lawn mower. All the same but for the freezer, against the wall in one corner, which was plugged into the receptacle of a heavy-duty extension cord that dropped down from the ceiling.

She hurried over, pausing only a second before opening it. Her head thrummed. What if Orson was in here? Perhaps Lisa had lied, and he'd never been cremated, and the Pious Body had given him to Nina to freeze again—or sold him to Nina, more likely. She bit her lip, thinking that the one thing she did *not* want to find was Mr. Whiskey—not whole, not flat. Not dead. She couldn't bear it.

It flitted through her mind as she pulled up the top that a freezer was really quite frightening until you opened it and saw all the white-wrapped chops and pork steaks. She closed her eyes. "Don't be in there," she whispered, meaning Mr. Whiskey. The lid lifted. The cold brushed her cheeks and evoked a flash of memory: a day in Chicago, walking briskly to work, in the original 1997. Pulling hard on the Homerun Donuts door and rushing in, clapping the cap on her head, and looking up to see Thomas.

She opened her eyes then and found herself gazing on a pile of gourmet frozen dinners and Italian ice pops.

The freezer wasn't hers.

THE WEEKEND PASSED, silent and lonely without the cat. She did not hear from Nina—she didn't expect to. The news from Kanz-_ ika was sparse. There was nothing from Howie.

Late Sunday evening, as she was slogging through the household tasks she should have done Saturday morning, her phone beeped in the living room. She put aside the shirt she was folding and ran to get it. It was a text from an unfamiliar number. She opened it urgently.

Thank you for trusting us with your companion. We took great delight in hosting him. *Emergit veritas ex solitudine.* He has seen the truth that eluded you both. We are returning him now; he is on his way to your place of residence, from where he will lead you forward into the past to put a patch on the future which is the present. Our chiphole prayers go with you. They are paid in full. Tap this link for delivery details of the *animalis beatus*: <u>8YPV45JNU530D</u>.

P.S. If you'd like a rate sheet for à la carte prices, we'd be happy to send one. Just reply YES to this message.

Chapter 28

Waiting up for the cat to arrive, Marcia found herself swinging wildly from one emotional pole to another. He was coming back! But in what condition? He might have died again; he might be *re*-reconstituted. He might not even be a cat anymore. He might be a blob of ectoplasm. That would be awful.

And what had the message meant by "forward into the past to put a patch on the future which is the present"? Before, when they'd "put a patch on the future" by saving Silvestro, it had ended disastrously, with Howie dead and her life a living hell.

Just after midnight, a car pulled into her driveway, activating the motion-sensing light over the garage. She stepped out onto the porch and saw that it was the same blue Ford Focus that had brought Mr. Whiskey's ashes in the beginning. She could not even guess now how many days ago that was. It seemed like twenty years, but it was probably less than two weeks. They'd tumbled through time so much that it was like Blindman's Buff after you've been spun around, only it wasn't a person she was stumbling after blindly; it was . . .

A home. The thought materialized out of nowhere. How long was it since she'd had a home? Not since Dale and Susan had died. The Noisetteses' had been a far cry from a real home. Chicago had always only been temporary. If Silvestro had lived, it might have been different; that might have become her home with Howie. But maybe not, as her ill-fated attempt to save him had proved. And Round Stone was definitely not home; it was why she wanted so badly to be freed from her life here.

This train of thought was interrupted when the driver got out of the Focus and retrieved something from the passenger seat. Marcia's heart raced. Not another bag of ashes, she thought. Not another vessel. A *live* cat, please.

It was the letter carrier, Marcia saw as the woman came up the walk with a bundle.

And then she made the connection: the letter carrier looked familiar because she was the same gender-ambiguous person who'd originally brought her Mr. Whiskey's ashes. Now, instead of a postal uniform, she (they?) was in a tunic like the one Lisa had worn at the church in Bixby, with the word *Lifted* in the same glorious script.

"But you're the letter carrier," said Marcia stupidly. She was groggy, having been half asleep when the car arrived.

"Letter carrier by day, disciple by night. Even Formally Doomed Souls have to pay the bills," said the woman and handed Marcia what she'd taken to be cloth but was actually the cat. He was curled up on a ridged blue pad that looked like it had been cut from a mattress topper. He did not wake or even stir a whisker when handed over to Marcia.

"Is he dead?" she said fearfully. She wanted to ask why he had been abducted and why he was now being returned to her, but it seemed too confrontational.

"No. He has been through a rigorous trial, though. He's sleeping it off. By tomorrow or the next day, he should be up and about. We've sent you a bill for the ordeal, by the way. It's \$459.00, and thirty-eight for pickup and delivery." She waited, and Marcia went and found cash for a tip.

Inside, in the living room lamplight, Mr. Whiskey appeared marmoreal and suspended, but she could see his fluffy side rising and falling faintly like the tiny motion of a fading moth, so he was alive. He felt cool to the touch but still furry and real.

"What did they do to you?" she whispered fearfully. She brought him into her room and laid his pad beside the dresser. All night she kept waking with fright, thinking he'd expired, but each time when she got up and put her hand on his side, there was breath. The last time she woke, she had the muddled idea that it was Howie whose vital breath she was checking for. Then she remembered it was the cat; that he was unconscious, was maybe never going to wake; and that her son was still on What Island, conducting the first-ever inquiry into the *real* culture of the living dead. She cried quietly.

When she woke for good the next morning, the cat was there, inert and unresponsive but a degree or two warmer. Reluctantly, she left him and went to work.

The courier's estimate was optimistic. For four days, Mr. Whiskey lay on the pad by the dresser like some feline Briar Rose in enchanted sleep. Marcia waited and went through the motions. Work, which was plodding—she'd heard nothing from Nina since the evening on her patio. Kirk must be back, and the Noisettes-Pettysaleses would be dining on cordon bleu from their garage freezer. From Kanz-_ika, the only news was the accelerating More-Tally, about which Limes had issued several self-congratulatory pronouncements. What kind of sociopath lived only to kill people? It wasn't anything like the declining population of "Coldernell, Alaska" in that old Droopy Dog cartoon. No gallows humor here. These deaths were real.

Every evening she put a dish of fresh water near the cat's pad in case he woke, and on the third day, a plate of small dried fish, which he'd professed to like when she'd picked some up on impulse once from the Asian market.

On Friday, a week after the debacle at Nina's, she came home with takeout Mexican, thinking she'd watch a movie on the computer in bed so she could stare at the cat and see if he moved. But when she went in the bedroom to change, the pad bore only his indentation and a few stray hairs; the dried fish had been nibbled at; the water dish was empty; the cat was nowhere.

Her panic was replaced with relief when, a few seconds later, he strolled unsteadily through the doorway, tilting sideways. She did not like to show emotion, so she just said, "You've lost weight."

He eyed her with annoyance. "Is that *really* what you want to say to me?"

"I missed you," she admitted. "I'm happy to see you. Are you all right? The mail person said you went through an ordeal."

"Crystal Harmony," said the cat.

"Is that like a vision quest?"

"It's the mail person's name."

"No way! They don't look like a Crystal."

"I know, right? And yes, it was an experience like only to death, and like death, it was both unwelcome and edifying."

"What do you mean?"

"I was subjected to certain discomforts, but I learned some things. About you. About Chicago. About my own enhanced capacities. I believe they will be needed soon. You know how they say that when humans die, they go into the light? Cats don't do that, by the way, or, at least, I didn't, but it could be because I was a blackguard in those days. But this was more like being dropped into a dunk tank of flaming benevolence. Those chipholes are not the innocuous little two-person tents they look like. They're tents on the outside, but inside, they are cavernous chambers that go from sweltering to tepid to arctic in seconds, like a Finnish sauna or a sweat lodge on steroids. They don't just remove sensation—they suck it out of you, and then they scrub all your senses to purity and flood them back into you. It was like getting a whole-body drain-and-flush at the same time as being a blind kitten again, nuzzling my mother in search of a teat. And then my eyes opened. A tongue of light washed me like cosmic sandpaper, and the universe suckled me and baptized me with random and compendious knowledge."

"They drugged you?"

"I don't think so," said the cat. "But I can't be sure."

"Well," said Marcia, "what now?"

First he insisted on a meal. Eating, he started to purr, and somehow that sound, even more than his physical presence, made her feel that if she wasn't actually home, it wasn't far off.

"I missed you," she said again.

He looked up from his plate on the chopping block. "Ditto. The only thing I couldn't learn in that chiphole was who *he* is, the man I loved. Or where he is. I guess I have to find him myself. But it will be hard to go."

"How will I bear it?"

"Don't get all emotional on me," he said and jumped down and spent a while washing his face and pulling bits of something sticky off his tail. Then he looked up at her. "I've got the inside scoop on some stuff I didn't know before. For starters. That freezer you found at Nina's? It wasn't yours. You know that already. It's her old one that she put in the garage. She told you about it. Remember?"

Marcia found that she did have a faint memory of a conversation in which Nina had discussed remodeling and buying all new appliances; she just hadn't paid attention because it was more of Nina's materialistic boasting. "So who stole my freezer?"

"The Pious Body. They'd been needing a deep freeze."

"They took it just because they needed a freezer? Aren't they supposed to be pious?"

"They have a different interpretation of piety. You said you weren't using it anymore, and they saw an opportunity to fill a gap in their appliance inventory and relieve you of a material burden."

"They could have asked me," said Marcia, annoyed.

"Could have, yes—except they don't think the way we do. But you're right that Kirk was hanging around your house and broke in through your porch after Orson died. He just wanted to see Orson one last time."

More pressing questions rose up and burst out of her: "Howie? He's okay? He's still alive?"

The cat hesitated. "Alive depends, you know. Look at me. Am I dead? Or alive? The line is more permeable than people like to imagine. It's not an either/or proposition, Marcia. Is it?"

Her heart dropped in her chest. "Are you saying he's dead?"

"If he is? He was dead before, and then he was alive again. Remember when I told you that you needed to stop worrying and focus on the greater good? That you needed to do what was set out for you?"

"Sort of," said Marcia.

"Well, it's time now. What's set out for you is more time-traveling. If you come with me and do what you're supposed to do, things will be better."

"Howie?"

"Will be all right. Want to see him first?"

She nodded.

"Go for it." The cat stared at her phone.

She found she didn't want to see him, just in case he was dead and rotted or something, but her whole being wanted to hear his voice. She redialed the alternate number. To her surprise, he picked up immediately.

"Mum. Mum."

"Howie."

"Mum, who ear yay? Who's tho ket?"

"I lost him. But I found him again. He went through an ordeal, but he's fine now. Howie, why are you speaking What Islander? I'm trying to get you out of there. To bring you home."

"Mom, I told you. I'm staying here." He was still speaking island speech, but she was able to translate.

"Just so you know, Mr. Whiskey and I—"

"Who's that?"

"The cat. We're going soon."

"I know. Mie told me."

"Mie?

"Crumb."

"Wait." Something was dawning on her. "Is Mie Mae? Is she a wiry old woman?"

"Mie is My, Mom. My is Mo. Mo is Moo."

"That's not what I'm asking."

"I know what you're asking. I know where you're *going*. I'm proud of you, Mom. I hope I see you again sometime. Take the gun. Remember when I told you not to use it? You can use it. It's OK if you have to shoot someone. I've grown up a lot here. I've learned so much from the dead. They know things no one else does."

"Howie? Are you dead?"

"No. Yes. Not always. I'm both. I've been both. You know that, right? I love you."

Chapter 29

SHE PUSHED THE button to end the call.

"It's time to go," said the cat.

"Will I see Howie? Is he alive?"

He didn't answer. Instead he said, "There are a couple of things you need to do. First, get the gun. Then open your investment account statements."

"You mean the things from PPP?"

"Prophetic Portfolio Planning, yes. Now, get the gun."

She went to the closet and found the left Langgrønfod boot. She dug around under the stuffing and pulled out the Beretta.

"Bullets are in the toe of the other boot."

More wads of boot stuffing. She tossed them on the floor and kept digging. The cat was right; there was a small box of 9mm rounds with full metal jacket. "How did they get here? Did I do that?"

"A lot of planning has gone into this. It's a difficult endeavor, guarding and sustaining life; it's easier to just kill people. Look how well Jaytie Limes has been doing with that."

"If I'm taking a gun along, how is that going to sustain life?"

"It's not your job to ask questions, Marcia. Load the magazine. You won't have a chance once we get there."

Marcia did as he said. Then she laid gun and magazine on the bed while she restuffed the boots and put them away. "Langgrøn-fod means 'long green foot,'" she said. "Who would name a brand of boots that?"

"Who would name a cat Cinders Friday?" said the cat.

She changed into the same jeans and azure top with the white piping that she'd put on for their first trip to Chicago.

"You look very nice," said the cat. "Now, open that mail."

With all the coming and going she had been doing lately, her floor basket of mail had gotten quite full. She rummaged through and found eight statements from PPP. They had irritated her with their repetitiveness, which was partly why she'd ignored them. Now she opened the most recent one.

She remembered sitting on Nina's patio, calculating the probable return on $25K invested for twenty-one years with no additional contributions. The number she was looking at was quite different. Not even close.

"What's wrong?" said Mr. Whiskey.

"It's almost $2 million," said Marcia. "It's supposed to be about $120,000."

"You must be a good investor," said Mr. Whiskey. "I did not know this about you."

"It shows I bought some stock in the IPO of *that* company. The online e-commerce bazaar everyone despises but keeps using because it's the only place to get budget-priced grapefruit spoons with free shipping," she said.

"Silvestro was dead and you already had blood on your hands by the time you bought the shares. What's a little more moral compromise?" said the cat philosophically.

She tossed the envelope back in the floor basket. "I'll deal with it when we come back. I can give it to charity. We *are* coming back, aren't we?"

The cat didn't answer this directly, either. He stared at her and swiveled his ears. "You know the man I love? His house does not have two stories. You asked me about it once when you said I was good on stairs. I couldn't remember at the time. But later, I remembered. It has one story. It has a kitchen, like yours, and it has that same big box of cold food."

"A fridge," said Marcia.

"A fridge, yes. He has one, too. He has a door in the front of his house and a door in back, like you. He does *not* have a neighbor boy who kills squirrels, though. And his furniture is different. He brings it home in his truck. It does not look as nice."

"Shabby chic?" said Marcia.

"That could be. I don't know much about furniture styles. He stands up when he eats, like you do when you're being lazy and don't want to get a plate. He does not have money to feed me such good food as you, but I can eat mackerel because I love him. I remembered more about his truck, too. It's the same color as my fur."

"Gray? Old Mrs. Stowe has a white truck," said Marcia.

"Is her cat white?"

"She doesn't have a cat. She has a husband who plays war games."

"Is he white?"

"So far as I know," Marcia said.

"Are you ready to go now?"

"I guess so. I'm afraid."

"I'll be with you. You have the gun?" he said.

She nodded, put the clip in the pistol, checked the safety, and slipped it into her bag. While she was doing this, the cat had hopped up on the bed. He laid his paw on her pillow and then, in a thoroughly basic-cat gesture, marked it with his cheek. "I'll miss sleeping on your bed," he said.

A leap, and he was beside her, twining around her leg like a choking vine. His gray tail switched wildly. They were starting through the straw. She thinned into nothing but a string, then a thread. It was such a long way, wherever they were going—too long. Could he do it? He was just a twelve-pound cat, and it was a rigorous journey, this trip, compared to all the others. But he was doing it; he was trying, at least, and she was thinner than thread, thinner, thinner, thinner than spider silk and farther in than she had been on any trip yet.

Her thoughts whirled as they traveled. Howie, I love you, she thought. Howie. Howie.

They went deeper and deeper and deeper—but then, just as they seemed to have attained maximum momentum and thrust, came a rough jolt. They'd stopped! They were stuck! She was stretched to a thinness one tick on the dial from nothing, and there was gray all around her, sticking in her mouth like walking into a cobweb. The cat's direction was accurate, but he lacked the strength to go all the way. A cacophony assaulted her ears: engines roaring, thunder hammering, and the sound of a million coins being spilled out of an overflowing piggy bank. She heard Orson, barking. "Orson!" She knew his bark.

The chaos diminished to a whisper. Orson's bark became a blue dog singing, "Oh, my darling, Clementine." Now there were dogs yipping everywhere, and then it turned into human singing: long, dry, soulful notes like the sounds they'd heard coming from the Pious Body in their chipholes.

It *was* the Pious Body. She'd know their chanting anywhere. They were intoning. Praying. For her. For the cat. And there was another voice, too. Someone humming a bit of tuneless Ian Matthews or Grateful Dead.

Suddenly there were others with them in the straw. Something powerful. No, two. A force of two. Beings so powerful that Mr. Whiskey was to them as a wheat kernel to a loaf. As yeast to the whole, risen galaxy. As a drop of wax to every candle ever burned. As death to love.

And they were there.

FOR THE SECOND TIME, Marcia emerged from the straw to find herself in a moving vehicle, though this time she wasn't driving. The sounds coming to her were muffled, but there was the chugging purr of the engine, the sigh of wind through half-open windows, and the humming she'd heard while going through the straw. Even though she'd been expelled from the straw and was back to her normal width, she felt unusually small. Also, she was blind.

"I'm blind!" she complained above the engine noise.

"Hang on," said a voice. Not the cat's.

A pop, and a weird, floaty feeling, and she could see. They were rattling over a desert dirtscape. It was late in the day, and the off-road vehicle, which she took to be a Land Rover, was rolling into a smeary, glowing twilight. It wasn't hot, but the air was chokingly dry. Marcia yearned for a liter of Gatorade.

"When is this? *Where* is this?" she asked the cat.

"Tunisia, 1970-something. We've gone back to where your parents met."

Now that she could see, she knew that she was in the back seat. The humming was coming from the front. It was indeed Grateful Dead. There were three men in front; from behind, they looked young. It was the man in the middle who was humming. He was dark-haired. The man on his right was preternaturally blond. The driver wore a ball cap.

Dangling from the rearview mirror was a vintage Huckleberry Hound puppet in a top hat, its fuzzy blue arm waving what looked like a billy club. It was suspended by a tight noose of green ribbon around its neck and secured to the mirror by a perfect green bow, as if Huckleberry had been hanged by a giftwrapping specialist. Marcia stared at the puppet and wondered what it meant. What was happening? Was that puppet the reason she'd heard Huckleberry Hound on the difficult journey through the straw? Despite being quite clear that she was in a Land Rover in Tunisia, her thinking was, at the same time, occluded.

"I can't think right," she whispered to the cat, wherever he was. Again, the voice spoke and said, "Sorry," and an instant later, her head felt much clearer.

Now that her mind was sharp, she looked around the car. The interior was black and dusty. "I never expected I'd ride in a Land

Rover. Shouldn't the steering wheel be on the right?" she said aloud to no one, and the blond man in front turned around, appraised her for a moment, and said sarcastically, "Life is *full* of surprises, isn't it, Brenda?" He continued to stare at her, which gave her a chill, and she was glad when he turned back to watch the road.

So far she had paid no attention to the person riding with her in the back seat. But now she looked over and sucked in her breath. Susan! Her mother! She was so young, just a girl—the age Marcia had been when she had Howie. Marcia studied her, comparing the young woman next to her to the mother she had missed for so many years. This young Susan was thin and coltish. She wore flared, faded jeans and a billowy white poet shirt. Her long, straight hair was parted in the center. The more mature Susan, Susan the wife and mother, would not have worn anything like this. That Susan's clothes came from secondhand stores and clearance racks; the shirts were often pilling by the time she got them, and the pants seldom flattered her. She'd kept her hair in a midlength pageboy, trimmed every two months by one of the students at the cosmetology school a few blocks away for four dollars and fifty cents, plus a dollar tip. This twenty-year-old Susan was hardly like her. She was a mystery: a prototype for a million women she might someday be. There was not even a whisper of the one she did become—poor, resourceful, fatally accepting of her handsome husband's proclivity for marijuana and his deficiencies as a provider. She was staring at the way ahead, so Marcia could see her only in profile in the fading light, but at this moment, it was one of the loveliest silhouettes Marcia had encountered.

"I can't believe it's you, Mom," said Marcia. "I've missed you so much."

Her mother ignored her. Probably she couldn't see or hear her. This saddened Marcia but was also a relief—what if Susan was disappointed in how she'd turned out? Her mother looked a little washed-out and bilious.

The cat was here, too. He had crawled into the front of the Land Rover and was crouched on the dash, just to one side of the mirror, so the Huckleberry Hound puppet wouldn't hit him as it spun and swayed. His tail slapped up and down. His eyes flashed with feral excitement. He looked down. "What's that orange ball?" he said and flicked at it with a paw.

"The knob of the stick shift."

"Why doesn't your car have one?"

"Mine's an automatic."

"No, it's not."

"It is."

"Then why do you have to push on that floor thing to make it go?" the cat demanded.

"It doesn't move automatically, but it shifts gears without me telling it to." Marcia hoped he wouldn't ask more, as she was fuzzy about the workings of transmissions.

But he'd noticed something else. "Why aren't any of you wearing car harnesses?"

It took her a minute. "You mean a seat belt."

"A car harness."

"That's what they're called. Seat belts. They're not standard yet. I guess Land Rover didn't have them in . . . are you sure this is 1975?"

"Positive."

"I thought you could only take me to times I've actually lived in," Marcia whispered. "How can we be in 1975 if I'm not born yet?"

"Not born, but alive. Your mother is pregnant. That's why she looks like she's about to throw up."

"Oh." It dawned on her. "So that's why I couldn't see at first? Or think? I'm a fetus?"

"At the moment, you're two Marcias. Fetal and perimenopausal. You're in utero because that's where you're supposed to be in 1975, but you're also out here."

It was true. She could feel it. It was different than Chicago, when she had been one body, one twenty-two-year-old Marcia but with the memories of her older self. Now she was more than one: she was the girl not yet born and the woman on the other side of midlife. It was not a bad feeling, not troubling or upsetting. It felt normal. She was large in a way she could not have imagined.

"Did you do that?"

"Me? Hardly," said the cat. "I don't have that kind of power. I couldn't even get us here. It was your friends from the desert. They make my abilities look like paint-by-number."

At this, Marcia started noticing the others. Mae was in the jump seat, looking just as she had in Chicago, but without the ball cap. The third man in front, with the cap, the driver, was Thomas. She was not surprised to see them again; probably she'd known all along that Chicago wasn't the end of things. Her heart flip-flopped when Thomas turned to look at her, but she checked her emotions. With the dim light and jolting of the Land Rover, she couldn't tell if he still had the acne. Perhaps the desert had cured it.

"Thanks for coming," he said.

"Where are we going? And why am I here?"

"We're going to see some wind sculptures," said Thomas. "Me and Mae and you and your cat and your parents and Socraties Love. It should be an enjoyable trip for everyone: a memorable desert adventure. And then, I'm afraid, we will need you to help us again."

"I'm going to help you?"

"I knew you'd say yes."

Chapter 30

As they rolled through the stark landscape into the twilight, the sky purpled and the temperature dropped. Marcia started to shiver, and Thomas tossed her a jacket. The cat climbed off the dash and over the seat back and curled up in her lap for warmth. He seemed very tired, and her fear that the jolting motion might make him sick turned into a fiercer worry that he'd worn himself too thin on this final trip, that this had been even harder on him than the chiphole ordeal, that he might not make it back—though what that meant, since he was already dead, she couldn't imagine.

She dreaded him leaving her—she'd learned to depend on him and to care for him more even than for Orson—but she also wanted him to be reunited with the man he loved. He'd done so much for her; he deserved to find his friend (though Marcia felt a prick of envy, picturing them bopping around on some carefree time-travel bro tour).

She'd figured out that Thomas and Mae were the guides who were taking them to the wind sculptures. She wanted to ask Mae if she knew Howie and whether he was all right. She wanted to ask what the two of them were *really* doing here. And why Socraties Love was along for the trip. Also, could her parents' prematurely cut-off lives somehow be restored to them? All these things she longed to know, but she dreaded the familiar retort, "It's not your job to ask questions, Marcia. It's your job to . . ." What *was* her job, though? To help them how? She hoped it was not to shoot someone again. But apparently this part would remain a mystery for now; she'd just have to wait to find out.

At least waiting gave her a chance to absorb her parents, whom she hadn't seen in a quarter century. From the back seat, not much of Dale was visible, but he'd turned around a couple of times to ask Susan how she was feeling, and she was struck by how handsome he was and how his face lit up when he saw anyone—it didn't matter who—and his voice lifted. He was, as she remembered, the gentlest and sweetest of human beings.

It turned out that he knew she was there. So did Susan. They could see and hear her; however, they couldn't hear anything she said about them being her parents, so she was forced to pretend she was just another tourist going to see the wind sculptures, a person named "Brenda." That was why the blond man had called her that. He was Socraties Love, and he'd obviously taken an interest in her, though it was hard to discern what kind, as she was at least fifteen, if not twenty years his senior. There was definitely something "sick" about him; his ice-blondness wasn't the half of it. His face was bizarrely smooth with no visible pores. The cheekbones were high, the brow prominent; the deep-set eyes were a paint-box blue; and his lashes were so pale they disappeared: a face like a skull wrapped in white latex rather than human skin with all its imperfections. A creepy face with ultramarine eyes. His sneering expression didn't help any.

None of them perceived the cat except Mae and Thomas.

When it was almost full dark, they stopped. Their two guides got out and by the light of a high-powered camping lantern set up some musty tents that were lashed on top of the Land Rover. The tents reminded Mr. Whiskey of his chiphole ordeal, and he started making a fearful commotion, but Mae promised him that these were just ordinary tents; he was not going to be subjected to an ordeal again.

"I choose to believe you," he said. "But if it turns out not to be the case, I am leaving forthwith."

They ate bread and cold kefta, which the cat would not touch. Even though he was invisible, he still needed to eat. Thomas produced some tinned fish for him and some water, and there were bottles of Vimto that didn't do much for Marcia's thirst. Then she and the cat climbed into a sleeping bag in one of the tents. Socraties Love was no fan of the desert and said he'd sleep in the Land Rover. Her parents shared a sleeping bag in the second tent. This confused Marcia. Which tent was she in? And which sleeping bag? Hers and the cat's? Or her parents'? It had seemed less problematic to be fetus and woman both when they were in the Land Rover, with all the distractions of the scenery and trying to figure out what was happening. Alone with the cat, she began to wrestle with her identity.

"Quit that," growled the cat. "You're Marcia. You're still not getting this, are you? You are who you are, and all phases of you are the totality. Call it a 'soul,' if that helps. Chronological age doesn't matter. Life stage doesn't matter. Today's date doesn't matter. Only essence is essential. I am still Mr. Whiskers, even in a new incarnation, with a new name and new abilities. You are still Marcia, whether floating in the amniotic sea or boasting about your instant transmission."

"Automatic," corrected Marcia.

"Look at Thomas and Mae. Are they still who they were in Chicago?"

Marcia admitted that they were, though they seemed more at home in the desert; also that her child-parents, despite being less formed and serious than they would later become, were quite clearly her parents, the ones who'd fed her Spam and filled out her permission slips. Perhaps he was right: all the pieces and stages and times of something were comprised in a totality that was not as easy to dissect as it might appear. In which case, Silvestro was not all that dead, and Howie was safe at home; Orson was not yet ash, and Chicago was Round Stone; the Warehouse College and Holliday were one, and she was daughter and mother, lover and killer, student and office worker, dog owner and cat traveling partner, millionaire and financially strapped single mom.

Finally, Marcia drifted to sleep, and her whirling thoughts settled like the flakes in a snow globe when you stop shaking it. Thomas and Mae either didn't sleep or slept on the ground outside. When she woke the next morning to Mr. Whiskey rumbling against her cheek, the two of them, Mae and Thomas, were confabbing in the cold vermilion dawn and charring winged insects over a fire.

"Are those a desert delicacy?" she asked. She was the first one up, having awakened to the smell of burning exoskeleton and hurried out of her tent in case there was an emergency.

"No, they're an invasive bug species. We burn them up wherever we find them," explained Thomas.

More Vimto, instant coffee, and powdered eggs over a campfire (the eggs tasted like burned bug and must have been made in the same pan), and the tents came down and they were on their way. Susan was feeling super queasy, so today she sat in front with Dale and Thomas. Mae was still on the jump seat. The cat sat on the back-seat floorboards. And next to Marcia, Socraties Love. She had a chance to study him closely now. It wasn't just his appearance and facial expressions that were creepy. An awfulness seeped out of him and saturated the air around him. She scooted closer to the door and wondered how her father could have befriended someone so abhorrent.

"Your father is pretty cool," said Mr. Whiskey, answering the unvoiced thought. "He would never kick a cat. He probably wouldn't swat a fly or shoo a raccoon out of the house."

"He wouldn't. He didn't," Marcia confirmed. "Susan had to do it for him."

"That's why he's friends with Socraties Love. The one man in the world no one can love met the one man in the world who loves everyone and everything. How often does that happen?"

"It's pretty rare," Marcia concurred.

In the front seat, her father was telling Thomas about the similarities between Astro and Scooby-Doo, how both had been designed by the same Japanese American animator who had honed his drawing skills in an internment camp and later gone to work for Disney and then Hanna-Barbera. Socraties leaned over and whispered confidentially to Brenda/Marcia/fetus, "Our friend Dale here knows more than anyone would want to know about animated dogs. He can tell you who voiced them and who drew them. He can tell you every single episode they ever appeared in. It's a pretty narrow niche, but he's got it mastered. I'm not much of a cartoon guy, but it's still impressive. I'm more of a numbers man. We don't see many American cartoons where I'm from. Which do *you* like, Brenda? Numbers or cartoons?"

A numbers man? Marcia's skin pricked all over, and she didn't reply. All those NooNews updates and *Post* headlines and articles from *The Information Hatch* reared up in her mind, and she knew, suddenly, who he was. He was Socraties Love, but he was Jaytie Limes, too. All phases of the totality. Limes, whose early history had been deliberately erased from the Internet. Who'd changed his name along the way. Love = Limes.

She was sitting next to the designer of Cor-Spamkeer! The man responsible for the More-Tally! Over a million were dead, and the numbers were rising—*would* be rising, in forty-one years. Her pulse was racing, and she wanted to jump out of the car, but they were in the desert, and there was nowhere to go. She was stuck. Here. Now. Only inches away from him. Sick was Limes. Limes was Sick. Sick was sick. A monster. Destroyer of innocents, for no reason other than that watching his Cor-Spamkeer death toll climb gave him a perverted sense of achievement. Builder of a killing-works. Author of a nightmare. What she didn't understand was how Dale could like him—love him, even. All the times her father had talked about Socraties Love while Marcia was growing up, never once had he said that Sick was too warped to be friends with; he'd only said that others had found him warped. "My friend Socraties," he'd said with affection in his voice. The closest thing to a loyal lifelong companion. The friend who got away.

What would Dale have said, though, if he'd lived to see Cor-Spamkeer?

Now Dale turned around and started talking to Marcia and Sick: nothing important, just chattering about how much he'd enjoyed sleeping out in a tent and whether they were stopping for lunch or snacking along the way; either would be great. He was excited about the sculptures. He offered them nuts from a baggie of almonds. His earnest, happy warmth was the antidote to the vileness that oozed out of Sick.

And maybe she imagined it, but she thought she could feel Sick's sickness ebbing. How could it be that he loved her dad? How could he be capable of it? A man who reveled in slaughter? But she guessed if Sick could love anyone, it would be Dale. There was no one who wasn't drawn to her father. He possessed a bottomless reservoir of cheer. No one was as delighted about everything as Dale. And no one could be as kind to people who didn't deserve it.

Eventually Dale turned around again. A few minutes later, Thomas and Mae started telling them trivia about the salt lakes and ancient underground dwellings and caves, but Love's words keep repeating in her head like a gong. *I'm more of a numbers man. We don't see many American cartoons where I'm from.*

Mae was watching her, and Marcia saw that she knew that she knew.

The cat had been asleep again, but he woke up long enough to say, "It's fine, you know. He's why you brought the gun."

BY THE TIME they were nearing the wind sculptures, just after midday, Marcia was a nervous wreck from bumping across the desert next to a genocidal sociopath. What the cat said had not been lost on her. She had a gun; she knew how to shoot it because she'd done it before. It was already loaded; the clip was in it. If she chose the right moment, she could shoot Socraties Love dead through the heart, just like she'd done to Silvestro. Then he would never become Jaytie Limes. There would be no Cor-Spamkeer. Thousands upon thousands upon thousands would be saved, their lives allowed to roll out and roll on as they'd been intended to. And honestly, who would miss Love if no one loved him? Probably only her dad.

But to shoot Jaytie Limes to prevent his atrocities was a staggering prospect. How might it affect . . . *everything*? If saving Silvestro, a man of little consequence with no family in the picture, could result in Howie being mauled to death and Marcia consigned to a hell-life, what might happen if she killed someone like Limes? Someone with money, who would rise to power in his part of the world? What vacuum would it leave? What—who—would fill it? What worse awfulness could potentially ensue by her disturbing some cosmic balance?

In the midst of these thoughts, she heard the cat say, "How strange that I was reconstituted because of emotion. Grief brought me back from the ashes. I wonder if it could happen to someone else?"

"Maybe, but probably not," she said absently. "Listen, I need your help. I don't know what to do."

"A good strategy when you are beset is to hiss loudly and prick your hair up so you look like a giant," the cat advised.

"That won't work."

He changed the subject. "What's the story on that nasty little dog?"

"What dog?"

"That blue barbarity hanging from the forehead reflector."

"That's Huckleberry Hound. And it's not a forehead reflector. It's a rearview mirror," said Marcia.

"I'll never get the hang of these automobiles," said the cat.

Chapter 31

WHILE MARCIA IN the back seat had been discovering the truth about Socraties Love and fretting over whether to shoot him, fetal Marcia in the front seat had been causing no end of disruption to her mother's peristalsis, though she didn't feel bad about it because she didn't know she was creating such awful nausea. It was pleasant to float here, fed and housed, sensing—not really knowing yet—that there was something beyond this, a place she would arrive that was full of light and space; that there were others, like and not like her. Vibrations surrounded her; they constituted a great deal of her awareness. Close-by vibrations that were intermittent, sometimes strident: watery burblings and gassy groanings that were coming from inside, where she was—whatever she was inside of. There was the ongoing vibration of motoring, which she did not have a name for. And a vibration from farther off, bell-like, which she couldn't perceive as a voice yet; it was her voice, her adult voice. It was afraid, full of apprehension, frustration. And there were other vibrations from *much*, much farther off that were like it, but there were more of them, many more, and they were extraordinarily clear. They were sacred and urgent but quite loud and demanding all at once. Fetal Marcia knew none of the words that would have described the voices, but she didn't need to. She was essence and totality. Soul. Everything she didn't know, she knew. She even half sensed that there was another part of her, a complement of gestating Marcia, just a few feet away.

It was her extreme alertness that was causing Susan so much trouble while Marcia in the back seat was sorting out what to do. For some reason that adult Marcia could not fathom, maybe just because she was randomly connected through her father, she had been given the chance to eliminate one of the world's most notorious murderers before he could begin his horror-campaign of slaughter. But without a crystal ball, deciding whether she *should* do this was like playing roulette with possibly far-reaching consequences.

"I want to go home. I don't care if I'm stuck in Round Stone for the rest of my life. I can put up with Nina. And Kirk. I just want things to be normal again. I don't want to be here. I want my son. I want Howie," wept Marcia. "Can't we just go back to the beginning?"

"Poor Brenda," said Socraties. "I can tell you're having a hard time. We all do, until we reach the end of the road. But tell me, how do you *feel* about death? Do you admire it? Fear it? Does it invoke a marvelous shiver when you hear the word? Especially when you think of a LOT of death?"

"No," said Marcia angrily. "Not at all. Not a bit. I know a lot of dead people. Every single one of them would rather be alive."

"But that's your view as a member of the tribe of the living. What if the dead have no preference? Or what if their greatest desire is for more company?"

"They do have a preference, and it's *not* for more company," said Mr. Whiskey, but Sick didn't hear him.

"What if someone were to master death? To adopt death as both life's work and the ultimate competition? To produce *more* death even than the plague? More than cancer and heart attacks and car wrecks all together? Could that not be sublime? Would it change your opinion?"

"No," said Marcia. "It wouldn't."

"Deaths 'as numerous as the stars in the sky and as countless as the sand on the seashore'?" he said.

"I was a history major in college," she said.

"I like intelligent women. My mother was not," said Socraties. "She was shallow and cruel, and she abandoned me."

"Well, that's no reason to kill a ton of people," said Marcia/ Brenda. "And you interrupted me. I was going to say that I was a history major, and one of the things I found out was that people don't really care very much about history unless someone rubs their nose in it. Almost no one in my classes could tell you about Mao and the millions tortured and killed in the Great Leap Forward. They couldn't even *name* Leopold or tell you what he did to the Congo. 'Stalin? Totalitarian Russian dude, right?' You know what people really remember? Things that make them laugh. They remember cartoons. Your friend Dale is onto something. More people could tell you the plot of their favorite *Scooby-Doo* episode than about the Holocaust. I bet in another forty years, there will be people who don't even *believe* in the Holocaust; but they'll still believe in Scooby-Doo."

Socraties turned away, and his ice-white ears grew very red. He was either furious or blushing. He stared out the window and didn't speak again, but now and then he glanced at Brenda/Marcia when he thought she wasn't paying attention.

THEY'D ARRIVED NOW. Her father and Susan jumped out, and Dale led Susan behind a rock. It was one of the wind sculptures, an outcropping etched by thousands of years of windblown sand to the shape of an ibis with a hole in its middle. Dale held Susan's hair back while she vomited behind the ibis. Everyone could see them through the hole. By the time they came back to the group, Mae and Thomas were handing around disposable cameras and bottles of Vimto, and the group began to weave among the sculptures, except for Susan, who had found a shaded rock to sit on. Dale was oohing and aahing with all the persistent, purposeless happiness Marcia remembered that had made him such a problematic husband for Susan: a little like Silvestro, but even Silvestro had had a few dislikes and some ambition. Marcia was not impressed by the sculptures. She'd spent many an afternoon in the Chicago Art Institute back in the day, and as they strolled over the dust and rock, she concluded that nature did a creditable job for a mindless force that never intended to make art, but that humans would always have the upper hand over accident when it came to aesthetics. The little group of tourists made note of a fish, a parrot, a three-legged wolf. There was a pinheaded bird that Mae called a gosling. Also a pig with a fin and slippers.

"This is incredible!" Dale exulted.

Thomas drifted over beside Marcia and put his arm casually around her shoulders. Mae appeared on her other side. Together they did their best to explain. "We're sorry we had to kill Silvestro, but he might have interfered with our access to you. As a rule, we try not to kill people," said Thomas.

"Our friend Fortress was the go-between with the college. He also engineered the settlement and, later, your successful investments. We needed to keep an eye on you by making sure you stayed in Round Stone. The Pious Body eventually settled near there; they've been indebted to us for some years, since we rescued them from Cor-Spamkeer and saved their lives and transported them. We didn't know Nina would follow you there or that having to put up with her would make you so miserable."

"Wait. What? You rescued the Pious Body from—" said Marcia.

"From Cor-Spamkeer. You heard right," Thomas said. "They were an unusually cowardly bunch who made a godawful commotion about dying, and it occurred to us that if they were teachable, we could show them a few tricks and use them as on-the-ground guardians for you and an all-purpose prayer squad for whatever we needed them for. We didn't bank on them being quite so money-grubbing, though. Sorry about your dog's ashes. But it led to the cat, and that all worked out unexpectedly . . . well."

Mae shot him a look.

"Better than we expected, anyway," he amended.

"And don't ask why we couldn't rescue *everyone* from Cor-Spamkeer," he added. "Do you know how many people Limes had locked up there? There simply wasn't anywhere to put them all. We needed to deal with the source of the problem; that's why we needed you."

"You *are* Desert People, aren't you? Why didn't you just eliminate him yourselves if you're so powerful?" said Marcia.

"We couldn't. It had to someone ordinary. Specifically, it had to be a big-breasted beautiful orphan. An orphan with a stoner father who loved cartoon dogs and had a prior relationship with Limes. We looked all over and only found one of those: you."

"It had to be you," Mae agreed and then continued, "Howie's fellowship was our doing, too. We made all the arrangements. It was no accident that his assignment was close to Kanz-_ika. We knew he'd be all right on What Island, but we didn't want *you* to feel too sure. We had to give you a reason to do what we needed done: to put a stop to all this death. The only motivation we could count on was your desire to protect Howie. You're a good mother, Marcia. And Howie is a fine young scholar. I'm sorry we couldn't offer him a better population to study—but he seems to have embraced our island scavengers."

"Are you Crumb?" Marcia asked her. "Can you convince Howie to come home?"

"I'm Mae. Mae is Mie in dead-speak. Mie is French for Crumb. So maybe I am, but only Howie can decide whether to stay or go."

Marcia thought of another question. "Where did you get the money? Howie got a stipend and a round-trip plane ticket and fees for ground transportation Who paid his fellowship expenses?"

"You did," said Thomas. "As you've guessed, we're very powerful, but in fact, we didn't have any money to speak of. Unlike in your messed-up homeland, wealth does not equal power where we come from—quite the opposite, most of the time. But we knew someone with money: you. The return on your investments was excellent, as we predicted it would be. **PPP** isn't Prophetic Portfolio Planning for nothing. You paid for Howie's fellowship as well as your scholarship to the Warehouse College."

Marcia frowned. "But that was before I knew I had that much money. The scholarship was before I even *had* the money. How could I unknowingly pay for a scholarship with money I didn't even have yet? And why would I fund my own scholarship to a third-rate diploma mill? Why not Brown? It doesn't make sense. I didn't authorize anything. I didn't sign anything."

"Sign, authorize, sense—you're getting awfully jurisdictional on us," said Thomas. "What happened to the young woman who took a job at my donut shop and didn't bat an eye when she found out about the 9mm under the old-fashioneds?"

"You also, quite generously, bought a horse incinerator for the Pious Body and a food truck for Old Mrs. Stowe so she can keep making sandwiches now that the store is blown up. And you paid for a *lot* of chiphole prayers," added Mae.

"But I didn't buy those things. I haven't paid for them. The Pious Body doesn't have a horse incinerator, only a firepit and my freezer. Old Mrs. Stowe's in the middle of a lawsuit; she doesn't have a food truck."

"It depends on when you're talking about, Marcia. The Pious Body may not have a horse incinerator in your 2018, but it's not always your 2018, is it? You should know that better than anyone."

"But I never told my broker to sell any shares."

"Your broker!" laughed Thomas, and Mae laughed, too, but they both quickly grew sober again, and she knew they were thinking about death.

"Who *are* you? Both of you?" she demanded of Mae and Thomas.

Thomas exchanged another look with Mae. "Maybe just call us 'donut people'? Your son knows the legends. We've been through a lot. Death and worse, and it gave us new abilities. Like your cat, but on a larger scale."

"We didn't expect the cat, but he came in handy," said Mae. "It would have been nice to avoid the detours with Silvestro, but at least it gave you some practice time-traveling."

"The sex with Silvestro was phenomenal," recalled Marcia wistfully.

Thomas changed the subject. "Speaking of the cat, where is he?"

"He didn't get out of the Land Rover," Marcia said with a jab of panic. She glanced to her parents—her dad chatting with Sick and her mother still sitting in the shade—then sprinted to the vehicle, Mae and Thomas trailing.

Mr. Whiskey was in the back seat, pacing in tight circles. "I've been waiting for you," he said sharply. "You need to take the gun now, Marcia. And I need to go. It's time."

He sat down full on his haunches. His green eyes drilled into her. Then he opened his mouth and ululated with a shrillness that outdid anything she'd heard from him yet.

Just as suddenly, he stopped. "There," he said. "Got that out of my system. That's how much I don't want to leave you, but I have to. I remembered his name. It's Randall. I know where he is."

She wanted to carry on the way the cat had—to yowl and howl with pain. But Thomas put his hand on her forearm, and Mae dug around in Marcia's bag and found the gun and handed it to her.

The cat watched her take it. He looked wispier and vaguer. There was no tail switching, just a slight fading. He said, "You're right that it's a bad idea to shoot Sick. It's Dale you need to shoot."

"My father? That's not funny," she snapped.

"I didn't mean it to be."

"If you shoot Sick, there's no telling what might happen," said Mae. "But if you kill Dale, Sick will lose his only friend. He'll grieve for him. So will you. And so will your mother."

"A vortex of grief, like the one that transformed me from a heap of ashes to your traveling companion," said Mr. Whiskey.

The truth of it socked her in the gut. She could see how right it was. How the uncertain and potentially terrible repercussions of shooting Socraties might be avoided altogether simply by killing her own father, a death that would barely make a ripple. She said slowly, "You mean, if I do this, Sick will be changed into someone who won't want to kill anyone? Cor-Spamkeer will never exist?"

"That's the idea," said the cat.

"I'm not sure I believe it. *You* had to die before you were changed," she argued.

Thomas and Mae were firm that it would work. "A lot of planning has gone into this," Mae said. "The Pious Body have been chanting in their chipholes for a *long* time. A lot of chanting. Very loud chanting. A long, loud time. They've received a lot of money for it."

"Let me guess. I paid for *that*, too," said Marcia. "Paid them to shout to the hills for me to kill my father so everything would be hunky-dory."

"You don't have to put it quite like that," said Thomas.

THEY WENT BACK toward the wind sculptures. The cat came along, but he was barely there. She could see him but not.

"Howie's okay?" asked Marcia as they walked along.

"Having the time of his life," said Mae.

"I'll see him soon?"

"If he decides to come back."

The air was hazy but also ridiculously dry. The sun was very intense and seemed to ricochet off everything like it was coming from a million directions. Fetal Marcia-in-Susan had no sense of this. Her world was dark and placid, but to adult Marcia, there was a shrillness in the atmosphere and a sharp thirst in her throat that made her testy. The gun was lighter than she remembered.

They reached the sculptures and found Susan sitting in the shade of some wide stones, a short distance from Dale and Soc, who were talking and laughing. There was plenty of space between the two men. It was a cream-puff shot. Dale was telling Soc about Underdog's super-energy pills. She knew this because he was pointing to an imaginary ring on his hand. He'd given her the same lecture about the pills and the ring, with the same pointing, more times than she could count. Her handsome, cheerful, silly father. The gentlest person alive.

It was a very easy shot.

In her mind, she saw Silvestro fall. And then she saw him alive and hearty in the house with the shiny faucets, twenty years older, singing and smiling. So maybe her father would come back. Live in another dimension. Death was not always final; sometimes it was interim or stand-in. Sometimes, even, a start.

"Now you're seeing what I saw in that chiphole," said the cat. He was just a patch of translucent gray by her ankle. He grew a notch fainter, and then he was gone entirely, but for a few seconds, a picture flashed in her head: she could see the cat cradled in one arm of the man he loved. They were, indeed, standing by a gray pickup. Mr. Whiskey had mind-messaged her a selfie! I bet you didn't know you could do *that*, either: send mind-selfies, thought Marcia.

I am the same and not the same, came the reply, and her heart contracted. But there were lives to save, and Howie to recover.

"Here goes," said Marcia. She raised the gun. *Howie. Howie, Howie, Howie. Howie.* She pointed. Sighted. Fired.

She clamped her eyes shut and turned away as the report rang out and echoed.

When she looked again, Dale and Soc were both sitting there as if nothing had happened. They were oblivious to the fact that she had been shooting at them. She looked for the gun. It wasn't in her hands. She must have dropped it.

It wasn't on the ground. Not anywhere. It was gone. What had happened? Had she dreamed the whole thing?

But Thomas and Mae were there, and from their faces, she knew she'd shot something.

Her father saw her and waved. "Brenda! Come over here! We've got an idea!"

"What the—?" said Marcia to no one. The sickness that had overwhelmed her right before she fired was subsiding. Her heart had stopped hammering. Somehow, she'd missed, and her father was still alive. And so was Socraties.

A hand grabbed hers. "Well done," said Thomas.

"But I missed!"

"No, you would have hit him in the chest, but we rerouted the bullet. And got rid of the gun."

"*I* rerouted it," said Mae, appearing beside her. "Very well done, by the way."

"But I didn't kill him, and Sick won't grieve, and he'll be the same monster he's going to be, and hundreds of thousands of people will die, and I'll never see Howie again."

"No, no. That's not right. You *will* get to see Howie if he wants to, just as soon as we figure out how to deal with some unexpected developments," said Thomas.

"What developments?"

"Major revision of our plan. You changed Soc's mind," said Mae. "The right words at the key moment. Totally unforeseen by us, by the way. Back there on the road? When you told him that people would rather laugh at cartoon dogs than study history? That people would remember Scooby-Doo before they'd remember the atrocities of Mao or Stalin or Hitler? You convinced him. You won him over. Who would have guessed that all it would take was a smart, pretty, older woman telling him he was wrong to change his whole direction?"

"And that changes just about everything. Not the least of which is your entire future, from birth to the age you are now," said Thomas.

"My entire future?" said Marcia weakly. "What about Howie?"

"Quit worrying," said Thomas. "Don't you see how great this is? Sick doesn't know it yet, but he's given up on Cor-Spamkeer, and he and your father are brainstorming their own cartoon dog series. You made *quite* an impression on Sick. He's pushing for a lady-dog protagonist. He has the money to produce it, and your dad has internalized every cartoon plot there ever was. And your mom isn't a half-bad artist. She can't do the animation, probably, but she can sketch out the characters."

"Are you *sure* Howie is fine?" said Marcia.

"Having a blast," said Mae.

"Brenda!" cried Sick again. He was shouting excitedly. Dale called out, too. "Brenda! We've got something to ask you."

Thomas and Mae turned back toward the Land Rover. Marcia crossed the stretch of sandy dirt and rocks to where her father and Socraties Love were still laughing. Marcia-in-Susan was asleep now, but Marcia the elder was wide awake and curious. They were like little boys, they were so excited. They reminded her of four-year-old Howie, words pouring out of them. She could see a little of Howie in her father and, unexpectedly, a little something like Silvestro in Socraties.

"The way you said it back there in the Land Rover, it was crystal clear," said Soc. "You were so passionate, too. It was like something was switched on in me that had been turned off all this time. Can you believe it: I'd never heard anyone say that death is less attractive than laughter. But the minute you said it, it made perfect sense. *Perfect* sense."

"Did I ever tell you about that Droopy Dog episode?" said Dale, and she could hear him winding up to tell it again.

"Not now!" said Soc. "Don't get him started," he warned Marcia.

"Ask her, Dale," he said to her father.

"We were wondering, could we use your name?"

"Marcia?"

"No, Brenda. For our protagonist," said Dale.

"Brenda Bloodhound," said Soc. They both started babbling about it at once.

"Brenda Bloodhound. What's her thing?" Marcia asked when she could get a word in.

"Thing?"

"Her bit. Her gimmick."

Soc said, "She's got an incredible nose. She searches the world for her kidnapped pup, Brody."

"And sniffs out and crushes all the villains she encounters along the way," said Dale.

"Right," said Soc.

"*Crushes*," said Dale. "But she's only badass by accident."

"Right. By accident," said Soc. "Mostly she's just a mom who wants to find her lost kid."

Brenda Bloodhound was an animated TV series that first aired on American television in October 1978. It was produced by Farrar & Love Productions, which later launched the ill-fated and litigation-plagued *Mr. Friskey's Timely Tail*, an animated series about a time-traveling Scottie dog (Mr. Friskey) with a human sidekick, Orphan Maria. Farrar & Love was sued for copyright infringement by the producer of the *other*, earlier show about a time-traveling dog and his boy. The resulting publicity and out-of-court settlement ruptured the close and prolific friendship between Socraties Love (son of Kanz-_ ikan airline mogul Gordon Love) and Dale Farrar. It also permanently ended production of *Brenda Bloodhound*.

During its three-season run, *Brenda Bloodhound* achieved wide popularity for its eponymous feminist narrator, who searched the world for her kidnapped pup, Brody, and cleverly but unintentionally sniffed out and defeated a dizzying array of sadistic villains. The perverted (for a kids' show) behavior of Brenda's antagonists added a salacious note that drew children and adults alike. The warped villains were the creations of Love, while Farrar created the hero characters. The partners stated that *Brenda Bloodhound* was based on a beautiful tourist they met in North Africa in the mid-'70s. However, pop-culture critics have proposed that she was in fact an adult version of Farrar's daughter, Marcia.

As a side note, in her late teens, after the dissolution of Farrar & Love and Dale Farrar's death from an accidental fall, Marcia, Dale's daughter, married his ex-partner, Socraties Love, twenty-six years her senior; but two years later, they divorced when she became pregnant by Italian software genius Silvestro Marco, whom she'd met through Love's new media endeavors. Marco was murdered by an unknown assailant in Chicago shortly after the birth of their child, a girl, Holly. Love was initially a suspect but had an irrefutable alibi. He died of a heart attack in 2008, and the case remains open. At twenty, Holly Marco underwent gender reassignment surgery to become Howie, saying he'd known from the beginning that he was born the wrong sex with the wrong name. But he bore no ill will about it. "The totality of my self was always Howie," he said. "I held on to that knowledge, and it nourished me until I could become who I'd always been."

In her early forties, Marcia Farrar penned a memoir, *Real Life Is No Cartoon.* In it, she wrote about how the Mr. Friskey lawsuit, her parents' deaths, her abrupt divorce from Socraties Love, the unsolved murder of her sexually magnetic paramour, Silvestro Marco, and her son's disappearance and presumed death while doing research on an unmapped island changed her into a person who felt most at home staking out crematories to watch people picking up their departeds' urns. In the conclusion to her memoir, she wrote, "My life was really not that bad. I had a lovely home, and I got a feisty gray cat to keep me company. Almost everyone I'd loved was gone, even my dog. But I liked thinking about them all in their altered conditions and imagining what they might be up to."

—THE INFORMATION HATCH

About the Author

Evelyn Somers, a longtime literary editor, has loved stories and cats since before she could read. She lives in Central Missouri with her extraordinary family and cats.